OPERATION
SHATTERED
ICE

An
Andrew
Russell
Novel

THAD
DUPPER

Published by
Kilshaw Press LLC
717 Golf Club Drive
Castle Rock, CO 80108
www.attackonack.com
attackonack@gmail.com
© Copyright 2021 Kilshaw Press LLC

This is a work of fiction. Unless otherwise indicated, all the names, characters, businesses, places, events, and incidents in this book are either the product of the author's imagination or used in a fictitious manner. Any resemblance to actual persons, living or dead, or actual events is purely coincidental.

eBook ISBN: 978-0-9983476-7-7
paperback ISBN: 978-0-9983476-8-4
hardcover ISBN: 978-0-9983476-9-1

Content editor: Jennifer Fisher
Copyeditor: Eileen G. Chetti
Cover design: Chris Berge, www/bergedesign.com
Interior book design:
Deborah Perdue, www.illuminationgraphics.com

Printed in the Unites States of America

To my parents,

Melvin and Marion Dupper

For their many sacrifices

that made our childhood in Bay Ridge, Brooklyn

happy, healthy, loving, and inspirational

Principal Characters

Andrew Russell: President of the United States (POTUS)

Kennedy Russell: First Lady of the United States (FLOTUS)

Lisa Collins: Director of the CIA, VP nominee

Sterling Spencer: Chief of Staff for POTUS

Sergey Latsanych: SVR Agent

Svetlana Ivanovna Zlovna: Director of Russian SVR

Dr. Alma Thomsen: Denmark Geologist and Mineralogist

Lauren La Rue: CIA Analyst

Chris Samson: Command Master Chief, USCG

Salman Rahman: Son of Saudi Sheik

How hard it is to keep from being king

When it's in you and in the situation

Robert Frost, 1951

FOREWORD

Thrillers come in many forms. Some place their action and adventure in a past era, adding nostalgia to the mix. Some are set in science-fiction futures. Some are the wolves in the sheep's clothing of romantic yearnings.

Thad's Andrew Russell novels live in what I would call "alternative present" settings. That is, the world largely as we know it, except right around the main characters. Russell is the 46th US President, leaving such personages as Donald Trump, and Joe Biden aside – and with them, our hyper-partisan domestic politics. But the international challenges remain: China, Russia, North Korea, Iran, Saudi Arabia, and the rest.

And technology reflects our real world in Thad's alternative reality. Thad is a past master of bringing modern military technology into your summer beach read, particularly the watery world of aircraft carriers with their attendant flying machines and submarines with their deep-sea skullduggery. But this read adds a key, though less glamorous, aspect: icebreakers, the plug-ugly shepherds that keep the cutters of commerce moving in difficult Arctic and Antarctic waters.

Thad makes no judgment as to whether global climate change is a bad thing or a good thing: it's just there. And it makes icebreakers more important as the Northern sea ice retreats. This could open up year-round shipping lanes north of Canada and Russia, significantly reducing the time for goods to move around the world. And a race would be on for strategic dominance!

For the other aspect of Thad's brave new world, we need a chemistry lesson.

The Machine Age depended on large quantities of metals such as steel and aluminum to make the cars, ships, buildings, bridges, railroads, yada, yada, yada, that constitute Twentieth Century infrastructure. But we've moved into the Information Age. Now we depend on metals we formerly considered valuable for money or personal adornment: copper, silver, gold, and platinum. Instead of treasuring them for their pleasing appearance, we require them as the best conductors of electricity. These elements connect the transistors on our chips, the chips on our circuit boards, the boards in our systems, the systems in our world.

But we have come to depend on a new set of metals, with strange names and even stranger properties. Unlike the structural metals like steel, or the conductive elements like gold, it only takes a minute amount of these elements to give the magic to our latest technology. And that's good, because these elements are scarce. So scarce that they are referred to as "rare earths".

And the New Gold Rush for these elements give Thad's latest story, the novel in your hands, its motivation. For those of you who want to get right to the action, skip the rest of this Foreward and dig in. For those who would like a little more background, more than enough to appreciate the headlines Thad rips right out of the Wall Street Journal, The Economist, and the New York Times, read on.

So, here is a bestiary of elements. All are metals. All make modern technology possible. And thus, all are the center of the New Geopolitical Game.

First, we encounter Lithium. Atomic number 3, the name comes from the Greek for "rock". Lithium is the key ingredient in the rechargeable batteries that have become ubiquitous in our game machines, cell phones, tablets, computers, not to mention just about every kind of electronic tschotke. Oh, yes, and Electric Vehicles. A man-made isotope of Lithium is in hydrogen bombs.

Lithium is not rare. There's probably Lithium in the soil or rocks of your back yard. It's just not very concentrated, except in a few places in the world where it's economical to mine and refine.

Scandium, atomic number 26, named for Scandinavia, is also not technically a rare earth, although it shares many chemical properties with them. Scandium makes structural metal alloys stronger. With it's expense, it's used primarily in aluminum alloys for aircraft.

Yttrium, atomic number 39, is named for the village of Ytterby, Sweden. A jack-of-many-trades, Yttrium is in lasers, superconductors, dental crowns, spark plugs, telescope lenses, microwave filters, high-temperature ceramics in jet engines, compact fluorescent light bulbs, and even cancer treatments.

Then we come to the true rare earths. The first is Lanthanum, atomic number 57, from Greek meaning "hidden". Scientists refer to the whole set of rare earth elements as "lanthanides" after the group's first member. Lanthanum is used to make battery electrodes, camera lenses, and catalysts for oil refining.

Cerium, atomic number 58, named for the dwarf planet, in turn named for the Roman goddess of agriculture, finds its way into glass as a yellow color, as a catalyst in oil refineries and self-cleaning ovens, and coatings for turbine blades. And in the flint of your Bic lighter.

Praseodymium, a real tongue twister, atomic number 59, means "green twins". Used in the powerful magnets that make your earbuds and smart speakers produce thumping bass, welding goggles, and the optical amplifiers that make your long distance calls possible.

Neodymium, atomic number 60, meaning "new twin", gives glass violet colors. It finds its way into lasers and magnets, particularly the magnets in the motors of Electric Vehicles.

Promethium, atomic number 61, is named for the mythical Titan who brought fire to humans. You will see its magic in luminous paint.

Samarium, atomic number 62, is named for the mine official who must have found the stuff. It's in lasers, magnets, and the control rods of nuclear reactors.

Europium, atomic number 63, named for the continent, is in the phosphors that make the red and blue colors of your various screen devices, from smart phones to televisions. You see its magic in the fluorescent lights of your office building or the mercury-vapor street lights that let you drive home at night.

If you ever had an MRI with contrast, you swallowed some Gadolinium, atomic number 64, named for a chemist who worked on rare earths.

The naval sonar systems, which will figure prominently in the story you are about to read, depend on Terbium, atomic number 65, also named for the village of Ytterby, Sweden.

My favorite rare earth name is Dysprosium, meaning "hard to get at", which say it all for rare earths. Atomic number 66 helps make the hard disk drive that stores these words as I write them.

Lasers and magnets employ Holmium, atomic number 67, named for Stockholm, Sweden.

Erbium, atomic number 68, also named for the village of Ytterby, finds its way into hard steel alloys, fiber optic cables, and lasers.

Thulium, atomic number 69, named for the land of Norse mythology, makes portable x-ray machines possible.

Ytterbium, atomic number 70, is the fourth element named for that quaint berg. No other place in the world can claim to name so many elements. It helps make the stress gauges that monitor earthquakes or weigh your truck.

Finally, we come to Lutetium, atomic number 71, from the old name for Paris, France. It's in your new LED light bulbs.

Rare earths occur in extractable concentrations in just a few places in the world. China has some of the largest reserves, and has been the most aggressive in mining, refining, and marketing these new strategic materials. Mining rare earths is difficult. Refining them either results in huge ecology-threatening waste, or high cost. China suffered the ecological damage, and has tried to contain the cost by forcing rare earth ventures to merge.

As a result, China has cornered the market for rare earths. Leaving high tech industry in the rest of the world, including us, pondering what to do about it. To find out, keep trolling the headlines. Or turn the page and start Thad's latest action-packed adventure.

—Dr. Philip M. Neches
Caltech PhD in Computer Sciences
Founder of Teradata Corporation
Friend of Thad

PROLOGUE

Command Master Chief (CMC) Samson was preparing to board one of the two Dolphin helicopters on the deck of the USCG Polar Star, one of only two heavy icebreakers in the Coast Guard fleet.

"Captain, we'll set the probes with Dr. Thomsen and be back before first watch"—8 p.m.—shared the CMC with Captain John Marohn, the master of the Polar Star.

"Make sure you are, CMC. The weather lieutenant says we're expecting blizzard conditions tonight. Also, be advised Jig Saw 2 is down with a mechanical," added the captain, referring to the second helicopter the Polar Star carried.

"Copy that," replied Samson as the captain departed the hangar deck on the well-past-its-prime icebreaker.

Celebrating his twenty-second year in the US Coast Guard, Chris Samson had ascended to his current billet of E-9, Command Master Chief, the highest noncommissioned rank in the service.

Samson next turned his attention to their gear. "Check the survival packs and load them on the helo," he ordered the members of his team who would be setting a series of electronic meteorologic probes, an assignment they had performed almost daily over the last month.

"CMC, what makes setting these probes such a big deal?" groaned E-3 Seaman Taylor Jacobs as he lifted the survival equipment into the chopper.

Boarding the matte-gray HH-65 Dolphin helicopter, Samson turned to his team and said for the third time that month, "Jacobs, don't let Dr. Thomsen hear you, and besides, we've been over all this. These sensors will track the ice melt and tell us when the Northwest Passage becomes navigable for commercial shipping. If ships can transit the passage," said the CMC with a grunt as he lifted one of the heavy packs onto the helo, "it'll cut thirty percent off the transit from Asia to Europe. That may not sound exciting to you, but it's a game-changer for about two dozen countries." Samson concluded, "He who controls the passage and can keep it open—wins. And President Russell has told the Coast Guard he expects the US to win."

Samson was referring to Andrew Russell, the immensely popular commander in chief. Russell, a US Naval Academy grad and ex-fighter pilot, was the forty-sixth president of the United States and had taken a personal interest in the Northwest Passage mission as a main tenet of his administration's economic plan.

Ninety minutes into their helicopter trip, Samson sat alongside his team of Jacobs and Hector Ruiz, petty officer second class (PO2). Also accompanying them was Danish mineralogist Alma Thomsen, PhD, from the University of Copenhagen, an expert in geochemistry, mineralogy, and petrology. She was assigned to a joint US-Denmark mission to better understand the origin and evolution of the earth's biosphere and hydrosphere and how tectonic processes were shaping our planet—Whatever that meant, thought Samson.

The airman turned to Samson. "CMC, we're fifteen minutes out." Samson nodded and turned to his team and Thomsen, holding up his left index finger and five fingers on his right hand to indicate they were approaching their touchdown location.

Dr. Thomsen and the coast guardsmen acknowledged Samson with a nod.

Samson turned his gaze back outside the helicopter and saw a streak of light shooting up from the snow-covered surface, but before he could alert the pilots, there was a tremendous flash of light. An alarm sounded as the helicopter started to violently whip around. They had lost the helo's tail.

In addition to rotating wildly, they started to oscillate as they careened toward the white snow-packed surface.

"Mayday, Mayday, Jig Saw 1," called the pilot.

"We're autorotating," yelled the copilot. "We lost the tail rotor."

The pilot yelled to his crew and passengers, "Prepare for a hard landing."

"Jig Saw 1, Home Plate, what is your emergency?" came the call from the Polar Star.

The pilots were adhering to the age-old adage that aviators around the world followed in an emergency: aviate, navigate, communicate. But the pilots of the Dolphin never got the chance to acknowledge the Polar Star's radio call.

As the snowy surface approached, the Dolphin pitched forward, causing the main rotor to strike the ground, which in turn caused the fuselage to flip violently as it impacted with great force.

There was a flash as fire leapt from the engine exhaust, which was showered with the remaining fuel from the copter's tank.

■

"Captain, we've lost Jig Saw 1," said the Polar Star's radioman.

"What do you mean you lost them?" the captain replied.

"We got a Mayday call from them. That's all we have, sir."

"What's their last position?" asked the captain in a terse tone.

"I'll have to replay the tapes to get an accurate plot, sir, but according to the flight plan they were about fifteen minutes from Probe 17, sir."

"What's the status of Jig Saw 2?" asked the captain of his executive officer.

"Sir, still down. Estimated time to repair another two hours," replied the XO.

"That storm's coming in and it's freezing out there. They won't last two hours," barked the captain. "What other assets are in the area?" he asked.

"Sir, the Canadians have an icebreaker eighty miles away, and the Russian Arktika is less than fifteen miles from the crash site."

There was silence for a moment, as the CO and XO knew calling for assistance from the Russians would be their option of last resort.

"What about the Navy?"

■

Representing one of the US Navy's newest and most capable attack submarines, Colorado was patrolling, submerged, approximately forty-five miles from the Polar Star but only twenty miles from the helicopter crash site.

"Skipper, we have a PAM coming in on the ELF," said the executive officer of the Colorado.

The XO was referring to a priority-alert message sent via the extreme-low-frequency, or ELF, radio transmissions that allowed the US Navy to communicate with its submarines deployed under the ice in the Arctic regions.

The XO handed the message to Commander Matthew Pryor, the first Black commander of a Virginia-class submarine.

From: COMSUBLANT
To: USS Colorado (SSN-778)
Subject:Priority Action Message

Remarks: 1. Coast Guard helicopter down 82.466, −118.375. Proceed at best possible speed for search-and-rescue operation.
2. Lend assistance to USCG Polar Star in recovery of helicopter crew.
4. Believe Russian Federation icebreaker Arktika and Yasen-class submarine in your AOR.

Captain Matt Pryor was an academy grad and a native of Kirkland, Washington. Pryor recalled what he'd said to his crew at his commissioning ceremony at their home port of Groton, Connecticut:

"When I walked on board, I was greeted by 140 steely-eyed killers of the deep." A year and a half later, nothing had changed, other than he had earned the respect of his crew as they patrolled the Arctic Circle in complete stealth. Pryor was known for mentoring his young shipmates. He would go out of his way to spend time with his junior sailors, knowing that many had chosen the Navy to escape a live of strife. He would advocate to his young shipmates, "The Navy can set you on a life of success and self-confidence, if you put the time and effort in."

Pryor went over to the navigation charts and called the officer of the watch (OOW). "Neal, I want a speed course to this plot."

"Aye, aye, sir."

Picking up the 1MC, the captain addressed his crew. "We've just been informed the Coast Guard has a down helicopter on our AOR. We're headed to lend assistance. Prepare to receive survivors. We'll be on station in approximately twenty minutes."

"Captain, I recommend course 088. Depth 150 feet," called the navigator.

"Copy that," replied Pryor. "Make your course 088 degrees, ahead flank. Diving Officer, make your depth 150 feet smartly."

The diving officer and the chief of the boat (COB) both repeated the captain's order, as was protocol. "Aye, sir. My rudder is standard at 088. All ahead flank. Making my depth 150 smartly."

Next Prior called, "Navigator, what is the thickness of the ice?"

"Sir, we are reading ice at three to four and a half feet," replied the navigator.

Captain Pryor knew he could break through ice three feet thick, but four and a half feet would be a test.

"Sonar, Con," called the captain. "Start a track on that Russian ice-breaker. Also, SUBLANT reports there's a Yasen in the area. Stay sharp."

"Aye, aye, Captain," replied the sonar lieutenant.

"Select discrete mode on the Barbeque 10," said the lieutenant to his sonarman, using the shorthand for their AN/BQQ-10 A-RCI sonar system.

The sonarman nodded as he adjusted his settings, saying, "Come on, baby, find me a Granny," using the nickname for the Russian Yasen.

The USS Colorado (SSN-788), which had entered the fleet in 2018, was one of the new Block III Virginia-class nuclear-powered attack submarines. She was the fourth ship to be named for the state of Colorado.

At 377 feet and displacing seventy-eight hundred tons, her

armament included Mk 48 Mod 7 torpedoes capable of being fired from one of four torpedo tubes, as well as Tomahawk missiles, which were fired from her vertical launching system (VLS).

Pryor next went to the communications station. "Send Polar Star: We are making best speed to crash site. Will apprise you of our rescue operations. Pryor Colorado."

It only took a few minutes before the navigator called, "Sir, we're at the crash location."

"What is the reading of the ice?" called Captain Pryor.

"Sir, the sounding shows a little over four feet thick, sir."

"Well, we have no choice. Come up to seventy feet," ordered the captain.

The submarine slowly rose toward the ice sheet.

"Captain, we are at seventy feet," replied the diving officer.

"Ten degree up angle, decreasing," ordered Pryor next.

The diving officer replied, "Aye, sir, point seven up velocity."

As the seventy-eight-hundred-ton submarine made contact with the ice sheet, the sound of air being forced into the Colorado's ballast tanks overtook the control room.

Captain Pryor called out, "One one thousand, two one thousand, three one thousand."

The sound of the hissing air increased.

"Again," ordered the captain, as the Colorado continued to press against the thick ice above its sail.

Counting again, Pryor could feel a slight rise, but they still hadn't broken through the ice.

"One-two-three again," ordered Pryor.

The diving officer now reported in a loud voice over the sound of the hissing air, "Breakthrough."

A few seconds later the officer of the watch added, "Stable ship, sir."

"Sail detail topside to clear ice," next ordered the XO.

Sailors climbed the ladder and emerged into the cold, dark Arctic air. Their duty was to push the four-foot-thick ice blocks off the top of the Colorado's sail, being careful not to let any of the giant blocks fall on them.

"Sail's cleared, sir," came the report after a short time.

"XO, COB, deploy search-and-rescue team," instructed Pryor.

The chief of the boat and XO were already wearing their Arctic foul-weather gear, and they ushered their sailors up to the sail.

Once topside, the XO surveyed the scene. He saw the remains of the Dolphin helicopter lying on its side about thirty yards away, still with slight flickers of flame emanating from its engine areas.

The rotor section, or tail, was nowhere to be seen.

As his team climbed down the ladder from the sail, they deployed across the wreckage scene. The forecasted blizzard had started to arrive, making visibility a challenge.

"Con, Sonar. We have an air contact. It's heading away from us."

An air contact? Pryor had been told the Polar Star's backup helicopter was down with a maintenance issue.

"Con, Sonar. It's a helicopter. It's heading to Sierra One," said the sonarman, using the designation for the Russian icebreaker.

Just then the XO radioed Pryor, "We aren't finding any survivors, sir. No bodies, nothing."

CHAPTER ONE

Rescue

As his eyes started to focus, CMC Chris Samson could tell he was lying in a berth, but it wasn't one from the *Polar Star*. Something was different. Then he heard a voice say in Russian, "On prikhodit v sebya. Predupredit' kapitana" [He's coming to. Notify the captain].

Next Samson felt a hand on his forehead. It was the chief medical officer of the *Arktika* checking Samson's pupils and pulse before saying, "How are you feeling? You're on the Russian Federation icebreaker *Arktika*."

Samson blinked a few times to clear his vision as he absorbed what he had just heard. Next, he felt a constraint on his left arm.

The doctor added, "Your arm is broken. It was a clean break, so I don't anticipate any long-term effects."

"How did I get here?" Samson asked.

"We saw the fire from your crash and sent our helicopter to rescue you and your party."

"The crew? Are they all right?"

"The pilot has a collapsed lung and we're attending to him. One of your sailors is fine other than some cuts and bruises. The lady also is fine other than some bruises. Unfortunately, the other pilot and two of your crew did not survive the crash."

Samson closed his eyes, processing the doctor's words.

"The names. Can you tell me the names?" asked Samson.

"Of course, our captain will brief you soon," replied the doctor.

■

A sailor handed the captain of the *Arktika* a report informing him that the senior member of the survivors was now conscious.

Captain Komarov was the master of the *Arktika*, one of a new class of Russian icebreakers known as the Project 22220 icebreakers.

The *Arktika* was a monster. At more than twice the size of the *Polar Star*, she weighed more than thirty-three thousand tons and was 570 feet in length. Furthermore, the *Arktika* was nuclear-powered and shipped more than eighty thousand horsepower, allowing it to sheer through ice that was more than nine feet thick. By comparison, the *Polar Star*, at four hundred feet long and thirteen thousand tons, was conventionally powered and could break through ice of only six feet.

It was now time for the *Arktika* to inform the Americans that they had rescued the downed Coast Guard crew.

Captain Komarov handed the message to his radioman, who called on the international emergency channel, "This is the Russian Federation icebreaker *Arktika* hailing the US Coast Guard icebreaker *Polar Star*."

Onboard the *Polar Star*, the radioman alerted his captain of the Russian contact.

With the captain and XO of the *Polar Star* at the radio station, the captain nodded to the radioman to acknowledge the Russian call.

The *Arktika* captain responded, "This is the master of the *Arktika*, Captain Komarov. We saw the fire from your helicopter and immediately launched our helicopter to conduct a search and rescue. I am pleased to inform you that we have successfully rescued your crew."

Captain Marohn of the *Polar Star* responded, "Thank you, Captain, for your assistance. What is the condition of the crew?"

Komarov suggested, "Captain, I suggest we first switch to channel 10 for more secure communications."

"Agreed, Captain," replied Marohn. "Shifting to channel 10."

Komarov then provided Marohn with status on the survivors as well as a list of the deceased.

With the blizzard now at full force, they agreed that no attempt should be made to return the survivors to the *Polar Star*. In addition, the surviving pilot was currently in no condition to be moved.

Marohn thanked the Russian captain again for his assistance and agreed to daily status calls.

■

The *Polar Star* was showing her age, witness her nickname, *Polar Spare*. Having entered service in 1972, not only was she well past her prime, but the US Coast Guard had to get by with table scraps when it came to budget allocations, making maintenance of the *Star* a never-ending challenge.

While it was true the US Coast Guard, now part of the Department of Homeland Security, had seen its budget increase since 9/11, the pace of its increases was always secondary to those of the other services. It was common knowledge that the current occupant of the White House favored all things related to naval aviation—almost to a fault.

That was about to change as the commandant of the US Coast Guard along with the chief of naval operations (CNO) met with

Andrew Russell and his chief of staff, Sterling Spencer, in the Oval Office to address a matter of national security.

"Mr. President, today we only have two heavy icebreakers, and while we have three under construction, that compares with seventeen for Russia, nine for Canada, and eight currently under construction for China," stated Admiral Steven D. Parrish, the four-star commandant of the Coast Guard. "Sir, the Russian commitment to its icebreaker fleet is a clear example of the Arctic's geostrategic importance to them, which has long been a priority of Soviet leaders."

"Yes, Admiral, I understand," replied an empathetic, but impatient, commander in chief, who did not appreciate those who stated the obvious.

Detecting the president's mood, Spencer intervened. "Admiral, let's get to the matter at hand."

"Understood," replied Parrish. "Sir, what brings us here today is that the CNO and I have worked out a plan to address our near-term shortage of icebreakers. We believe this proposal will support your Northwest Passage initiative as well, sir."

This was the cue for Admiral Jacobsen to enter the discussion. "Mr. President, we can take seven of the recently mothballed *Ticonderoga* Aegis cruisers and re-hull them, turning them into medium-class icebreakers similar to the current *Healy*. This will stem our shortage as we await the completion of the three new *Polar Security*–class heavy icebreakers." CNO Brian Jacobsen clicked the mouse on his laptop to show an animation of the Navy cruisers morphing into icebreakers.

President Russell, who was well briefed on the strategic importance of an open Northwest Passage, watched as the animation rotated the images of the cruisers turned icebreakers.

"How long and how much?" asked Russell.

"Sir, we can have them operational in eighteen months at a cost of $500 million per unit—$200 million to re-hull and $300 million to update the systems and propulsion," said Parrish.

The president raised his hands to his chin, which was always a good sign. "No one comes to this office asking for something without a 'but.' What will we be giving up to make this happen?"

"Sir, it's the *Harry Truman*," CNO Jacobsen replied, referring to CVN-75, one of the Navy's eleven aircraft carriers. "She is slated to enter RCOH this year—if we move ahead with this plan, we'll need to use the graving bay in Newport News that was intended for the *Truman*."

RCOH stood for "refueling and complex overhaul." Each carrier, when it reached twenty-five years of service, went into the yard for a two-and-a-half-year extensive refit and refueling of its nuclear reactors.

"Admiral, what will delaying the *Truman*'s RCOH mean for fleet readiness?" asked the president.

"Since we already planned to RCOH the *Truman*, she isn't in the current deployment rotation. We can keep her active in the Atlantic Fleet—but keep her close to home. The delay basically moves all RCOHs out two years."

"Won't that eventually leave us one carrier short?" asked Russell.

"Not this year or next, sir. It will, however, impact FY 2024, sir. We'll be down a carrier then," replied Jacobsen.

Returning to the subject of the cruisers, Russell said, "Tell me how seaworthy and effective these re-hulled cruisers will be as icebreakers."

Parrish launched another animation. "Sir, the *Ticonderogas*, at 566 feet and thirteen thousand tons, are already capable warships.

The design, which some of the engineers at Newport came up with, adds this extended hull." Again he clicked his laptop. "We'd add a ten-foot extension to the existing hull as well as incorporating bow thrusters. They won't win any beauty contests. That said, icebreakers never do, but the most important point is we can get them online quickly."

Jacobsen added, "Sir, there's another benefit to this plan. Icebreakers never have the firepower that Aegis cruisers have. By having cruisers deployed in the Arctic Circle, we get an offensive capability we've never had even with our subs. Plus, we can link their Aegis systems to create a surface and air active radar net. We'll have more command and control of the surface and air than the Russians, the Canadians, or the Chinese."

The president looked over to his chief of staff. "Sterl?"

"It's creative, sir. We know how important controlling the Northwest Passage is to our economic plan. This idea helps us even the playing field in the Arctic with the added benefit of surprise. No one, not even the Canadians, expect we can pull off this sort of feat in this aggressive a timeframe. But at $500 million a ship, that's almost as expensive as new *Polar Security*–class icebreakers, sir."

Admiral Parrish interjected, "The benefit here is getting them online in only eighteen months. It would take us seven years to add seven *Security*-class icebreakers."

The president had heard enough. "Gentlemen, work out the details and get this plan in front of the Senate Armed Services Committee. Code word it so I don't read about it in the *New York Times*, and keep me apprised of your progress." This was the cue for Parrish to close his laptop. Both admirals stood, smartly saluted their commander in chief, and quickly exited the Oval Office.

After they left, the president turned to his chief of staff. "Sterl, work with the Senate to find the funding for this, and do it behind closed doors. Make it a supplement to the Navy budget so it'll move faster. Also, look into getting additional funding to advance the completion of CVN-80"—the USS *Enterprise*, the latest Ford-class supercarrier. "I don't want to be down a carrier come 2024."

CHAPTER TWO

Singapore

At the age of forty-two, Sergey Latsanych was pleased with what he saw as he peered into the mirror in his Singapore hotel room. Latsanych was a senior member of the SVR, or the Russian Foreign Intelligence Service. It was the Russian version of the CIA.

A voice from the bedroom called, "Darling, come back to bed."

There, covered only by six-hundred-thread-count cotton sheets, lay an exquisite thirty-something Asian woman.

Sergey, a towel wrapped around his waist, leaned over and kissed his guest. "Sorry, my dear, but I have an appointment."

Letting off a noticeable sigh, the nude woman with jet-black hair stood and flitted by Latsanych on her way to the shower. For a moment Latsanych thought about joining her, but he knew his business couldn't wait.

As he finished dressing in a suit with an open-collar shirt, which was now the accepted dress in Asia, Latsanych called, "How about dinner tonight at the Marina Bay?" It was the most popular spot in Singapore, with its fifty-seventh-floor rooftop club.

"That sounds wonderful. Shall I make us a reservation for seven?"

"Better make it eight," replied Sergey as he grabbed his briefcase and exited the room.

Latsanych was meeting with officials from the Indonesian government to conclude what had been an eighteen-month effort negotiating a new fair-trade pact that would give Russia control over a large portion of Indonesia's rare-earth mineral mines.

"A fair-trade pact." Sergey laughed to himself, knowing there was no such thing, but that was the way business was done in countries like Indonesia—or in the broader Asian markets. People like Sergey would negotiate with a high-ranking general or minister with direct ties to the country's president. It went something like this: "General, my country is interested in negotiating a mutually agreeable arrangement for" whatever—be it the country's wireless spectrum, mineral rights, or even the contract to print the country's currency.

What would ensue was months of meetings so Latsanych could be vetted to ensure he wasn't part of a sting or a counterintelligence operation. This would often include joint family vacations with the principal as well as meetings across many countries with the goal of the eventual building of trust.

Once trust had been established, many millions if not hundreds of millions of dollars would be transferred to a series of private bank accounts in Zurich, Bermuda, and Anguilla. More recently, cybercurrencies like Bitcoin and Ethereum were used, as they were practically impossible to trace.

The result of all this work was something as opaque or seemingly innocuous as the notification of the release of an RFP, a request for proposal, for the rights to purchase a country's rare-earth metals or 5G spectrum.

Then Russia would participate in responding to the RFP just as many other well-intentioned governments and businesses would. However, these other entities would never know, although they might suspect, that the decision had already been made many months prior as to who the eventual winner of the RFP would be.

Of course, there were attempts to clean up the process. In 1977 the United States passed the Foreign Corrupt Practices Act (FCPA), whereby any American company involved in trying to bribe a foreign official would find itself in violation of the law and fined many millions of dollars.

Many US companies, especially technology companies, looking to close deals in the emerging markets had either intentionally or inadvertently run afoul of the FCPA, usually via the work of a local partner, agent, or introducer. It had become increasingly difficult to protect one's company from the FCPA because it not only extended to payments made directly by the company, but also included payments made through an agent. In practice, it meant that a local reseller offering something as generic as an Intel server, or a license of Microsoft Office or Red Hat Linux, could trigger a violation by making what is known as a "grease payment" to secure the order.

And it was always hard to determine exactly what had occurred. Say the US company contracted with an in-country partner to assist with importation duties and taxes related to the purchase of some hardware or software. In addition, the local partner might also provide local support, installation, and training. For that, the US tech company would pay the agent fifteen percent of the overall contract value. But you never quite knew where that fifteen percent was going. You expected the local agent to use the money to pay their staff to conduct the training and install the products, but you never were one hundred percent sure if some of those funds weren't going to an official or executive to influence their decision in awarding the contract.

More recently, the UK also tried to address this problem via their 2010 Bribery Act. It worked like the FCPA but was even more restrictive, in that it applied not only to government officials but also to any foreign executives or employees.

But while both attempts were virtuous in their goal, neither seriously prevented activities on which the likes of Sergey and many others around the world spent a large majority of their time.

And this case involved rare-earth minerals and lithium, which were becoming increasingly strategic materials. Originally discovered in the small Swedish village of Ytterby in the 1780s, rare-earth elements (REE), or rare-earth metals (REM), were a collection of seventeen elements of the periodic table. With exotic names like cerium, yttrium, and scandium, these elements were eventually considered essential to the production of smartphones, solar panels and computer chips. And while not a rare-earth mineral, lithium had become a highly coveted resource as one of the main components of the batteries that powered electric vehicles or EVs.

The United States, China, and Russia were actively working to amass controlling interests over the world's supply of rare-earth minerals and lithium. It was an arbitrage of the highest level, and the US, late to the game, was losing. Indonesia, long considered a top source for mining these minerals, had been mishandled by the US for years, going back to the Clinton and Bush administrations, and then continued under President Obama. That left President Russell far behind in the race for Indonesian rare-earth minerals.

Which was why Latsanych, one of the most skilled SVR agents, had spent the last year and a half working exclusively on this deal with the increasingly left-leaning government of Indonesia. It was considered a personal coup that Latsanych had edged out the US in securing the deal. Completing this arrangement would serve to not only enhance Latsanych's already well-regarded reputation within the SVR, but also justify his lavish lifestyle and exorbitant expenses, which he typically submitted to Moscow in a belated fashion.

With the end of his assignment in sight, Latsanych felt a bit of remorse over the thought of leaving the City of Lions, as Singapore was known. Singapore, with its heat and humidity, was, without question, the financial center of Asia. The London of Asia, Singapore was home to every major bank's Asian operations. As such, it was a beehive of capitalism and banking—most, but not all, of which was legitimate.

As a reward for his hard work, Latsanych's first stop this morning was to the exclusive mall at the Marina Bay Sands.

"The Rolex always makes a statement," said the salesman as he slid tray of Submariner-style Rolex watches for Latsanych's review.

Sergey picked up a few of the watches and tried them on, "Too big, too flashy," he dismissed them. "What about the Pateks?"

"Ah yes, you are quite correct that the Patek Philippe sends a subtler, if not more impactful impression."

After fifteen minutes of trying on different watches, Latsanych chose the blue-faced Nautilus 5740 Patek. He knew he couldn't wear a $120,000 watch in the Kremlin, but it would help with his image while on assignment, plus he liked it. Next, he selected a silver Rolex with a surround of crusted diamonds, the Pearlmaster 34, as a surprise gift for his dinner companion. In all, he spent more than US$170,000 on watches that morning.

By the time he was ready to leave, the valet had pulled Sergey's Audi R8 to the entrance of the Sands.

As Sergey drove away, advancing through the gears, the

unmistakable opening riff of the Eagles' "Life in the Fast Lane" blared. It was a song that seemed to encapsulate Sergey's lifestyle.

Blowin' and burnin', blinded by thirst

They didn't see the stop sign

Took a turn for the worst.

She said, "Listen, baby,

You can hear the engine ring.

We've been up and down this highway

Haven't seen a goddamn thing."

CHAPTER THREE

Camp David

Just as the Federal Reserve Bank held its annual retreat of leading economists in Jackson Hole, Wyoming, so too President Russell had taken to holding an invitation-only retreat at Camp David. This year's guests were:

Jeff Bezos CEO, Amazon
Tim Cook CEO, Apple
Larry Ellison Chairman, Oracle
Jensen Huang CEO, Nvidia
Elon Musk CEO, Tesla
Thomas Rosenbaum President, Caltech
Ed Holland Presidential Senior Economic Adviser
Sterling Spencer President's Chief of Staff

Also, in attendance was Lisa Collins, the director of the CIA and soon-to-be-announced nominee for vice president, replacing the current VP, Jack McMasters, who had been diagnosed with leukemia and whose prognosis had taken a turn for the worse over the past months.

Lisa Collins, a career CIA spook, at forty-nine years old and five foot ten cut a confident and striking figure. With more than a passing resemblance to the actress Bridget Moynahan, she had been given the Secret Service code name "Javelin."

Walking along the path to the main house, Andrew Russell chuckled as he said, "Sterl, these individuals all have homes and compounds that make Camp David look like a Hampton Inn. I think Larry Ellison owns his own island in Hawaii, doesn't he?"

Sterling Spencer tilted his head in agreement before adding, "That may be, sir, but there isn't a CEO on the planet who wouldn't give his eyeteeth to be here. Mark Benioff"—the CEO of Salesforce. com, who was increasingly showing an interest in politics—"called me trying to get an invite."

"I like Mark. Maybe we should include him next year. He very well could be the next governor of California," replied the president.

As President Russell entered the conference room, which more accurately resembled a hunting lodge, everyone stood. "Good morning, and thank you for coming," began Russell waving to everyone to be seated.

After pleasantries were exchanged, Sterling Spencer called the meeting to order. "Our topic for the morning is rare-earth minerals. We will be talking about what essentially amounts to *economic statecraft*. As such, I remind you that our conversations are confidential, classified and not to be shared outside this room." Everyone in the room nodded, then Spencer looked to Jensen Huang, the CEO of Nvidia, to kick off the discussion.

"Mr. President, the US will face a severe shortage of rare-earth materials and lithium in the coming year, if not months. China has put a stranglehold on the supplies from both Asia and Africa," said the Taiwanese American billionaire businessman and electrical engineer.

"Mr. President, as you know, we rely on rare-earth minerals and lithium for everything from iPhones to our laptops to batteries," added Tim Cook, with Elon Musk nodding in agreement.

The president responded, "We're in final discussions with Indonesia to procure access to a large portion of their rare-earth mineral supply."

That caused Larry Ellison to enter the conversation. "Mr. President, this is extremely confidential and sensitive information, but I have it on good authority that the Indonesians are going to award that contract to the Russians."

"And just how do you know that?" asked Ed Holland, the president's senior economic adviser.

"For this room only," Ellison said, "we have a mole inside the Indonesian military."

This prompted Russell to look to Collins. "Lisa, tell me Oracle doesn't have better intelligence on Indonesia than we have."

"Mr. President, I don't know the accuracy or validity of Mr. Ellison's declaration, but I can tell you our people are saying we have a good chance to secure the contract."

Ellison was curt. "The deal is dead. Indonesia won't happen for the US."

"I'm building three giga-factories in China right now," added Musk. "By doing so, we guarantee access to enough rare-earth materials to meet our needs. Tim, you manufacture most of your iPhones in China. Why not just leave it to the Chinese to supply you with what you need in terms of materials?"

President Russell looked at Spencer.

"Gentlemen, Lisa, we believe having access to an unlimited supply of rare-earth minerals, including lithium and cobalt, is of strategic importance to the United States. We cannot rely on China—or any other nation for that matter—to provide us with such critical resources. Not even Europe. If China were to wake up one morning and decide to cut off the supply of rare-earth minerals, it would cause at the very least an economic crisis."

"We simply will not allow that to happen," added the president.

Bezos said, "It's true our supply chains are intertwined, but I agree, you don't rely on someone who is a potential competitor, or for that matter a rival, for a critical resource. The Japanese taught us that lesson when we cut off their supply to oil in 1941."

Russell was still absorbing Ellison's revelation regarding the Indonesia deal when Thomas Rosenbaum, the president of the California Institute of Technology and a professor of physics, interjected simply, "*Greenland.*"

■

Exhausted after a long flight from Singapore, Sergey Latsanych stretched as he rose from his bed and gazed down on the Moskva River from the eighteenth floor of the fashionable Radisson Hotel, which occupied one of Moscow's buildings referred to as the Seven Sisters.

Identical in their elaborate Baroque and Gothic styles, the Seven Sisters—a series of seven buildings built in the post–World War II era—are Moscow landmarks. Today, three of the Sisters are used as government buildings, one houses Moscow's state university, one has been converted to apartments, and two have become fashionable hotels, one of which Latsanych found himself a guest on this cold February morning.

After showering and getting dressed, Latsanych took the elevator to the hotel's five-star restaurant on the very top floor. There he nodded to the maître d' and said something in a whisper, after which he was shown to the private dining room.

Positioned on either side of the doors were bodyguards, one of whom raised his wrist to his mouth to announce the arrival of Latsanych while the other opened the door.

Sitting at the table was Svetlana Ivanovna Zlovna, the director of the Russian Federation's Foreign Intelligence Service, or SVR, the department that had succeeded the KGB.

Unlike the Russian Federal Security Service (FSB) which was the equivalent of the FBI, the SVR is tasked with intelligence and espionage activities outside the Russian Federation.

Trim and just forty, Svetlana Ivanovna Zlovna was a formidable combination of beauty and guile. Intimidating in many ways, she had more than a passing resemblance of an older Margot Robbie, with a personality more akin to Nikita Khrushchev's. Wearing a fitted Alexander McQueen suit, Zlovna commanded attention in the private dining room. The white linen tablecloth set off her black suit and her immaculately coifed blond hair. She remained seated as she welcomed Latsanych: "Ah, the hero of Indonesia. Congratulations, Sergey."

Latsanych smiled and bowed slightly before sitting down. "Thank you and good morning, Madam Director. It's always good to be in Moscow and I'm pleased it's on the back of a successful mission."

"Yes, but I suspect it'll take some time for you to get reaccustomed to our winters after the warmth and comradery of Singapore," said Zlovna as she noted Latsanych's custom suit.

Sergey took note of the director's comments, as she never chose her words indiscriminately.

The Moscow of 2021 was a far cry from Stalin's Moscow. In

today's Moscow, capitalism and prosperity were alive and well and wealth was clearly evident. The people in power, be they in government or business, all took care of themselves in terms of luxury.

"Sergey, I have another assignment for you," said Zlovna, getting right to the business at hand. "Our success procuring the mineral rights in Indonesia has the Americans panicked. They'll have to secure another source. That means only one thing—Greenland. We need you to head to Copenhagen. In addition to the diplomatic steps we're taking, we need you to get close to the key Danish decision makers as you did in Indonesia. Your expertise in rare-earth minerals makes you the perfect choice for this assignment."

Zlovna reached below the table into her bag.

Handing an envelope to Latsanych, she said, "These are the Danish individuals of influence regarding Greenland and its natural resources. We need you to do—what you do best." Svetlana Ivanovna Zlovna smiled.

"Madam Director, I'll make plans to leave immediately," said Latsanych. You didn't become one of the SVR's most effective and reliable agents by taking time off—especially when there was work to be done, and there was always work to be done.

"But before heading to Copenhagen, let me ask you, have you ever been on an icebreaker?" asked Zlovna.

Their conversation continued, centered on the icebreaker portion of the mission. Eager to get started, Latsanych moved as if to leave, but Zlovna reached across the table and held his hand, adding with her irresistible smile, "Don't leave just yet, Sergey. I've ordered breakfast for us."

With breakfast finished, Sergey returned to his room, where he opened the envelope and reviewed the bios of the targeted people for this mission. As expected, most were Danish diplomats or military flag-rank officers, but two stood out: Søren Larsen, the CEO of shipping giant A.P. Moller-Maersk, and a Danish mineralogist from the University of Copenhagen, Dr. Alma Thomsen.

Latsanych called his administrative office and had them book a two-leg flight originating in Moscow and terminating in Newfoundland, Canada. From there he would continue on his odyssey, which would end with him eventually joining the *Arktika*. With his business out of the way, Latsanych turned his focus to more social matters.

"Katja, yes, it's Sergey. I am in town but only for the night."

"How does Artel Bessonnitsa at nine sound?" she asked, suggesting they meet at one of Moscow's most exclusive nightclubs, catering only to the ultrarich.

"Perfect, see you then, Kiska," Sergey said, using her pet name.

Changing into workout clothes, Latsanych headed to the Radisson's gym for a hard workout. Inserting his AirPods, he turned up the volume to get in the mood for exercise...

He was a hard-headed man; he was brutally handsome
And she was terminally pretty.
She held him up and he held her for ransom
In the heart of the cold, cold city.
He had a nasty reputation as a cruel dude.
They said he was ruthless; said he was crude.
They had one thing in common: they were good in bed.
She'd say, "Faster, faster, the lights are turning red."

CHAPTER FOUR

Back at Camp David

The president of Caltech, Dr. Thomas Rosenbaum, expanded on his Greenland exclamation.

"The sine qua non for a cleaner America—for a cleaner world—is access to REMs," said Rosenbaum using the shorthand for rare earth minerals.

"We understand we need them for everything from lighting to magnets to turbines and chips, but they are costly and dirty to mine. As a result, we have become dependent on China for eighty percent of our supply of REMs," added Spencer.

"And that needs to change, Sterl, if we want to decarbonize," directed the president.

"Quite right, Mr. President, but it's Greenland, not Indonesia, that's the prize, sir," said Rosenbaum. "It's estimated that Greenland holds one-quarter of the earth's REMs. As we move toward a future dominated by electric vehicles powered by lithium batteries, as well as smartphones, and laptops, which all require significant quantities of cobalt, not to mention lanthanum, terbium, and gadolinium, we'll need steady access to those materials. Mr. President, simply put Tesla and Apple cannot survive without an abundant supply of these elements," said Rosenbaum matter-of-factly, with Elon Musk and Tim Cook nodding in agreement.

"Mr. President, it is clear the economy is decarbonizing as we transition to EVs. And an essential part of that is having adequate access to REMs, lithium, and cobalt," added Musk.

This wasn't the first time President Russell had heard the name Greenland mentioned in connection with REMs. Just one month earlier he'd met with his secretary of state to open discussions with Denmark about a more expansive trade agreement between the two countries.

"Sterl, what's the status of State's progress with Denmark?" asked the president.

"It hasn't been a top priority, but given the Indonesia news, we can make it so."

The president nodded and added, "Ed, I want you to get involved with these trade talks. Let's make sure we expand the scope of the talks to focus on Greenland."

"Understood, Mr. President," responded the president's senior economic adviser.

"In the meantime, what can industry do?" he asked, looking around the table.

"Sir, we've seen the European Union form the European Battery Alliance, or EBA. The companies in this room can be the founding members of a US version of the EBA," proposed Bezos, with many of the CEOs in the room nodding in agreement.

Over the next two hours the president heard various other ideas of how the companies represented at the meeting could collaborate and invest in ways to position the United States to become a leader in the production and mining of *clean* REMs and lithium.

Ed Holland said, "Returning to the topic of Denmark. We will need to be careful that our actions and investments in Denmark and

Greenland don't ignite runaway inflation there. Denmark is a relatively small economy, and some of the plans I just heard will clearly impact their economy. We need to coordinate our actions."

These men, men of unfathomable wealth who were not accustomed to being restrained, especially where their businesses were concerned, next heard the president's caution.

"Ed's running point on this. Please coordinate your plans with him to avoid superheating the Danish economy. The last thing we need is a reluctant Denmark," directed the president.

"I'll leave you and Ed to work on the details, but I'll rejoin you for lunch. Thank you. Sterl and Lisa, I think we have another meeting."

■

After boarding a Russian fishing boat in St. John's, Newfoundland, it took Latsanych the better part of a day to reach the Russian submarine *Kazan*, which was cruising undetected about one hundred miles south of the *Arktika*.

The *Kazan* was the newest version of the Yasen-class nuclear submarines, which were replacements for the feared, but aging, Akula-class attack subs and represented a giant leap forward for the Russian navy.

More correctly categorized as missile submarines rather than attack submarines, the Yasen class's technical classification was SSGN, with the *N* standing for nuclear.

Coming in at a price tag of $1 billion per copy, the Yasens were intended to compete with the Virginia-class American submarines.

Equipped with a fourth-generation nuclear reactor, the single-hulled Yasen-class submarines are significantly quieter than their Akula predecessors. The US Navy has assessed the Yasens as capable of twenty-eight knots while running in silent mode, which is comparable to the Seawolfs and Virginias, which can run at twenty-five knots in silent mode.

With a crew of only eighty-five, the Yasen class employs an array of highly automated systems. By comparison, the newest US Virginia-class submarines have a crew of 134.

The master of the *Kazan* greeted Latsanych, welcoming him to the pride of the Russian submersible fleet.

"Comrade Latsanych, my orders are to deliver you to the *Arktika* as soon as safety allows," said the senior Russian captain.

"Thank you for your welcome, Captain. That is correct, as soon as you can get me to the *Arktika*, it would be appreciated," said Latsanych, who was happy to be off the decrepit Russian fishing boat.

"The *Arktika* is only one hundred miles from our position. We should have you there within a few hours. That is, if we don't run into any Americans. In the meantime, Senior Agent Latsanych, please make yourself at home in our officers' wardroom," said the Russian captain.

■

"She's bruised and will be sore for a while, but other than that she's fine," reported the chief medical officer to the captain of the *Arktika*. Joining the captain for the medical briefing was also the *Arktika*'s political officer, or *zampolit*, Yuri Borodin, as well as its chief scientist, Dr. Nicholai Petrov.

With that information in hand, Petrov made his way to Dr. Thomsen's cabin. Unlike on the *Polar Star*, Thomsen was given a VIP cabin on the *Arktika*.

Petrov nodded to the guard posted outside the cabin as he knocked lightly. "Dr. Thomsen, may I come in?"

Thomsen, who was resting, responded, "Just a minute," as she rallied her body off the bed to open the door.

"Dr. Thomsen, I am so sorry to hear about your ordeal. Although it does provide this unplanned opportunity to finally meet at long last. I am Dr. Nicholai Petrov of the National Research Tomsk State University," he said warmly.

"Dr. Petrov of the gadolinite disorder research? I know of your work," a now animated Thomsen replied.

"You flatter me, Doctor. That was some of my earlier research," said Petrov, clearly pleased.

"I read that work with great interest, Doctor. I've done some of my own work on gadolinium and terbium and used some of your formulas," said Thomsen, falling right into a technical discussion as Petrov had hoped.

"May I sit?" asked Petrov. "Perhaps you would like some tea or coffee?"

"I would love some, but first how are the others?" asked Thomsen.

Before responding, Petrov pressed a number on the handset and asked for refreshments, then asked, "Doctor, what happened on the helicopter? Do you recall or mind talking about it?"

A grimace formed on Thomsen's face. "It all happened so fast. We were approaching our test location when, all of a sudden, the helicopter started to shake and gyrate violently. There was yelling and then we hit the ground. I don't remember much after that other than being helped onto a helicopter, which I assume brought me here."

"I am afraid there were some casualties, including the pilot and two of the crew members. However, the copilot and two of your party are with us and receiving medical care. I believe they will recover."

"Do you know their names?" asked Thomsen.

"No, unfortunately, I don't, but I'll get them for you," said Petrov, observing Thomsen's concern.

Just then there was a knock on the door and an orderly brought tea, coffee, and biscuits.

"In the nick of time," said Petrov with a smile, as he took the tray and arranged the items on the table between them.

As he poured Thomsen some strong Russian coffee, he added, "I hate those things," referring to the helicopters. "I fly on them only because I must—but I'm never at ease. Give me an Airbus any day—then I sleep like a baby."

Petrov then asked about Thomsen's research.

"We're conducting research on ice melt," replied the Danish doctor.

"Ah yes, the effects of climate change on the Arctic. It seems we humans are doing everything possible to accelerate a climate crisis. Finally, the scientists are convincing the politicians that we must act on climate change. Hopefully it isn't too late," confided Petrov. "My passion leans more toward rare-earth minerals that I studied so extensively in university."

Thomsen replied, "Interesting. When I'm done here, I'm headed to Greenland to work on RE minerals."

"To be in Greenland during the summer, I envy you. It's so much better than the seemingly endless nights of the Arctic." Petrov smiled. "What's the nature of your Greenland research, Doctor?"

"I've been given a grant to survey the amounts of yttrium, lanthanum, and lithium the island possesses," said Thomsen.

Petrov's interest was piqued, but he knew it was time to wrap up and instead said, "Doctor, you must rest. I have already taken up too much of your time. I will leave now. I'm certain plans are underway to get you back to your ship once this blizzard subsides."

Then he added, "I know your ordeal was awful, but I'm pleased to have made your acquaintance. If you're feeling up to it, I'd like to give you a tour of our facilities on the *Arktika* and introduce you to my staff. In the meantime, if there's anything I can do, please do not hesitate to let me know." And with that Petrov made a small bow and left the cabin.

The Russian captain was checking with his officers about the other part of the mission. "Are you sure the team collected all the critical pieces of debris?"

"Sir, they found the rotor and as many of the missile fragments as they could. They loaded it into the cargo net, which they dropped in our wake before coming on board. Anything that they didn't pick up will no doubt be buried under five feet of snow from this blizzard."

"Just as planned. Very well," said the captain, now turning to Petrov, who had joined him along with Zampolit Borodin.

"How is she?" asked the captain, referring to Thomsen.

"Considering everything, she's quite well. Tomorrow, I'm going to give her a tour and introduce her to my team. Everything's progressing as planned."

Borodin said, "I'm meeting with the servicemen who survived the crash in a few minutes. We'll need to keep them separated from Thomsen for now. After I have completed my interrogations, I'll brief Moscow," he added, just to remind everyone of his importance.

■

Submerged at a depth of 150 feet and barely making headway, the USS *Colorado* was shadowing the *Arktika* as ordered. As long as the Coast Guard personnel were on the *Arktika*, the *Colorado* was ordered to remain on station ready to lend assistance.

The *Arktika*, which didn't care about stealth, was throwing off a cacophony of sound as it smashed through the ice sheet while traveling at three knots. At that speed, the *Colorado* could easily remain undetected, which wasn't hard for one of the newest attack submarines in the US Navy.

At the sonar station on the *Colorado* the supervisor was both the shift leader and responsible for training his junior sonar operators. To that end, the supervisor was instructing his third class on the latest state-of-the-art AN/BQQ-10 A-RCI sonar system. "Diego, remember the Barbecue 10 employs both active and passive sonars, which allows us to identify both surface and submerged contacts. Copy?"

"Copy, Supe. The BBQ-10 lets us track other submarines, surface ships, and detect mines," said Diego.

The supervisor was pleased that his operator included mines in his answer. Often that tripped up his junior sonar operators.

"And by using frequency modulation, we can filter out all that noise Sierra One is throwing off," added the sonar lieutenant, who had overheard their conversation. Sierra was the nomenclature used on submarines to track targets. They would never use the proper name of a ship like *Arktika* since they rarely knew the name of a target.

As the lecture continued, the display on the sonar system changed. Immediately the sonar supervisor grabbed the microphone. "Con, Sonar. We're picking up a new contact."

The sonar operator called out, "Starting a track on Sierra Two."

The supervisor started to tighten up the aperture on his bow array sonar while the BQQ-10 identified the contact.

"Con, Sonar. The BQQ-10 identifies the contact as a Russian Yasen-class sub."

"Sonar, Con. Give me a track on Sierra Two," responded Pryor.

"Con, Sonar. He's close, sir, bearing 288 degrees."

"Con, Sonar. Sierra Two is coming around. Sir, he's headed right for us. I doubt he sees us," said the sonar supervisor.

And why would the Yasen detect the *Colorado*? She was drifting at barely three knots, and at that speed she was just a hole in the water not making any sound.

Nearby in the control room, Captain Matt Pryor didn't hesitate. "Left full rudder, all ahead full. Twenty-degree down bubble. Diving Officer, make your depth four hundred feet now. Maneuvering make turns for twenty-five knots."

The chief of the boat put his hand on the back of the pilot, who was seated with the yoke in his hands that controlled the submarine's depth, and began to yell, "Take her down, take her down now, fast. Come on, we gotta go."

Pryor next ordered, "Sound the collision alarm."

A clanging rang out throughout the submarine and crew members quickly started to dog the hatches that separated each compartment, making the submarine more likely to survive a collision.

The control room was alive with the officer of the watch (OOW) and the chief of the boat (COB) repeating and yelling commands to the planesman, navigator, and pilot.

The 377-foot *Colorado* started to turn to port as it accelerated and dove to vacate the ocean where the Russian Yasen submarine was fast approaching.

"Con, Sonar. Sierra Two bearing 266 degrees, range one thousand yards. She's continuing to close."

At a twenty-degree down bubble everyone on the *Colorado* was hanging on to something to keep from falling over.

The captain refined his bearing. "Come left to 170 smartly," he said in a cooler tone.

The *Colorado* had just passed 220 feet on its way to its ordered depth of four hundred feet.

"Sonar, Con. What's the range to Sierra Two?" called the captain.

"Con, Sonar. I have Sierra Two bearing 270 degrees, range seven hundred yards, still closing. Sir, I'm getting hull popping sounds."

"Sir, she's surfacing," reported the sonarman.

With that last bit of news, Pryor knew that the crisis had passed. He brought the *Colorado* onto a parallel course with the *Arktika* at a depth of four hundred feet and matching her speed. The *Colorado* would continue to shadow but now at a standoff distance of one mile.

"Sonar, Con. I want updates on Sierra One and Two every five minutes," ordered the captain.

"Aye, aye, sir," replied the sonar operator.

Similar to piloting an airliner, commanding a Navy attack submarine can best be described as countless hours and days of boredom and routine interspersed with a few minutes of total exhilaration and adrenaline.

The captain turned to his XO. "So, a Yasen just surfaced behind the *Arktika*. Why?"

They didn't have to wait long for an answer.

"Con, Sonar. Sierra One and Sierra Two are slowing," called the sonar supervisor.

"Sir, they're stopping," updated the sonarman.

"XO, let's take a look," ordered Pryor.

"OOW, bring us in behind them quietly, five-degree up bubble, make your depth seventy-five feet," ordered the captain.

Once the *Colorado* was behind the two contacts, Pryor ordered, "All stop, raise the photonics mast." The photonics mast had replaced the periscope on modern-day submarines.

As the captain trained the mast on the surfaced Yasen, he pressed the button on the mast to start recording the images.

Zooming in, he saw crew members from the Yasen securing a boat from the *Arktika*. Then a figure dressed in black dropped into the boat before it headed back to the *Arktika*.

"The *Arktika* is picking up a passenger," said the captain to his XO, letting him take a look through the photonics mast. "XO, let SUBLANT know and send the video file with it," ordered the captain.

"Sonar, Con. Let us know when Sierra One and Two start moving," ordered the captain, which was just for added effect because he knew his sonar team would do so. Even the captain was still operating under an adrenaline surge.

Speaking to his OOW, he said, "When they start moving, give us some distance. I want to still shadow Sierra One, but with Sierra Two at close station we need to give ourselves a larger safety zone. We'll trail Sierra One on an orthogonal course. A mile behind and two miles amidships. And report on Sierra Two as she dives."

The captain, XO, and OOW spoke for a few more minutes with the COB joining them to review the details of the planned maneuver.

After taking a sounding of the ocean floor and doing a sweep of the surrounding ice, they decided to maintain a depth of 250 feet.

Just then the culinary specialist (CS) entered the control room carrying a tray with two thermoses of coffee, four cans of Red Bull, and four cans of Monster for the crew. The CS rightly predicted that the control room crew would be manning their stations for many hours and they would need the energy drinks.

Every US Navy ship goes to sea with an inordinate amount of energy drinks. It causes some withdrawal when the deployments are over, but while at sea it doesn't matter if you're on board an aircraft carrier, a destroyer, or a submarine: Everyone drinks these beverages constantly. Everyone was addicted to caffeine and adrenaline in the Navy.

Next Pryor went to the radio station to compose the message to SUBLANT along with the video file from the mast.

CHAPTER FIVE

Back on Board the *Arktika*

The *Arktika*'s chief medical officer pointed to the X-ray of the radius bone of Samson's right arm. "With immobilization it will heal with no lingering effects. You were lucky."

That caused Samson to ask, "The copilot and my crewman, how are they?"

"The pilot has a collapsed lung. We had to intubate him but I'm confident he, too, will fully recover in time. The young sailor is fine; he has no injuries."

"And Dr. Thomsen?"

"Other than some bruises, she, too, is fine."

"I'd like to see them," Samson replied, more as a statement than a request.

"I'll pass your request on to the captain," responded the medical officer as he left the small medical room. Upon leaving he ran into the political officer of the *Arktika*, Yuri Borodin.

"The chief is awake and asking to see the rest of his crew," said the medical officer. Borodin just nodded before entering the room where Samson was sitting. "I am Yuri Borodin, the *Arktika*'s deputy commander for political matters," he said, asserting a certain authority. "I'm happy to share with you that the members of your party are being well taken care of by the excellent medical staff of the Russian Federation's *Arktika*."

Samson nodded at the *zampolit*.

"Chief Samson, I am curious. Why would you be out on a mission with a blizzard bearing down on you?"

"The blizzard was still several hours away. Our mission was short, and we felt it was well within our safety envelope."

"Well, obviously that wasn't true or else you wouldn't be here," said Borodin with a bit of an edge.

"I thank you and your team for rendering assistance to us," said Samson, taking a different tack.

"It is fortunate, indeed, that we were able to rescue you before the blizzard hit. We wouldn't have been able to use our helicopter had it been a few hours later."

"I'd like to radio my ship to provide them with an update," said Samson.

"Yes, of course," replied the *zampolit*. "Unfortunately, the weather is interfering with radio communications. It'll be a while before you'll be able to speak to them, I'm afraid. Your Coast Guard seems to have a great deal of interest in the Arctic, no?" needled Borodin.

"I would say no more so than Russia's interest in the Arctic," replied Samson.

"Chief, you forget, Russia is a country of snow and ice. We're a winter-hardened people. Your Coast Guard seems better suited to the warm waters of Florida and California. You should leave the Arctic to those with experience of living *and fighting* in the cold."

Samson did not reply.

Borodin was satisfied with this first conversation and closed with, "Chief, you asked to see your men. I'll see to it." And with that, Borodin exited the room, passing the guard who was stationed outside Samson's cabin.

A few hours later Borodin was as good as his word, and Samson was escorted to see his team members. First was E-3 Jacobs.

"CMC, are you okay?" asked the young coast guardsman, seeing Samson's sling.

"I'm fine, Jacobs, how are you?"

"Not a scratch, CMC, can you believe that? How are the others?" he asked.

"Ruiz, the airman, and the pilot didn't survive the crash."

That hung in the air for a moment before Jacobs asked, "What about the doctor and the copilot?"

"I'm going to meet with them next. I'm told she's fine and the copilot has a collapsed lung," stated Samson.

"CMC, when can we return to the *Star*?" asked Jacobs.

"We'll need to wait till the storm passes. I would say we'll be here for another couple days. In the meantime, rest up. Also, if they ask, don't tell them anything more than your rank and that we were on a meteorological mission."

Jacobs replied, "Copy that, CMC." Samson patted the guardsman's shoulder and left to meet with the copilot.

Samson was escorted to the medical facility, where the copilot was being attended to in an open room with each bed separated from the next by a pull curtain.

As Samson entered, he saw the copilot was still intubated.

Getting close to the copilot, Samson asked softly, "Lieutenant, how are you doing?"

The lieutenant nodded slightly to Samson.

Samson updated the copilot on his condition as well as that of the rest of the crew and the casualties.

Samson's next stop was with Dr. Thomsen.

"Doctor, how are you holding up?" asked a concerned Samson as he entered Thomsen's quarters.

"Better than you, I see," said Thomsen.

Samson looked at his arm. "Oh, this. I'll be fine. How have they been treating you, Doctor?"

"Very well, Master Chief," replied Thomsen, not getting Samson's rank correct.

"Have you spoken with anyone?"

"There's a research professor whom I spoke with—a world-renowned mineralogist. Other than him just medical staff and the orderly," answered Thomsen.

"What did you talk about?" inquired Samson.

"I think he came by as a courtesy to introduce himself. I know his work. He's a brilliant scientist," stated Thomsen.

"The officers I've met seem very interested in our mission. Just to remind you—the less you share with them, the better, Doctor."

Thomsen didn't know whether to be insulted by Samson's last line or curious. "Master Chief, what do you recommend I say?"

Samson considered correcting the doctor as to his rank of command master chief but thought better of it.

"Keep it cordial but don't tell them anything more than we were on a meteorological mission to check the ice melt. With this storm we're going to be here another couple days. I'll try to check in on you regularly," said Samson as he exited.

A few minutes later there was a knock on the door and a Russian sailor brought a note to Thomsen: "Doctor, I hope you will join me for dinner tonight. Nicholai Petrov."

■

During the morning break the president was given his Presidential Daily Briefing (PDB) by the Joint Chiefs and intelligence heads.

With the Joint Chiefs teleconferenced in, the chairman (CoJC) began, "Mr. President, we had a helicopter go down in the Arctic. It was a Coast Guard helicopter, sir."

After discussing the casualties and survivors, the CoJC added, "Mr. President, the Coast Guard team was working on Caesar II," using the code word for the operation to install a modern-day SOSUS network in the Arctic.

The president knew Sterling Spencer, not having a naval background, was at a disadvantage where SOSUS was concerned. Also, it was fairly routine for the president to show off to his staff his knowledge of Navy technology.

Russell turned to Spencer and Lisa Collins and began, "Sterl, Lisa, the Sound Surveillance System, or SOSUS, was a passive sonar system developed by the Navy to track submarines. The Navy funded a research project, I think it was in 1949, led by a Dr. G.P. Hartwell of the University of Pennsylvania. Hartwell's group recommended the Navy hire Bell Laboratories to leverage their work in speech analysis and spectrographs in order to develop a long-range passive-detection system. This led to a network of hydrophones being placed on the seabed or towed along the sea bottom. Through the 1960s and '70s it allowed us, and our allies, to detect and monitor the movement of Soviet submarines."

While everyone knew the president was an ex–naval officer, the amount of detail in his soliloquy on SOSUS surprised even the admirals and generals of the Joint Chiefs.

Unable to resist, he added, "In the sixties a project code-named Caesar was funded to outfit four cable-laying ships, known as the Caesar Fleet, to install SOSUS equipment along the ocean floor. The team said they were doing research on whale migration. Which brings us to today and Caesar II."

With a smile the president concluded, "Full disclosure, I wrote a paper on SOSUS while at the academy."

That got a laugh, with the CNO adding, "I'm going to get a copy of that paper and distribute it before tomorrow's PDB, sir."

"But seriously, with this team working on Caesar II, is there any concern of foreign involvement in the crash?" asked the president.

"Well, sir, that's just it. Our icebreaker wasn't able to rescue the team since their backup helo was down. A Russian icebreaker in the area picked them up, as weather was setting in. The team's still on the Russian icebreaker."

"When do we expect to get them back?" an alerted president asked.

"The weather's set to clear in the next forty-eight hours," said the CoJC.

"Okay, keep me apprised. What's next?" said the president, turning to Lisa Collins for the CIA update.

■

The next morning back on board the *Arktika*, Borodin was meeting again with CMC Samson.

"Command Master Chief," said Borodin, extending the courtesy to Samson before getting to his point, "what can you tell me about your installation of a sonar net in the Arctic?"

Samson didn't react and replied in a flat tone, "Our mission was a meteorologic one, to measure the ice melt."

"Yes, I'm sure that's what you would like us to believe," replied Borodin, his tone tightening. "But in addition to recovering you and your crew, we also found your so called ice-measuring devices. Mixed in with your ice-measurement equipment we found a curious device, different from the other items. Now, I'm not an expert in such things, but I would say that what we found was an underwater passive sonar system. Does that help your memory, Chief?"

"I know nothing about sonar. Our mission was and still is to measure the Arctic ice. The United States Coast Guard does not conduct military operations beyond our territorial limits," replied Samson in a tone similar to Borodin's.

"This is becoming tiresome, no?" said Borodin. "I'm sure I'll get better results from your young sailor and Dr. Thomsen."

"Deputy Commander Borodin, I request you allow me to communicate with my ship."

"Of course, Chief. But it seems our radio communications are still being affected by the storm," said Borodin, who rose and exited without another word.

Samson took stock of the situation. Neither Jacobs nor the pilot knew anything about Caesar II, but both were young and open to coercion. Nor was Dr. Thomsen aware of Caesar II; nevertheless, she was a risk. Thomsen was smart and she was on all the missions to deploy the ice probes. It was possible she'd deduced the purpose of the missions. Plus, Samson had no insight into what conversations she may have had with others on board the *Polar Star*. More than a risk, Thomsen represented a wild card—an unknown. Samson knew the sooner he could get them all off the *Arktika*, the better.

■

After having breakfast in her room, Thomsen waited for Dr. Petrov, who had sent a message saying he would come by at 10 a.m.

Alma Thomsen, PhD, was one of the premier mineralogists of Denmark. Having graduated with honors from the University of Copenhagen, she was renowned for her work in geochemistry, mineralogy, and petrology. As such she was eager to learn about the work being conducted on the *Arktika*.

"Good morning, Dr. Thomsen, are you ready for our tour?"

"Good morning, Doctor. Yes, I am," she replied.

"And how are you feeling this morning?"

"Still a little stiff, but I think it'll do me some good to get out of this cabin and walk some."

"Of course," replied Petrov with a smile as he held the door for her.

"Your facilities on this ship are amazing," said Thomsen. "And your accommodations—each scientist getting their own stateroom. I wish we had that on the *Polar Star*."

"This ship is dedicated to scientific research, Doctor, and it was designed with that in mind," Petrov said with a smile. "Now, if you are up to it, I would like to introduce you to my staff and share with you some of our research."

"I would love to meet your team," said Thomsen with enthusiasm.

They descended two decks and entered a corridor marked with signs denoting each lab.

Their first stop was the marine biology lab, where a young doctor explained his work. "We're measuring the Arctic microbes' reaction to warming water. We have a series of tanks with microbes from the Arctic in water of increasing temperatures, oxygen, and salinity levels."

Thomsen asked a few questions and then they continued on to

the oceanography, glaciology, meteorology, and hydrology labs. It was a collection of scientific resources the likes of which Thomsen had never before seen on a ship. It far, far surpassed what the Americans had on the *Star*.

The tour and lab visits took them well past lunch, so Petrov had arranged a private meal for Thomsen, where Borodin would join them.

"Allow me to introduce Deputy Commander Yuri Borodin," said Nicholai Petrov.

"It is a pleasure to meet you, Dr. Thomsen," said Borodin. "Dr. Petrov speaks very highly of you."

Dr. Thomsen smiled as they all sat down and ordered from the menu. Thomsen was rather overwhelmed by her morning—and now ordering from a menu. The *Arktika* was more like a cruise ship than a research ship. She started to dread going back to the more primitive conditions of the *Polar Star*.

"I trust you've found your time on the *Arktika* pleasant and educational?" asked Borodin.

"Very much so. The facilities on this ship are beyond anything I've seen," said Thomsen, being truthful, as was her nature.

Borodin continued, "The Russian Federation values Arctic research, Doctor. The very fact that this ship, and four others like it, exists proves that point. As a Nordic country, Russia, much like Denmark, has a vital interest in understanding and protecting the Arctic."

Petrov added, "Dr. Thomsen, perhaps you'd be interested in joining us on one of our future expeditions?"

"Thank you, Doctor, that sounds very interesting." Then, being the perfectionist she was, she added, "The balance of my year is spoken for. First, I need to conclude my work on the *Polar Star*, and then, as

I mentioned yesterday, I have a project in Greenland set to begin this summer."

Borodin changed the subject in a rather casual manner. "I hope it's scientific research, Doctor, and not focused on weaponizing the Arctic as the Americans seem committed to do."

Petrov continued, "I detest any military interference with scientific study. This ship never gets mixed up in military operations. My scientists and I would never stand for it."

As the food arrived, Borodin said, "We keep our military separate from research work. This ship and its crew are dedicated to the advancement of science in the Arctic and Antarctic."

Thomsen, feeling a little defensive, responded, "My mission was focused exclusively on ice melt and the capture of CO_2 in the Arctic."

Borodin said offhandedly, "Is that so? We were under the impression your work involved the installation of a passive sonar network."

Looking at Petrov with some bemusement, she replied, "I don't know anything about that. My work is focused strictly on climate and ice melt."

"I don't know how you put up with it, Doctor," said Petrov. "The self-righteous arrogance of America. Their 'we're always right' attitude. Their condescension toward others—it's so insulting; it's so unsophisticated."

Alma Thomsen didn't respond.

Having achieved their goal, the two men felt no need to press any further. Borodin simply said, "Isn't this sea bass exceptional?"

The seed had been planted.

CHAPTER SIX

Back at Camp David Day Two

After taking the morning off to enjoy the amenities of Camp David, President Russell's guests prepared for the afternoon session, which would focus on the navigation and policy recommendation of the Northwest Passage.

An admiral from the Office of Naval Research, headquartered in Arlington, Virginia, teleconferenced in to give the briefing.

"Good afternoon, Mr. President," began the admiral as he brought up his first slide. "As climate change causes the Arctic Sea ice to retreat, the Northwest Passage, or NWP, becomes more open to shipping. This represents the potential for a shorter shipping route through the Arctic and a boon to international trade. Specifically, the NWP can decrease the trip from Asia to North America and Europe by one thousand nautical miles as compared to the Panama Canal route. This would cut four days off the average trip, saving an estimated US$200,000 per voyage."

This wasn't news to the people listening, as they had all read the pre-meeting material, but it did frame the discussion.

The admiral continued, "Currently travel via the NWP is not at all possible without an icebreaker escort, but due to climate change, it's expected that it will soon become navigable in the summer months without an icebreaker. However, making the route navigable year-round would require constant icebreaker grooming of the route, sir."

The president nodded to Sterling Spencer, recalling their recent discussion about converting mothballed Ticonderoga cruisers to icebreakers.

The admiral turned the presentation over to the secretary of state, Mark Holloway. "From a sovereignty perspective, Mr. President, the NWP passes through the waters of three countries: Canada, the United States, and Greenland. However, both Russia and Canada assert policies holding navigation of the NWP under their exclusive control. The United States, of course, differs in its interpretation of the status of these waters. Similarly, the international community has cited the UN Convention on the Law of the Sea, as the NWP connects two major bodies of water."

"I think our voice to date has been rather muted on the subject," added the president.

"Quite correct, sir," replied Holloway as he advanced to a new slide on the topic. "The last diplomatic progress point on the NWP occurred in 1988 with the signing of the Agreement on Arctic Cooperation, which states that the US will ask for Canada's consent any time we send an icebreaker through the NWP. However, in practice, we've never asked Canada for permission before we've sent our icebreakers through the passage. Nor have we ever requested permission for transit of our submarines."

Holloway's next slide addressed the indigenous people. "I should also mention, sir, the Inuit Circumpolar Council contests Canada's claim of sovereignty over the NWP. They say that the ice and water in the NWP is their territory."

Holloway then moved to his final slide.

Policy Options

1. *Charge a fee to transit the NWP similar to what Panama does with the canal.*

This would reduce the traffic through the NWP while generating fees that can be used to support the icebreaker fleet needed to keep the NWP open year-round. Furthermore, some of the funds could be used to assist the indigenous people of the region.

2. *Allow free passage of the NWP*

By opening the NWP to free trade, we would be seen as promoting global trade and the free navigation of the world's oceans. This could be an important precedent should China look to exert control in the South China Sea around the Spratly Islands or the Russians in passage through their Northern Sea Route.

Recommendations

1. *Immediately begin negotiations with Canada for the free transit of the NWP while advancing parallel talks with Greenland.*
2. *Create a fund to assist the Inuit people in the region through the State Department's US Agency for International Development (USAID).*
3. *Provide a significant increase in the size and staffing of the Prudhoe Bay Coast Guard Station in Alaska. Consider creating a new Coast Guard station at Nuuk, Greenland.*

"I should add, Mr. President, that Russia's interest in the Arctic centers much more around what they call 'the Northern Sea Route' than the Northwest Passage," added the admiral from the Office of Naval Research.

Bringing up a backup slide, the admiral continued. "Just as the Northwest Passage is becoming navigable due to climate change, so, too, are the passages north of Russia. This area comprised of the East Siberian, Barents, and Kara Seas is entirely uncontested Russian waters. This, more than anything, explains their large investment in an icebreaker fleet. Russia sees the 'Northern Sea Route' as more strategic and delivering a larger economic benefit. By way of example, a ship traveling today from Yokohama to Rotterdam covers seventy-five hundred miles and has to transit the Suez Canal. Were the Northern Sea Route to open, that trip is reduced to forty-five hundred miles. The duration of the trip would decline from forty-five days to thirty-three days. The Northern Sea Route promises about the same savings in transit as the NWP does, although it caters to an entirely different trade route. It is for these reasons I do not think Russia will present a deterrent to our opening and controlling the Northwest Passage."

The admiral's information regarding Russia's Northern Sea Route helped put the Northwest Passage discussion in a more complete context.

In closing, the admiral added, "Due to the thicker ice above Russia, it is projected it will take ten years longer for the Russians to open the Northern Sea Route than for us to open the NWP."

"Questions?" the president asked, formally opening the topic for discussion.

Ed Holland had a point to raise. "Mr. President, returning to our earlier discussion about incenting Denmark to give us access to Greenland's minerals. If we did charge for transit through the passage, as an incentive, we could provide free passage to all Maersk ships. That would be a sweetener that would help us on the Greenland issue."

The president thought about it for a moment. "Ed, it's true providing a chit for free passage to Denmark would be a good negotiating tactic, but free navigation of seas is a more important issue. The notion of charging for passage through the Arctic Ocean sets a precedent that is guaranteed to come back and bite us with either China in the Yellow and China Seas or Russia with their Northern Sea Route. No, no, we cannot charge for passage through one of the world's oceans."

Jensen Huang, the CEO of Nvidia, asked, "Mr. President, what makes you think Canada will relinquish territorial control over the passage?"

"Larry, do you have any 'special' relationships with Canadian generals or politicians?" joked the president as he looked at Larry Ellison as the room laughed.

"No, Mr. President, other than competing against them in the America's Cup races, I don't have any influence," responded Larry Ellison, chairman of Oracle.

Mark Holloway responded, "Our relationship with Canada is multidimensional, as you might expect. We're confident we have the levers necessary—trade, defense, and immigration—with Canada to get them to agree to our position."

Sterling Spencer added, "Russia doesn't have much to gain from the passage becoming navigable unless they thought they could generate revenue from it. Furthermore, they really aren't in a position to dictate control over the passage. Yes, they have an effective fleet of icebreakers, but they have much higher priorities to address than getting involved in controlling an international waterway. Plus, we can dangle lifting our sanctions on the German/Russian gas pipeline Nord Stream as an inducement. That's a much higher priority for them."

The discussion continued for another ninety minutes, after which the president's chief of staff adjourned the meeting as scheduled, with President Russell closing with, "Thank you again, everyone, for taking time from your extremely busy schedules. I trust you found the conversations enlightening and I look forward to spending more time with you this evening at dinner."

Again, they all stood as the president, Sterling Spencer, and Lisa Collins exited.

Ed Holland remained to continue his discussions with the group.

■

Later that evening, with dinner now over, everyone adjourned to the main living room of Aspen Lodge at Camp David at the president's invitation. Here the president looked forward to unstructured conversation with this elite group of business leaders.

That said, everyone waited for Andrew Russell to begin the conversation, which he did by asking, "Tim, how is your business in India?"

"It is going very well, sir. We've released a more affordable iPhone specific to the Indian market and we are having trouble keeping them on the shelf."

"We don't talk about India anywhere as much as we do China, but with almost the same size population, it clearly is a huge market opportunity," Russell commented, further seeding the conversation.

"Yes, sir," said Ed Holland, "but their GDP is a fraction of China's, barely $3 trillion compared to China's $14 trillion. Of course, they all trail our GDP at $21 trillion."

"Jeff, I'd be interested in your thoughts on China and their growth potential," said the president, speaking to the founder of Amazon.

"Mr. President, China represents a market four and a half times larger than the US, and their economy is growing at twice our rate. Any company who doesn't aggressively pursue both the Indian and Chinese markets will find themselves a minor player within ten years."

Tom Rosenbaum was listening to the conversation and working on his iPhone's calculator.

"It's true, Mr. President," added Elon. "To put it in perspective, we have 331 million people, and the EU has about 450 million. India and China each have 1.4 billion. Now, their economies are nowhere near as developed as ours, but both are growing at a compounded growth rate twice ours. Add to that the need to become cleaner in terms of the environment. China is and will continue to be key to Tesla. India is another story—we'll only sell ten to fifteen percent of the volume there that we'll sell in China."

Having completed his calculations, Tom Rosenbaum now entered the conversation. "Mr. President, I'm sure you've seen these figures, but if we take today's GDP figures—the US at $21 trillion and China at $14—and we apply growth rates of three percent for the US and double that at six percent for China, by 2034 China's GDP will equal ours. If we look out twenty-five years, assuming constant growth rates, our GDP will be $44 trillion, but China's will be thirty-seven percent larger than ours at $60 trillion, sir."

There was silence for a moment while everyone absorbed Rosenbaum's figures.

President Russell, showing how he had mastered his political skills since leaving the Navy fourteen years earlier, said, "And with that, I think I need another drink," to which everyone responded with a laugh.

"It's true that China's GDP will likely eclipse ours in twenty-five years or so but looking out further China's population is set to decline from 1.4 billion today to less than 1 billion by 2100. Plus, their population is aging quickly. It's another reason why our position on immigration is key to our own growth Mr. President," said Jensen Huang the CEO of Nvidia.

"Jensen's correct Mr. President," added Rosenbaum, "China needs to get wealthy before it gets old. That means you can expect them to be hyper-aggressive over the next ten to fifty years."

Again, the president realized that the Caltech president provided some of the most insightful advice of the group.

The president now looked to get Lisa Collins into the conversation. As his assumed nominee for VP, he wanted to see how she interacted with these giants.

"Lisa, you worked with Tim before on the North Korea operation," said the president, alluding to a successful mission that had occurred the year before.

"Quite right, sir," replied Collins. The president was referring to a CIA operation that involved the SS *United States*, the famous American ocean liner Apple had acquired and refurbed into a floating technology lab. Having spent approximately $4 billion to acquire and update the *United States*, Apple agreed to make its inaugural trip to North Korea at the CIA's behest.

"Tim, where is the *United States* currently?" asked Collins.

"In the Mediterranean, where she'll spend the next twelve to eighteen months. We're doing a technology tour starting in Spain, then continuing on to all the southern European countries before heading to Turkey, the Middle East, and then coming back via the northern African countries. I'm scheduled to join the ship three times during the tour."

The president added, "Tim, that was such a magnificent PR move—acquiring the *United States* and refurbing it. I think Steve"— meaning Steve Jobs, widely recognized as one of the best marketing executives and technologists of our time—"would have loved it."

"No doubt," replied Cook. "I had to work to convince my board to support the plan to buy the rusting relic. But now they see how popular it is and what a win it's been for Apple."

"Jeff, do you have any plans for a similar project?" asked Collins, showing some moxie.

"I thought about raising the *Titanic*, but, you know, it's too far gone," replied Bezos with a laugh. Then he added, "But as you know, my plans and Elon's tend to focus on space."

As the evening concluded, the president delivered his closing remarks. "Again, I want to thank you all for attending this meeting. I realize it isn't easy for any of you to take time out from your empires. The topics we discussed—in addition to being confidential—will have a measurable impact on our world's commerce and climate. I value the insights you shared with me and my team. As you know, I'm a strong believer in government and business working together to achieve mutual goals. That is to say our goals are aligned, especially where Greenland and the Northwest Passage are concerned. From time-to-time Sterls, Lisa, Ed, or I may follow up with you on a particular issue. And I look forward to meeting with you again this summer in Aspen. Thank you, everyone."

And with that there were a series of photographs taken and individual good-byes said. The president then retired, knowing that Marine One would be returning him to the White House early the following day, as it was his daughter's fourteenth birthday.

■

"Dr. Thomsen," said Dr. Petrov, "would you be interested in remaining on the *Arktika* and assisting us with our glaciology and hydrology research? Last night I read the paper you wrote at university. I know this is an area of interest and importance to you."

The possibility hadn't even occurred to Thomsen. Yes, she was impressed with the *Arktika*, and Petrov had been nothing but kind to her, but this was something she hadn't contemplated. "Doctor, I am grateful for the offer, but I have unfinished work on the *Polar Star*."

"I understand," said Petrov. "I was thinking about the work you'll be undertaking this summer on Greenland. I think we could give you a head start on that project here on the *Arktika*. Our work on glaciology would provide you with an important baseline for your work in Greenland. And I was thinking if you joined us, you would be our director of rare-earth mineral research."

Petrov could see that Thomsen was interested, and she clearly saw the nexus between the work on the *Arktika* and what she would be doing in Greenland. Not to mention the title would also be an upgrade for her.

Not wanting to rush her—even though that was exactly his goal—he added, "Take some time to think about it. In the meantime, Chief Samson is working on the arrangements for the rest of the party to get back to the American icebreaker. But we would be so pleased to have you stay with us." He then left Thomsen to think over his offer.

The more Thomsen thought about Petrov's offer the more it appealed to her.

CHAPTER SEVEN

Semper Paratus—Always Prepared

Now, with the arrangements made, the USCG HH-65 Dolphin helicopter approached the stern helipad of the *Arktika*.

The deckhands flashed international hand signals to the Coast Guard pilots as they executed a three-point landing on the massive nuclear-powered Russian ice breaker.

With the Dolphin secured and its rotors stopped, the occupants disembarked.

First off was an airman who double-checked that the helo was secure. He was followed by the *Polar Star's* chief medical officer and Captain Marohn.

An officer from the *Arktika* welcomed and guided them into the interior of the ship, where Captain Komarov officially welcomed them on board. "I welcome you to the Russian Federation's nuclear ship *Arktika*."

"Thank you, Captain," replied Marohn.

With pleasantries out of the way, Marohn was taken to a lounge where Samson, Jacobs, and the pilot were waiting. As Marohn entered, Samson and Jacobs stood at attention and saluted. "At ease, CMC," said Marohn. The pilot was on a stretcher and simply nodded to the captain.

Marohn spent a few minutes with each man, asking them about their health and thanking them for their service. Next Marohn pulled CMC Samson aside and asked, "Where's Dr. Thomsen?"

Samson replied, "I don't know, sir. I told her we would be assembling here before we left."

A minute later a Russian sailor brought a note to Captain Marohn. Opening it he read, "Captain can you please come to my stateroom—number 121. Thank you. Dr. Thomsen."

Passing the note to Samson, Marohn could see concern in the other man's eyes.

"Come with me, CMC," said Marohn as he followed the crew member who escorted them to Thomsen's cabin.

Upon entering Thomsen's cabin, Marohn could see she was surprised to see him and CMC Samson.

"Dr. Thomsen, you look well considering the ordeal you've been through," said Marohn.

"Thank you, Captain Marohn, for coming. Master Chief, you look well," replied Thomsen.

Then Thomsen dropped the bombshell.

"I have been invited to remain on the *Arktika*, and after careful consideration I have agreed to do so. It turns out Dr. Petrov and his team are conducting research that is very important to the work I will be undertaking this summer on Greenland, and this offer gives me the opportunity to get a jump start on that work," briefed Thomsen.

Marohn and Samson just listened.

"I've already talked to my government and the university, and they are both supportive of my continuing on here," said Thomsen with finality.

Marohn asked, "But what about your work on the *Star*?"

"Captain, it was almost completed, and Drs. Quick and Wenig are more than capable of finishing the work," replied Thomsen.

Realizing she had already made her mind up and knowing Marohn had no authority over her decision, they accepted her decision. As they exited the stateroom and entered the passageway, Samson asked the captain to wait for a moment while he turned and reentered Thomsen's cabin.

"Yes, Master Chief. Can I help you?" asked a surprised Thomsen.

"Doctor, I just wanted to ask one-on-one if you are sure about your decision."

"Master Chief, it is very kind of you to come back and ask, but I assure you my mind is made up," said Thomsen.

"You're certain about this. No one is coercing you?" added Samson.

"This was my decision, Master Chief. I hope that at some time in the future we will have the opportunity to work together again. Thank you," said Thomsen.

Something about Thomsen's decision didn't sit right with the CMC. But with nothing left to say, Samson rejoined his captain and along with Jacobs and the pilot chopped back to the *Polar Star*.

■

The president's personal secretary entered the Oval Office and announced, "Mr. President, the first lady wanted me to remind you that Katie's birthday party will be starting within the hour."

The forty-sixth president of the United States was just finishing up with his chief of staff on some budget discussions and replied, "Yes, thank you, Miss Ahern. I'll be leaving momentarily."

Miss Ahern didn't believe it but just nodded and exited.

"Mr. President," continued Sterling Spencer, "I've made progress with the Armed Services Committee on funding the Aegis icebreaker conversion proposal."

"Good," replied the president. "What about accelerating the commissioning of the *Enterprise*?" he asked, referring to CVN-80.

"I think it'll work out, but the Republicans are going to want something in return."

"Have they suggested anything?" asked the president.

"They aren't going to push too hard since they're aligned with you on military spending," said Spencer. "I believe they're going to want to expand the Opportunity Zones."

"I don't have a problem with that, do I?"

"No, but I don't want to give it to them too soon. Let me run with it for a while, sir."

"Very well, Sterl. Now I have a very important appointment to get to," said the president with a smile.

"Of course, sir. The last thing I want on my ledger with the first lady is making you late for Katie's party," said Spencer.

"Good thinking, Sterl."

Having left the West Wing and now entering the residence, he checked in with his wife as he changed into casual clothes.

"Have the guests arrived?" asked the president.

"Yes, everyone's here. Tonight's easy. It's tomorrow that needs more work. The Secret Service still needs to clear two of Katie's friends for the sleepover."

"Do you need me to get involved?"

"No, I'm sure the Secret Service doesn't want to get blamed for ruining Katie's party," said Kennedy.

"I suspect you're right," said the president with a smile as he finished changing.

The president and first lady gathered the guest of honor and their sixteen-year-old son, Andrew, and headed to the Yellow Oval Room of the residence. There they welcomed their guests for the evening: Lisa Collins and her husband, Dick; Kennedy's sister Hailey, who was Katie's godmother; the president's brother Mark, who was Katie's godfather, and his wife Jane; and the bishop of Brooklyn and dear family friend, the Most Reverend George T. Deas.

Kennedy and Andrew Russell welcomed everyone, as did the children, displaying the politeness that their parents had instilled in them.

Kennedy caught up with her sister while Andrew Russell introduced Bishop Deas to Lisa Collins and her husband.

The addition of Lisa and Dick Collins to the invitation list was no accident. The president and first lady were still vetting Lisa Collins as the replacement for the current VP. And that included getting to know Dick Collins too.

"Your Excellency, may I introduce Lisa and Dick Collins," said the president in a cordial tone.

"Very nice to meet you," replied the prelate.

"Lisa, Bishop Deas and I met when I was a congressman back in Brooklyn. He was an auxiliary bishop at our parish before being appointed the bishop of Brooklyn. Do you know the Brooklyn Diocese is the largest diocese in the country? In fact, it's larger than many archdioceses," said the president with some pride. The president excused himself and went over to welcome his brother and wife.

Lisa Collins responded, "Your Excellency, it's a pleasure to meet you. Having attended Georgetown, my affinities skew more toward the Jesuits," she said in good humor.

"Well, we won't hold that against you, and please call me George," said the bishop.

"In time I suspect I could get comfortable with that, but for now, if you don't mind, I prefer Bishop," replied Lisa Collins, displaying a warmth and politeness at the same time.

Nodding his consent, Deas asked, "Dick, what business are you in?"

"I am a partner at Watson, Larkin & Pierce. My expertise is maritime law, Your Excellency," replied Dick Collins.

"Fortunately, we don't deal with many maritime issues in the Brooklyn. At least not at the diocese," said Bishop Deas, extracting a polite laugh from the Collinses.

"Lisa, the president tells me there may be some changes coming your way," the prelate said.

It wasn't a well-kept secret in Washington that Collins was at the top of the list as a possible—or even likely—replacement for the ailing vice president.

"Bishop, you seem to be well informed. I would just reply that it is an honor to even be considered as a possible nominee," replied Collins.

That was the opening the bishop was looking for. "Lisa, when I went from being an auxiliary bishop to becoming the bishop of the Brooklyn Diocese, I underestimated the amount of politics involved and the savvy I needed in order to be successful. Do you worry about that in the potential transition from the CIA to the political position of vice president?"

With a knowing smile, Collins contemplated her response. She also knew that when the president invited her and her husband to come to the White House for a social event, it would be part of the vetting process.

It occurred to her that Bishop Deas must, indeed, be a trusted confidant of the president's to be enlisted as part of the VP vetting team.

"Bishop Deas, I assure you that dealing with the White House and Congress, as well as the NSA, FBI, and Justice Department on a daily basis has sharpened my political acumen to a level that makes me very confident that I can navigate the waters of the Russell administration as well as those of the media," replied Collins.

The bishop responded, "Your response reminds me of a line from Shakespeare's *Lear*: 'Let me, if not by birth, have lands by wit. All with me's meet that I can fashion fit.'"

Next the bishop circled over to talk with Andrew Russell Jr., the president's teenage son.

"Andrew, my boy, how have you been?" asked the bishop, who was like an uncle to the first family. In fact, it was Bishop Deas, then Monsignor Deas, who baptized the Russell children at Our Lady of Angels parish in Bay Ridge, Brooklyn.

"Fine, Bishop Deas. I'm trying out for the lead in the spring musical," replied Andrew, happy to see the bishop and to share the news.

"What play are they performing?"

"*The Music Man*," said Andrew. "I'm trying out for Professor Harold Hill."

Bishop Deas smiled and replied, "But of course. When I was in the seminary, we used to sing all the songs from it. It is a wonderful play, and I can see you as Harold Hill."

Bishop Deas had always been supportive of the Russell children. He always was and would always be.

After meeting everyone and catching up with Kennedy and Katie, the bishop got some time alone with the president.

"George, how are things in Brooklyn? You know I miss it," the president said in an unguarded moment.

"Brooklyn is fine, but I'm afraid there is a lot of consolidation going on in terms of parishes," said the bishop, whose words denoted the stress of any person responsible for making decisions that impacted thousands of people.

The president easily recognized that tone and could relate, of course.

"There's some news I'd like to share with you in confidence," said the bishop quietly.

"Yes?" replied the president, now completely focused.

"It won't be announced until next week, but the Holy Father has made me a cardinal-designate, with the plan that I become the archbishop of Washington."

A large smile appeared on the president's face. "Congratulations, George, or should I say, Your Eminence? That's wonderful news," a clearly moved president responded.

"Thank you, Mr. President. I can't help but think our friendship factored into the Holy Father's decision," said the cardinal-designate.

"As it should," replied the president, adding, "George, can I share this with Kennedy and the family?"

"Of course, sir, but I would appreciate it if you could keep the circle small until it's publicly announced."

At that moment, the usher of the White House entered to let Kennedy know that dinner was ready to be served.

Everyone adjourned to the residence's dining room, with the customary seating of the president and first lady at opposite ends of the table, with Katie next to the president as the guest of honor and Andrew sitting to his mother's right. The rest of the seats were filled by the six guests.

With everyone seated, the president said, "I'd like to make a toast." As he stood, so did everyone else.

Raising his glass and standing, the president spoke. "On the occasion of our daughter Katherine Elizabeth Russell's fourteenth birthday. To our dear, dear Katie, as Bob Dylan so aptly put it years ago—'May you build a ladder to the stars and climb on every rung, and may you stay forever young.'"

Everyone stood when the president stood now joined in with calls of, "Happy birthday, Kate!"

While remaining standing, the president said, "Your Excellency, if you'd say grace."

Bishop Deas began, "Father, we thank you for your guidance and love as we come together to celebrate this gifted young lady's birthday. As her namesake, Saint Katherine Drexel, whose symbol was the heart, reminds us, 'Let us open wide our hearts.' Our Katie exemplifies this as a person who is charitable and always ready to lend a hand or to share a word of encouragement to others." The bishop noticed Katie blushing and added, "You'll forgive me, Lord, but I admit to being biased in this particular case."

The bishop then concluded as he blessed the table with, "God bless our nation and those who struggle and need our help. God bless our troops and keep them from harm's way. And God save our president."

Everyone joining in by saying, "Amen."

The meal then commenced, with small talk and laughter until it was time for the dessert. Before the staff turned off the lights and brought in the birthday cake, the president chimed his wineglass with his knife.

"If I might," said the president, standing, which caused everyone at the table to stand again. "We have another occasion to celebrate this evening," he said having picked up a leather folio placed next to his seat. "This afternoon I received this letter:

Mr. President,

I extend my best wishes on the occasion of your daughter's birthday.

I am equally pleased to share with you today I have elevated the bishop of Brooklyn, His Excellency George T. Deas, to cardinal-designate, archbishop of Washington, D.C.

Ego Franciscus Episcopus Ecclesiae Catholicae

Which, translated, is "I, Francis, Bishop of the Catholic Church."

Applause broke out and everyone toasted again with a clearly moved and embarrassed George Deas.

Shortly thereafter, the lights went out and the usher carried in a cake with fourteen candles and one for good luck as everyone sang "Happy Birthday" to a beaming, beautiful young lady.

■

On Sunday afternoon Andrew Russell had some time to catch up with his wife.

"Ken, what do you think of Lisa Collins?" asked the president.

Kennedy Russell sat on the couch in the White House's living room across from her husband, who was seated in an armchair. "I assume you're asking with regard to replacing Jack."

He nodded and she replied, "She's intelligent and clearly self-confident. Her job has prepared her well on intelligence and international affairs."

The president nodded. "Yes, she has all those strengths."

"And she's extremely photogenic," added the first lady.

"Is that a problem?" asked the president.

"Of course, not. It is an asset," said Kennedy Russell.

Kennedy then got right to the crux of the matter, which was her style. "But politically speaking she's inexperienced. That's your biggest risk. She's never run for office; can she manage all the trade-offs that come with being a politician?"

The president valued his wife's opinion more than anyone else's.

Before letting the president respond, Kennedy added, "On the other hand, a female VP would make a lot of people happy, like fifty percent of the electorate, and bring a lot of pluses. And you would be setting her up to succeed you, making her the first woman president. That would be another milestone for the country and another major accomplishment that you orchestrated."

"Well, I meet with her and Sterl tomorrow. If the meeting goes well, I plan to tell her that I'm going to nominate her to replace Jack."

The first lady asked, "How's Jack doing?"

"Not well," said the president with a grimace. "He's headed to Sloan Kettering tomorrow. Hopefully, they'll be able to start him on a regimen that he couldn't get at Bethesda. The update I received didn't have a good prognosis, though."

Kennedy replied, "I'll call Helen tomorrow to offer our support."

The president realized replacing his vice president would present an unplanned challenge for his administration, as well as an added effort to bring Collins up to speed, not to mention he was deeply concerned about his friend Jack McMasters. But the realities of life were forced on him as they were on everyone.

CHAPTER EIGHT

Psyops

On board the *Arktika*, the next phase of the operation was about to begin.

Sergey Latsanych entered Dr. Petrov's office, where he was meeting with Alma Thomsen.

"Dr. Thomsen, I would like to introduce you to Sergey Latsanych from our Commerce Directorate," said Petrov.

"Nice to meet you," replied Thomsen.

"Dr. Petrov speaks highly of you," said Latsanych, leveraging his charm on the Danish doctor.

"That is quite flattering, Mr. Latsanych. What brings you to the *Arktika*?" asked Thomsen.

"To be candid, you do," said Latsanych.

"I'm confused," Thomsen responded.

"Then allow me to explain. I've been put in charge of the Russian Federation's negotiating team for Greenland's mineral rights. I believe you will be instrumental in shaping your country's position on awarding that contract," said Latsanych.

"I think you overestimate my influence, Mr. Latsanych. I suspect I'll be asked to review proposals from an ecological perspective. But that's all. I seriously doubt I'll have any input into the terms and conditions of the trade agreement," said a rather modest Thomsen.

"Well, it's the ecological aspects of the agreement that have brought me to the *Arktika*. You see, Dr. Thomsen, Russia will be advocating for a restrained approach to mining the resources of Greenland. We think that will be philosophically opposite from what the Americans will propose," stated Latsanych.

"Restrained in what way?" asked Thomsen.

"We believe the Americans will propose an extremely aggressive plan to mine minerals from Greenland. And, in doing so, will do irreparable damage to the Greenland ecosystem. The Russian Federation, on the other hand, will be proposing a very restrained approach to mining on Greenland. We'll advocate for closing the American Air Force base at Thule, which, as you know, with their Camp Century Project, caused a blight on Greenland even to this day," continued Latsanych.

Thomsen was familiar with the Camp Century issue. Back in the 1960s the Americans built a base incorporating a series of subterranean tunnels in the tundra that would hide missiles from the Russians. The project was abandoned after numerous challenges presented themselves having to do with the constantly shifting glacial subsurface ice.

"I suspect you're also aware of the nuclear waste the Americans left behind on Greenland after their failed Camp Century project," added Latsanych.

"Yes, I'm aware," answered Thomsen. "During my master's studies I wrote a paper on the remaining American hazardous material buried under the ice and how it's become an environmental concern."

Petrov nodded, adding, "We must protect that ecosystem. It is so fragile; it must not go the way of the Brazilian rain forest."

"Dr. Thomsen, my presence here is to gain your insights on how we can tailor our proposal so that both Denmark and Russia can be model stewards of one of the last remaining wildernesses on the planet," said Latsanych in a convincing manner.

The next phase of Latsanych's plan was more devious and involved what is called psychological operations, or psyops.

With his meeting with Thomsen concluded, Latsanych departed the *Arktika*'s dining room to meet with the two psyops operatives who were on board.

Introduced during the Cold War, modern-day psychological operators rely on behavior-modification techniques and an array of psycho-psychotic drugs as well as environmental stimuli.

Psychological operations, an offshoot of psychological warfare (psywar), were often used to induce confessions or to modify attitudes or behaviors of civilian or government targets.

Experts in their field, psyops, or what are referred to as "black hat" operatives, specialized in employing unconventional techniques that often achieved rapid results, in many cases in just a matter of days.

Latsanych requested a briefing from the two operatives, who provided the following plan: "We'll slip Thomsen a barbiturate narcotic every evening at dinner. Then, once she is asleep, we'll bring her to our lab, where we'll conduct the behavior-modification therapy."

Upon entering their suite, Latsanych saw a setup of twelve ring lights on tripods, a bed that had restraints, as well as headphones and multiple video screens. Off to the side was an array of syringes and vials. Latsanych also noticed in the corner a car battery and a roll of duct tape.

"Our plan is to begin tonight and to continue every night until we're done," said the thirty-something dark-haired operative.

Realizing he had seen and heard enough, Latsanych said, "I will leave you, then. I would appreciate you providing me with a daily update as to your progress."

"Of course, Colonel Comrade Latsanych. We will keep you apprised of our progress," said the lead operative, utilizing Latsanych's formal rank, something very few people used. In addition, both agents were more than aware of Latsanych's rumored *close* relationship with Director Zlovna.

■

Early the next morning, Lisa Collins sat in the outer office of the Oval Office. She was understandably early, which gave her a few minutes to compose herself as she prepared to go into the most important meeting of her career—of her life.

As she sat there, she began an exercise to slow her breathing in order to clear her mind. Then she went over her goals for the meeting: communicate clearly, lay out how she could complement the administration, be confident but don't dominate.

Collins caught herself on the last point. She reflected on how disappointing it was that in 2021 women still needed to make sure they didn't dominate a meeting, as it would surely be seen as a negative. Then she she remembered the advice her father would tell her when she ran cross country in high school, "Lisa, run your race and let the others try and catch up."

She smiled and would follow her father's advice and, in this case, let the boys try and catch up.

Her attention was jarred back to the present when Alice Ahern said, "Director Collins, the president will see you now."

"Good morning, Mr. President," said Collins as she entered the Oval Office.

The president made his way to his armchair at the head of the two couches that framed the fireplace. On the president's left sat Sterling Spencer, while Collins sat to the president's right.

The president began, "Lisa, you know Jack McMasters has leukemia and his prognosis is not good. He plans to resign, and I support the decision. Not since 1973 with Spiro Agnew and President Ford has the country had to replace a sitting VP. The Twenty-Fifth Amendment allows for it, but both houses of Congress have to approve whomever I nominate. What would you say if I were to nominate you for VP?"

Pausing just a second, Collins replied, "I would say I would be honored, Mr. President."

Sterling Spencer got right to the point. "Lisa, as opposed to the Agency, the VP position is a political position. The president and I are very impressed with your work at the CIA, but this is a different assignment that requires a political finesse that, quite frankly, it's not clear you have."

Sitting with perfect posture, Lisa Collins was prepared for the objection and addressed it while looking directly at him. She had found that even when sitting, her five-foot ten-inch frame conveyed confidence. That plus the fact Sterling Spencer was shorter than Collins added to her advantage.

Collins's height would not be a problem for Andrew Russell, however, as he was six foot one. As a matter of fact, his staff had amassed an array of photos of the two of them together and were very pleased with the optics. However, neither the campaign nor the president's staff dared tell the president that one of the pluses of having Collins as VP was how photogenic they would be together.

"There's no doubt where political experience is considered I am at a deficit," replied Collins. "Although to suggest I've been immune to politics as director of the CIA is simply not accurate. More importantly, I believe my experience and position on material matters complement yours, sir," added Collins, now looking directly at the president.

"How's that, Lisa?" asked the president, eager to hear her thoughts.

"Mr. President, for example, your naval career has been a great asset not only in guiding you while in office but also while campaigning. Everything that comes with the persona of a fighter pilot makes you extraordinarily appealing to voters. In addition, your knowledge of military matters and capabilities is second to none and has been a great asset to the country," said Collins.

The president smiled and said, "So why do I feel there's a 'but' coming . . . ?"

"No 'but,' sir," said Collins, smiling. "My views are complementary to yours, with some important nuances."

"And they are?" asked the president.

"Sir, on defense—having led the CIA over the last two and a half years I've learned our biggest threats today are cyber in nature. Mr. President, you advocate for a Navy with twelve aircraft carriers costing $14 billion each. Sir, it costs us another billion a year to operate each carrier. We're also in the process of replacing the Ohio-class submarines with the new Columbia class at a projected program cost of at least $150 billion. Sir, if I were in your seat, I'd support a smaller carrier fleet and the same with the Columbias. I'd build eight of them, not twelve, and the dollars I'd save I'd put toward cyber, both offensive and defensive. To me, that would be the best use of our Department of Defense's $733 billion budget," said Collins.

"Let's say I agree with you—which I don't. How would you go about implementing your vision, Lisa?" asked the president.

"Sir, I would go to the Armed Services Committee behind closed doors and present the plan with supporting documentation," said Collins.

"Lisa," said Spencer, "the leading Democrats on that committee—people from our party—come from Connecticut, Virginia, California, and Washington. Where do you think we build and port those carriers and submarines? And how do you think the Joint Chiefs and the Pentagon would react to your plan?"

The president offered, "Lisa, you just laid out *what* you'd do. Sterl is talking about *how* to get it done. Trust me, politics is more about the *hows* and *whens* than the *whats*."

"My point, Mr. President, is that I envision our country's defense based more on software than your vision of steel—of carriers and submarines. The threat is changing; so must our response to it," said Collins.

The president brought his chin to rest on his folded hands, which was a sign he was mulling over Collins's words. Not only her words but how she presented them.

Next the president looked at Spencer, who imperceptibly nodded his support.

A moment later the president held out his hand and spoke. "Director Collins, I am pleased to nominate you as the fiftieth vice president of the United States."

After a moment to take in the historic nature of the president's words and offer, Lisa Collins took the president's hand and responded, "Mr. President, thank you, sir. I look forward to the opportunity to support our country as vice president. As always, I am honored to serve at your pleasure."

The president nodded, taking in the moment too.

"Sterl, lay out the schedule and next steps in the process," said the president.

"Tomorrow, the president will announce that he has accepted Vice President McMasters's resignation due to health reasons. That will set off the administration's search for a replacement. That will take exactly one week. Meaning next Tuesday, the president will nominate you officially as VP. That'll start a shortened three-week period where you'll be vetted by members of the Senate and House. You'll meet with members of all the critical committees as well as the majority and minority leaders. Three and a half weeks from tomorrow the House and Senate will vote to confirm your nomination. We expect the Senate will confirm you by a margin of no less than 93 to 7. The House margin is projected to be 407 to 28. The day after the vote you will take the oath of office. We don't want the country to be without a VP for any longer than is absolutely necessary."

"Who do you recommend replacing you?" asked the president.

Prepared for the question, Collins replied, "My deputy director, Dan McCauley."

The president nodded, having expected Collins's answer.

"Congratulations, Lisa. Let's keep a lid on this until next Tuesday," said the president as he stood, and they shook hands again.

"Congratulations," added Spencer, who also shook Collins's hand.

"Sir, we have a Sit Room meeting in ten minutes," said Spencer, getting on with the next item on the president's schedule.

With that Lisa Collins stood and left the room, leaving Spencer and the president alone in the Oval.

After she left, the president asked, "What do you think?"

"I think she'll be fine. Yes, she'll make some mistakes, but she brings a perspective that's different from yours, sir, which is what we wanted. Plus, she tested very highly with our focus groups," replied the chief of staff.

"We'll need to bring her along in terms of her political savvy and campaigning. Encourage her to keep Jack's chief of staff. Sean will be a big help to her," added the president as they left the Oval for the secure Situation Room, located in the subbasement of the White House.

■

It was the end of Thomsen's first week on the *Arktika* and she was beginning to feel more at home, although she was having trouble sleeping and seemed to be perpetually tired, which manifested itself in her being less sharp than she usually was.

When she joined Nicholai Petrov for dinner, their conversation tilted toward research, as it usually did. "Alma, did you notice today's ice crystals were arranged in layers of hexagonal rings exhibiting a c-axis basal plane?"

Thomsen replied, "I did, and it supports my work that glacier ice is built up from many individual ice crystals packed closely together."

"The real question," said Petrov, "is what impact does temperature have on basal gliding and crystal tensile strength?"

Thomsen replied, "It will be the square root of the basal crystal counts divided by the temperature deltas."

Petrov sat in silence, absorbing Thomsen's answer, and then replied, "Why, yes, of course, that would be the case. Alma, that is remarkable. Yes!"

Thomsen wondered if she had just shared some highly sensitive information. Her lack of sleep was affecting her.

"I'm going to get some dessert. Can I bring you anything?" asked Thomsen, getting up more to clear her head than anything else.

Petrov shook his head, still lost in thought. "No, no, thank you."

As Thomsen made her way to the buffet, Petrov took a small vial from his vest pocket and poured it into Thomsen's coffee.

When Thomsen returned to the table, Petrov couldn't help but ask, "But if the temperature deltas are asymmetric rather than symmetric, won't that mean the square root will also be asymmetric?"

Thomsen said in a mentoring tone, "Yes, that's correct, Nicholai, but remember—and this is key—the rings are hexagonal. That makes them fractals."

Petrov simply repeated, "Fractals," as he pondered the ramifications of Thomsen's words.

Finishing her coffee, Thomsen said, "I'm completely wiped out. Shall we start again tomorrow at nine?"

Petrov nodded. He would be up all night working through Thomsen's formulaic epiphany.

Thirty minutes later, the door to Thomsen's stateroom opened and the two SVR psyops operatives carried her unconscious body to their room.

Strapping her down to the bed, one of the agents inserted an IV into her vein and started a drip of a powerful psychosis-inducing drug.

A few minutes later they placed headphones on Thomsen's head and turned on the ring lights as they shook her into a semi-conscious state.

An audio track began, "America is a land of greed. Americans are selfish. When Denmark needed help, America was nowhere to be found. Russia is Denmark's friend and always has been." It went on like that for hours.

Tonight's phase was behavior reinforcement. There were no other stimuli other than the audio track that played on a continuous loop at varying volumes, accompanied by synchronized flashing lights to emphasize the words in the message.

At 6:30 a.m. the two SVR operatives carried a limp Thomsen back to her stateroom.

She would sleep for the next few hours and have to apologize to Petrov for showing up late for their meeting. Petrov, of course, was more than forgiving.

The next night Thomsen's ordeal moved to a higher level.

The lead SVR agent started talking to Thomsen, who was blind-folded, via her headphones.

"You will remember that America is evil. They are the enemy of the Danish people. America is trying to steal Denmark's resources. America is only after Greenland's minerals. They do not care about Greenlanders." This went on for hours, accompanied by electric shocks and an even more potent cocktail of psychotic drugs.

With the triggers planted, all the SVR agents needed to do was to continue to reinforce the message at increasing levels of stimuli.

Zlovna's expectation was that Thomsen would be influential in the upcoming Greenland negotiations, and as such the SVR director wanted to have as many advantages in those talks as she could gain. Now Thomsen represented one of those hedges.

∎

Sergey Latsanych had just arrived at the Russian embassy in Copenhagen, having completed his mission on the *Arktika*.

He was welcomed by the Russian ambassador to Denmark along with an intelligence team from Moscow. While weary from his trip,

Latsanych was eager to get on with the briefing.

"Comrade Latsanych, other than the ministers of finance and foreign affairs, these are the highest-priority targets that we believe can influence the Danish Parliament, the Folketing," said the Russian ambassador.

Having reviewed the list of potential targets, Latsanych wanted to focus on the CEO of A.P. Moller-Maersk.

"Tell me about the Maersk CEO," directed Latsanych.

"Søren Larsen is married with two adult children. He tends to go out for dinner on the weekends with his wife, sometimes with his children. Here's a list of the restaurants he frequents. He is a typical Dane—his work is very important to him. He doesn't smoke and drinks only moderately, and he is a loyal husband. He also has a passion for racing and belongs to a racing club where he keeps two Porsche race cars. However, given the time of year, he will not start racing again until May at the earliest. He belongs to a health club and typically goes there three times a week. Always after work. We've arranged a membership for you," said the officer, handing Latsanych the report.

The briefing continued with similar dossiers on all the targeted Danes.

With the intelligence briefing completed, a third person joined the meeting. "Colonel Comrade Latsanych, I am Petr Barkov and I work for the Russian Ministry of Finance," said the thirty-something finance expert, who was dressed in a tailored suit along with horn-rimmed glasses.

"I'll be supporting you and running the finance side of this operation. As you know, we are partnering with China to present a combined bid to procure the rights to Greenland's minerals. I must remind you that information is confidential, and at no point are we to reveal to the Danes that we have partnered with China," said Barkov.

Barkov continued his briefing. "In order to influence the negotiations, we will, through a series of accounts, acquire a material, if not controlling, interest in the shipping company A.P. Maersk. Once we've achieved our ownership position, you'll approach the Maersk CEO and inform him of our desire for him to advocate for our proposal."

Latsanych asked, "Are there enough public shares available?"

"Currently they have a $428 billion market cap their series A and B shares. I'll purchase a five percent position. That way we won't trigger any circuit breakers with the regulators here in Denmark or in the US, where their shares are listed. Working through partners, we'll continue to buy their stock, amassing a thirty percent ownership position, at which point you'll approach their CEO. You'll tell him we expect him to support our proposal on Greenland, and you will threaten to secure seats on his board of directors if he doesn't comply. And should he not agree to our demands, we'll threaten to dump our shares, sending their stock into freefall."

To be clear, what they were doing wasn't legal. That is, having a foreign group of investors take control of a company headquartered in another country—but it was very hard to expose. It took time and a lot of effort to track down stock ownership, and that always worked in the corporate raider's favor.

Latsanych knew the relationship between the two countries was positive based on the indebtedness Denmark felt toward Russia, which, along with the British, liberated the Danes from Nazi occupation during World War II. Plus, his ace in the hole would be Thomsen. With her behavior modification now almost complete, Latsanych was confident he would have an influential technical resource completely supporting the Russian proposal.

The next phase included introducing Latsanych to a group of influential Danes at a party hosted by their ambassador.

In preparation for the party, the Russian ambassador wanted to ensure that Latsanych was up to speed on several points. Besides, the ambassador knew of Latsanych's relationship with Zlovna and wanted to not only impress him but host him in a grand way.

"First, some background on the Danish government's structure. It is a traditional European-style parliamentary system. Led by the prime minister, who represents the Danish monarchy, the Parliament is known as the Folketing. It comprises 179 members, 175 of which represent Denmark proper, with two members each representing Greenland and the Faroe Islands.

"In addition to the Parliament, the Danish prime minister also heads the cabinet, which is made up of twenty-five ministers. Most are inconsequential, but Magnus Nielsen, the minister of defense, is key. He's responsible for not only the military but also the diplomatic service. He'll be attending our party Friday night, where I'll introduce you. In addition, there will be several other influential members of the Folketing attending."

The ambassador added, "I'm going arrange a separate meeting to introduce you to the CEO of Maersk."

Latsanych was pleased to be off to a quick start, especially when he recalled Director Zlovna's comment about there being a compressed timeline.

■

Lauren La Rue had become the CIA's most talented asset in the newly defined area of "economic statecraft," which wasn't surprising given her talents. That said, the way she came to the Agency was not via the usual route.

La Rue had been the financial principal for the Saudi sheik Abdul Er Rahman, who had masterminded the kidnapping of President Russell's family almost three years ago while they vacationed on the island of Nantucket.

But her cooperation with the CIA on that operation, as well as her later work exposing a cybergroup in Dubrovnik, had proven her worth, if not her trust, to the Agency.

Today found La Rue where it often did, in her office at CIA headquarters in Langley, Virginia, in front of her Bloomberg terminal as well as four other screens that employed proprietary technologies to mine hundreds of millions of stock transactions.

La Rue knew that if she could use this technology to trade stocks, she'd make a fortune on Wall Street. That said, she already was one of the wealthier employees at the CIA, if not the wealthiest, from her earlier work for the sheik. As her fingers flew over the keyboard, she knew that firms like Goldman Sachs and J.P. Morgan thought they had sophisticated systems, but they didn't come close to what the CIA and NSA had—not even close.

There were some days when she barely spoke with anyone. She just clicked away and sifted through terabytes of data identifying trading patterns. But today wasn't one of those days.

She had urgently requested a meeting with her director, Lisa Collins, regarding some information she had just uncovered. La Rue entered the director's office and said, "Lisa, look at this."

Lisa Collins, who valued La Rue's expertise and was something of a mentor, replied with a smile, "Lauren, you're going to have to give me a little more than that."

Laying out three spreadsheets, La Rue took a breath and said in a tone that declared victory, "Lisa, it's a wolf pack."

Collins still didn't grasp what La Rue was trying to tell her.

"In the last few days, trading activity in Maersk shares has soared, led by a hedge fund out of Copenhagen. But there are four other groups buying as well. One in Anguilla, one in Bermuda, and two dodgy firms out of New York."

"What's a wolf pack?" asked Collins.

"A wolf pack is a group of traders who work in conjunction with one another to amass a controlling position in a company without tripping any of the SEC circuit breakers. Someone is making a move on Maersk, I'm one hundred percent sure of it," said La Rue. "And look at the participants in this wolf pack. They aren't Bank of America and J.P. Morgan. This is a network of shady traders. I used to do the same thing for the sheik. Maersk is under attack and I bet they don't even know it."

"Lauren, start at the beginning and assume I'm not an investment banker," directed Collins.

"You can't buy more than a five percent stake in a publicly traded company without filing a Form 13 with the SEC. There are two types of Form 13s. A 13-G, where you own at least five percent of a company but you state you won't be an activist owner. The other is a 13-D, which means you *will be* an activist owner. And as such, you may press for board representation or to divest a business or to push for a dividend. When you file a 13-D, you're a corporate raider," said La Rue.

Collins asked, "So you think you've found a group that will have to file a form 13-D on Maersk?"

"No, no. I mean yes, there is a group out of Copenhagen that's going to have to file a 13, and I guarantee you it will be a 13-D.

But that's not the important piece. What's important is there are four other groups flying under the radar. They're buying up stakes in Maersk like crazy but just under the five percent threshold, so they won't have to file. However, these groups, if they act in coordinated fashion, will own more than twenty-five percent of Maersk, which is enough to exert enormous pressure over the company. Especially if the rest of your shareholder base is mainly retail shareholders, which is exactly what Maersk has," said La Rue, hoping she had explained it clearly.

Then she added, "In your briefing last week, you mentioned Greenland and the Northwest Passage are hot spots for us to keep an eye on. Well, Maersk is Denmark's largest company and one of the world's largest shippers. And given the traders in this wolf pack, I bet they aren't aligned with our interests."

That was enough for Collins. She called to her assistant, "Pascal, phone Ed Holland's office at the White House and tell him I'm sending Lauren La Rue over to meet with him today."

She turned to La Rue. "Lauren, Greenland and the Northwest Passage are top priorities for us—it's bigger than you even know. If you're correct and someone is trying to gain influence over Maersk, it may have something to do with what Ed Holland is working on. Tell him what you just told me and see how he reacts, and then report back," said Collins.

Pascal came into the office announcing, "Miss La Rue has a two o'clock meeting with Mr. Holland."

"Thank you, Pascal," said Collins.

La Rue, the financial wizard that she was, added, "Good, that just gives me enough time to create some more graphs."

Collins was once again impressed by La Rue. If, in fact, Collins became vice president, La Rue was someone she'd want to bring with her to the White House.

■

Latsanych pulled up to the Russian embassy in his brand-new red Porsche 911 GT3 RS and got out, letting the valet park his supercar.

Tonight's plan was for the Russian ambassador to introduce Sergey Latsanych to the power players of the Danish Parliament.

With the evening well underway, the Russian ambassador said, "Minister Nielsen, allow me to introduce Sergey Latsanych."

Magnus Nielsen, the Danish minister of defense, replied, "It is a pleasure to meet you, Mr. Latsanych. What brings you to Copenhagen?"

"Mr. Minister." Latsanych nodded. "Very good to meet you. I am part of the Russian team negotiating the Greenland mineral rights with your government."

"Well, then I suspect we will be spending a great deal of time together," said the minister.

"No doubt," replied Latsanych.

The ambassador suggested, "Magnus, perhaps you, Sergey, and I can meet in my study later this evening for an after-dinner drink?"

"I look forward to it," said the minister, who then circulated around the room.

Approximately two hours later, an aide brought Latsanych and Nielsen separately to the ambassador's private study.

With everyone comfortable, the ambassador poured three glasses from a $3,500 bottle of Louis XIII cognac.

"Magnus, Sergey is just back from Singapore, where he successfully negotiated a trade agreement for us with Indonesia for rights to their rare-earth minerals," said the ambassador.

"I was briefed on that transaction," said the minister. "That was your handiwork?" he asked, looking at Latsanych.

"It was, Minister," said Sergey, feigning no modesty.

"Please, in such surroundings, call me Magnus," replied Nielsen in a friendly manner.

"Very well. Magnus, as you might expect, Moscow is very interested in securing the mineral rights to Greenland. But our plan is much different from that of the Americans. Now that we have access to the Indonesian rare-earth minerals, our approach is for Greenland to keep those minerals for a future time when a need arises. As such, our hope is to carefully develop Greenland in a manner quite different from the American plan," said Latsanych.

"We will evaluate all proposals on an even basis," said Nielsen, getting down to business.

"As I expect you would," said Latsanych. "But I beat the Americans in Jakarta, and I plan to beat them here in Copenhagen too."

"We welcome all bidders," said Nielsen, showing no preference.

"And we welcome the contest," said Latsanych, showing no weakness.

At which point the ambassador, sensing the slight tension, interjected, "Magnus, what do you think of this Louis the XIII?"

Taking another sip, Nielsen replied, "Sublime, simply sublime."

Latsanych noted that Denmark's minister of defense appreciated the finer things in life. It was an important data point that he could make use of later.

■

"Good morning, Ed," Lisa said as she picked up her receiver.

"Morning, Lisa," replied Holland. "Listen, I'm calling about

Lauren La Rue. I want to add her to my Denmark team."

"You liked her wolf-pack analysis on Maersk yesterday?"

"I did," he replied. "She picked up on it before anyone on my team did. Given her background in international finance, she'd be an invaluable addition to our team. Sorry for the suddenness of the request, but we're headed to Copenhagen later this week. And you know how important this is to the boss," said Holland, referring to the president.

At least he was asking, thought Collins. Plus, having La Rue on the negotiating team would give her insights into what was going on. And Holland was right, this was critically important to the US and to the president.

"Ed, I'm on board, but you have to promise me that I'll get her back," said Collins.

"You have my word," said the pleased senior economic adviser to the president.

Collins replied, "I'm going to hold you to that."

Collins knew that the future security of the United States would be predicated on two imperatives: cyber capabilities—both offensive and defensive—and economic statecraft. And while Collins was adept in the former, she relied on La Rue's expertise in the latter. That meant she needed to keep La Rue with her.

CHAPTER NINE

Greenland

Cruising at thirty-seven thousand feet in the US State Department's 757 on the way to Copenhagen, Ed Holland thought he would take the opportunity to get to know Lauren La Rue a little better. "Lauren, I'm familiar with some of your CIA work, but can you tell me a little about your time in the Middle East?"

"After receiving my MBA from NYU's Stern School, I was recruited by all the familiar names: Goldman Sachs, Allen & Company, McKinsey, but in addition to them I was pursued by a secretive hedge fund. Or at least I thought it was a hedge fund."

Holland interjected, "And you were what? Twenty-five or so at the time?"

"Exactly. After interviews in New York, I was flown to Dubai, where they made me what I can only characterize as a very, very generous offer. So, I accepted and moved to Dubai. For five years I managed Sheik Rahman's Venture Fund. Over time as I was brought into the sheik's inner circle, I started to see a more complete picture of his operations and especially his ideology."

"Is that when the sheik hatched the plan to kidnap President Russell's wife and children?" asked Holland, referring to the 2017 event.

"Basically yes. But just to be clear, I never knew anything about that. I was involved in wiring some funds that turned out to fund the operation. Although at the time I had no idea what they were intended for," clarified La Rue.

Holland said, "I heard that the CIA had to rescue you in the middle of the kidnapping operation."

"The sheik would have never let me go. So, yes, the CIA did rescue me, which explains how I came to join the Agency," said La Rue.

Having achieved his goal, Holland changed the topic. "Lauren, the reception we get from the Danes will be very important. While they're a NATO member and supported the operations in Kosovo and Afghanistan with troops, their history is deeply intertwined with Russia. The Danes remember that they were liberated by the Brits and Russians in World War II and not the Americans."

"I realize that, Ed, but the package we can put together for them is far beyond anything Russia can offer. Maybe China can match us, but Russia—never," responded La Rue.

"No doubt, but before we get to the economics of the deal, we first have to convince them to want to do business with us. We need to establish a rapport, build a trust with the Danes, and that'll require a certain finesse," said Holland.

"Ed, having lived in Dubai for seven years, believe me, I know firsthand how American arrogance can derail a deal," La Rue responded.

"Quite right," replied Holland. "It's one of the biggest risk factors of this negotiation."

"In Dubai we used to refer to it as Ugly American or U Ass Syndrome," said La Rue.

Holland had never heard that before and chuckled. "The other thing to be sensitive of is what they call *samarbejdspolitikken*, or the cooperative policy they exhibited during the war in regard to the Germans," Holland said. "When Germany invaded Denmark, the Danes pretty much capitulated. Much more so than the other Nordic countries. It's all history now, but it's still a sensitive topic for them. So, any discussions of World War II are best avoided. That said, we can count on the Russians to play their World War II hand strongly." Holland finished with, "The Danes are extremely modest but also rather reserved."

"Other than the modesty part, they sound like Germans," said La Rue.

"Yes, they're like modest Germans. Modest Germans." Holland laughed. "Now, that's an oxymoron if I ever heard one."

The kidding aside, La Rue listened carefully to what Holland was telling her. She had thought they would show up with a financial proposal so overwhelming they'd knock the Danes off their feet, but now she realized the task would require much more aplomb.

Lightening the mood, La Rue quipped, "Look, I'll order herring salad and you order sturgeon and that will put us on their good side."

Holland laughed, pleased that he and La Rue were getting along well.

With that, they both tried to catch some sleep. Once they landed, they would hit the ground running.

After landing in Copenhagen, Lauren La Rue and Ed Holland were driven to the US embassy and escorted into a conference room for their briefing by the US ambassador to Denmark, James McGinley.

"Jim, nice to see you again. I want to introduce you to Lauren La Rue. She'll be working with me on the Greenland negotiation," said Ed Holland.

"Pleasure to meet you, Ms. La Rue. Director Collins speaks very highly of you," said the ambassador, who was an Andrew Russell appointee.

"Nice to meet you, Ambassador," replied La Rue. "Director Collins sends her regards," added La Rue, intending to remind McGinley that La Rue was part of the CIA.

"Should we begin?" said McGinley. "Our relationship with Denmark is sound. The Danes have been a supportive member of NATO since its founding. However, with regard to Greenland, it is a little more complicated," said McGinley.

"Isn't it always," replied Holland.

"First, some history. We've had a presence in Greenland since World War II. That presence today is most prominent in the form of Thule Air Force Base, located in the northern area of the country." McGinley brought up a slide with a map of Greenland on the flat-screen in the conference room.

Advancing to the next slide, McGinley continued. "Thule was constructed in 1953 with many expansions since then. It's home to the 821st Air Base Group, part of the Twelfth Space Wing out of Peterson AFB in Colorado. We have about six hundred Air Force personnel on-site. In addition to a weather squadron, there is a fighter squadron and, from time to time, during exercises, a bomber squadron that all operate from a single ten-thousand-foot runway. We also operate an advanced phased array radar station there."

La Rue was eager to get to the more pressing issues. "Ambassador, what can you tell us about Camp Century and Project Iceworm?"

Nodding, the ambassador replied, "Quite right, that's the area of recent controversy. Back in the 1960s we built a base known as Camp Century. It was designed to be a series of subterranean tunnels that would be hidden from the Russians. Project Iceworm was our plan to house intermediate range ballistic missiles, or IRBMs—modified Minuteman missiles—under the ice. But Iceworm was abandoned after recognizing the challenges presented by the constantly shifting glacial subsurface ice."

"I assume all this was top secret and kept from the Danes and Greenlanders?" asked Holland.

"Not entirely. We did disclose Camp Century to the Danes and said it was a scientific research base. But we never disclosed Iceworm. The issue, which is more of a public relations problem than anything else, is that when we abandoned Camp Century, we left some hazardous material buried under the ice, and that has become an environmental concern."

La Rue spoke up. "A public relations problem—why isn't it an environmental problem? My understanding is we had a nuclear reactor there and the water we used to cool it was just pumped under the ice. Plus, what about the two hundred thousand gallons of diesel fuel we also left there to seep into the ice?"

McGinley, clearly not used to being challenged in such a manner, responded, "I was going to get to those details, Ms. La Rue, but to be clear, we're not talking about Chernobyl here. As you correctly stated, we did use water to cool the reactor. But that produced a very low level of radioactive material in the form of wastewater that had a half-life of twelve years. Meaning every twelve years its radioactivity is halved. It's been fifty-three years since that reactor was removed. The radioactivity, which was of a low level to begin with, has now decayed to five percent its original amount.

"What created this 'public relations' problem was recent reporting on global warming that predicted the remaining radioactivity could be exposed to the air. But it is all just alarm journalism. The natural radioactivity of the Greenland soil is a much larger concern than anything left over from Camp Century. Just as many homeowners back in the States worry about radon, which is a naturally occurring gas, so, too, in Greenland do these rare-earth minerals produce more than a nominal amount of radioactivity. Just as Americans see the need to install radon mitigation systems, as part of our negotiations we can offer to mitigate the effects of the rare-earth elements we mine from Greenland, thereby protecting the people."

La Rue followed up with, "And Camp Century's remaining diesel fuel?"

"Ms. La Rue, do you remember the BP Deepwater Horizon oil spill in the Gulf back in 2010?" asked McGinley.

"Yes, of course," she replied.

"That oil leak, which flowed for eighty-seven days, released an estimated 4.9 million barrels of oil, or more than 210 million gallons, making it the world's largest accidental spill. That's a crisis. At Camp Century we're talking about two hundred thousand gallons of diesel fuel. That's one-one thousandth the size of the Deepwater Horizon release. So Camp Century is a very, very minor amount. But as a show of good faith, in 2017 the Pentagon issued a statement saying the United States 'acknowledged the reality of climate change and the risk the Camp Century waste poses,' and we agreed to 'work with the Danish government and the Greenland authorities to settle the issue in a mutually acceptable manner.'

"Now, to be honest, while we committed to clean up the Camp Century site, we haven't done anything in terms of actual cleanup yet. Therefore, it does open the door to put that as an action item in your negotiations," added McGinley.

"Jim," Holland said, "I understand your points and they're valid; however, we can't run the risk of winning the battle but losing the war here. As you said, this is more of a public relations issue, and where I come from, in DC perception is reality. So, if we're perceived as being stubborn on this Camp Century issue, it'll work against us. And why? For a few million dollars of cleanup work? No, cooperation with the Danish government remains our most pressing imperative today. Bear in mind, despite being a member of NATO, Denmark is opening dialogues with both Russia and China over the Greenland rare-earth mineral rights. As a result, we need to be sensitive and ultra-responsive to the Danes. To that end, the president wants a cleanup effort at Camp Century to begin ASAP."

Ambassador McGinley knew that when Andrew Russell used the term "ASAP," he meant it. Without any further debate, McGinley replied, "We'll start working on a plan immediately."

■

Svetlana Ivanovna Zlovna, the director of the SVR, was being briefed on the progress with the Greenland negotiations and the situation with Dr. Thomsen.

"Ma'am, we received an update from our psyops agents last night. They're progressing according to plan. They expect it will take another week and they will be finished with Thomsen. We plan to feign an engine problem on the *Arktika*, which will require that Petrov and his team terminate their research. Then we can release Thomsen and send her back to Copenhagen, where we expect she'll be brought in as a technical expert on the Greenland negotiation," said the reporting deputy director.

"Very well," said Zlovna. "And how is Latsanych progressing?"

"Madam Director, very well. He's been introduced to the minister of defense and also has a meeting with the CEO of Maersk. As you know, we have been successful in amassing a large position in shares of Maersk stock," added the deputy director.

Pleased with the progress report, Zlovna added, "We need to verify that the work on Dr. Thomsen was successful. Tell Latsanych to meet with her once she's back in Copenhagen and determine if our psyops team has accomplished their goal."

■

As the Chief of Naval Operations Admiral Brian Jacobsen entered the Oval Office and saluted the forty-sixth president of the United States, who returned the salute and then motioned for the admiral to have a seat alongside Sterling Spencer.

The president and the CNO had known each other since their days at the US Naval Academy, where they were classmates.

"Sir, I have the Major Command Selection List for your review." The CNO handed the president the list. While not routine for other presidents, President Russell always reviewed the Major Command Selection List before it was submitted to Congress for final approval.

The president nodded as he went down the list. "Good," he said. "Our first female CO of an aircraft carrier."

The president was alluding to Captain Amy Bauer, a helicopter pilot who had risen through the ranks to reach this history-making billet as CO of the USS *Abraham Lincoln*.

"It's been a long time coming, but Bauer's earned this command," said the CNO.

The other name on the list that caught the president's eye was Captain Mike Bartlett, selected to become the commanding officer of the nation's newest aircraft carrier, CVN-79 USS *John F. Kennedy*.

"Mike Bartlett's getting the *Kennedy*?" asked the president.

"That's correct, sir. He's currently CO of LPD-25 USS *Somerset* in the Indian Ocean with the USS *Makin Island's* ARG," said the CNO, referring to the amphibious ready group.

"Sterl, it's long been the Navy's policy to send aviator O-6s"— he used the shorthand for the captain rank—"who they expect to become commanders of aircraft carriers to spend a year on a deep-draft vessel like an LPD or LCC," explained the president to his chief of staff, who wouldn't be familiar with the intricacies of the Navy's promotions and commands.

"We do that to basically teach the aviators how to drive a large ship," added the CNO.

Where Captain Mike Bartlett was concerned, the president had a soft spot. First, Bartlett's wife, Kristin, was his deputy director of intelligence at the NSA. Second, it was Mike Bartlett, then a commander, who flew in the back seat of the president's F/A-18F that shot down Sheik Abdul Er Rahman's jet over the Mediterranean as payback for masterminding the kidnapping of his wife and children three summers earlier.

"The *Kennedy*'s set to join the fleet in six months, so he'll be its first active captain—a plankowner," said the CNO using the term given to every member of a ship's first crew.

"Brian, did you see what happened at the *Kennedy* christening with Caroline Kennedy?" asked the president.

"I did," said the CNO, shaking his head. Spencer looked confused.

"Sterl, Caroline Kennedy was asked to christen CVN-79, named after her father. But when she swung the bottle of champagne, it bounced off the bow, so she had to swing it again to break it. That same thing happened when she christened CV-67, the original USS *John F. Kennedy*. The only difference was that in 1967 she was nine.

Sailors think it's bad luck when it takes more than one swing to christen a ship," said the president.

"I remember telling the first lady when we went to New York to rechristen the SS *United States* that she had to make sure her first swing broke the bottle. Leaving nothing to chance, the kids and I got three bottles of champagne and had her practice in the Rose Garden. By the time we were done she had a swing like David Ortiz. At the christening she swung so hard she actually came out of her right shoe," said the president with a smile.

"I'll see that notes of congratulations are sent to all of the selectees," said Spencer.

"Brian, I hear the Coast Guard helo crew is back on our icebreaker," said the president, changing the topic.

"That is correct, sir," said the CNO. "Sir, the Coast Guard has debriefed the crew. There's a potentially important piece of new information. The command master chief thinks the helo was brought down by a surface-to-air missile."

"The helo was shot down?" asked the president in an incredulous tone.

"We have no confirmation of that, sir. We had no satellites in the area and the *Colorado*, which was nearby, didn't detect anything. That said, Admiral Parrish says his CMC is one of his most reliable chiefs," said the CNO.

"Why would someone shoot down our helicopter, and who would do so?" asked the president.

"The only ones in the vicinity were the Russians, sir," answered the CNO.

"The Russians. Why?" asked the president.

"That's just it, sir. We don't know. We do know that after the rescue the Danish mineralogist decided to stay on board the Russian icebreaker. The CIA thinks she will be a player in Denmark's decision on the Greenland mineral rights. But other than that, we don't have a strong narrative to support why the Russians would want to shoot down one of our helos in the Arctic," responded the CNO.

"What about Caesar II?" asked the president.

"It's still progressing, about a week behind schedule now due to the accident," said the CNO.

"No, I mean could the Russians have shot down our helo to get some information on Caesar II?" asked the president.

The CNO was caught off guard by the president's question. "I'll need to investigate that angle, sir, but it does present a problematical scenario."

"Brian, I want you to speak to this CMC too. See what you think of him and if he impresses you as being credible," added the president. "And let me know what your team thinks about the Caesar II linkage too," said the president.

"Aye, aye, sir," was the CNO's only response.

CHAPTER TEN

Something to Sell

Svetlana Ivanovna Zlovna opened the secure link to her conferencing software. On the other end appeared the image of Salman Rahman, the twenty-four-year-old son of Sheik Abdul Er Rahman, the deceased leader of the Islamic Front.

"Salman, how have you been?" she asked.

"Fine. I just returned from a six-month retreat where I received enlightenment from Allah," said the spoiled radical.

"That sounds very uplifting," said Zlovna, who then got down to business. "You mentioned you had something of interest for me."

"I do," said Rahman.

Several images of a nude woman appeared on the screen.

"Do you recognize this person? It's Kennedy Russell," said Rahman.

Zlovna saw images of a nude woman lying on a bed of pine needles. She was clearly unconscious. They weren't sexual in nature, but they were graphic.

"The images were taken when we abducted her on Nantucket," said the sheik's son. "How do you think the cowboy in the White House would react if we released these?"

Zlovna ignored his question and asked, "Other than you, who's seen these pictures?"

"Just a very tight circle of my top people. I can assure you these are the only images. There are no copies."

Zlovna was recording their conversation, as she did all her calls, so she would have screen grabs of the images if she needed them, but the resolution would not be good.

"What are you proposing, Salman?" Zlovna asked.

"I assume theses photos would be of great value to whoever had them. Am I correct?" he asked.

"We would be interested in them," Zlovna said.

"I'm sure you would. I have two conditions. First, I want Lauren La Rue delivered to me alive. The next is harder but just as important. I want the resignation of Andrew Russell," said Rahman.

Zlovna laughed. She thought getting La Rue was achievable, but the second demand was preposterous. And she was a person who did not make promises she couldn't keep.

"Salman, I think you may have spent too much time in the sun during your retreat," she said. "Getting you La Rue, we can do. But getting the American president to resign is virtually impossible. He's immensely popular, and the Americans would no doubt side with him if these photos ever came out. They certainly wouldn't force him to resign," said Zlovna.

"No, the Americans wouldn't force the president to resign. But would he resign to stop the photos from coming out? That's the gambit," said Rahman.

"Andrew Russell would never resign. He didn't even step down when his family was kidnapped, as you recall," added Zlovna. "Look, Salman, you're not wrong. In the right hands these photos are valuable. They can cause the US president great personal embarrassment. They can be leveraged to achieve a goal, but not his resignation. His embarrassment, and that of his family, will have to be enough for you," said Zlovna, repeating herself to ensure the young Saudi got her message.

"Maybe I'll just post them to the Internet tonight and see what happens," was Rahman's retort.

Zlovna was experienced at dealing with the Saudis and understood their temper and their impetuousness. The sheiks and princes, all of immense wealth, often acted like spoiled children if they didn't get their way.

As the one adult in the room, Zlovna replied, "Salman, you know you aren't going to do that. You're too smart to waste an opportunity like this."

"Well, then, maybe the Chinese or North Koreans will be more supportive of my demands," he responded.

"Salman, we can get you La Rue, and we can greatly embarrass the president of the United States and his wife. Isn't that enough?" asked Zlovna.

"I will want to know how and when you plan to use these pictures," said a relenting Rahman.

"Salman, why don't we speak next week when I can brief you on what our plans would be for these photos," said Zlovna.

Rahman nodded and closed the call with, "Mualaikumsalam."

That left Zlovna to reflect on their conversation. She knew her business was a dirty one. Almost anyone could be gotten to with sex, alcohol, drugs, or money, but this request particularly offended her. It's true that in today's world any picture could be photoshopped into the most vile image, but they were always dismissed as deepfakes. This was different, she thought. Embarrassing the first lady of the United States could potentially backfire.

On the other hand, she could imagine how these images could get under any husband's skin. Especially a man like Andrew Russell. After all, he personally flew the fighter that shot down the plane of the man who kidnapped his family.

Svetlana Ivanovna Zlovna wondered what Andrew Russell would do if these photos became public. And that's where the value was. That was the play, she thought.

As a next step she would need to create several scenarios of how she could use these photos. Once they were in hand, she would be in a position to brief her own president.

Her other worry was Salman Rahman. He couldn't be trusted, and he was unpredictable. She knew she had to act fast or else that sophomoric zealot could do something rash—probably with North Korea or Iran.

■

Kevin Mannix, a senior analyst located at the NSA's Fort Meade, Maryland, headquarters, was tasked with sifting through intercepted call logs from the NSA's watch list. That list included Salman Rahman.

After two days of close analysis, Mannix requested a meeting with his boss, Kristin Bartlett, deputy director of intelligence for the NSA.

"Kristin, do you recall our old friend Salman Rahman?" asked Mannix.

"The sheik's son? Yes, I thought he had gone quiet," she replied.

"He had, but he's not anymore. In the past week he's been in contact with the Russian, Chinese, North Korean, and Iranian intelligence principals. The last time we saw this sort of call pattern he was selling missiles to the North Koreans. It's a fair bet that if he's in communication with these folks, he has either something to sell or a mission in the offing," said Mannix, whose reputation at the Agency was made by his work during the Nantucket kidnapping.

Bartlett knew Mannix was ambitious, and where Sheik Rahman and his family were concerned, he was sometimes overeager. "Kevin, are you sure you aren't seeing things?" she asked.

Put off, he fired back, "Seeing things? I don't think so. Salman hasn't talked to anyone for six months. Now, all of a sudden, in one week he's been on calls with the intelligence communities of Russia, China and North Korea. No, Kristin, I'm not seeing things," he said emphatically.

That was what Bartlett was looking for—she wanted to hear Mannix's conviction. "What do we think is the nature of the calls?" she asked.

"That I don't know yet. But I'd like to employ the God Box," said Mannix, referring to the NSA's most secret decryption technology.

"You know I'll need director-level authorization both here and with the CIA director to use it," said Bartlett.

"And that's why they pay you the big bucks, Kristin," said Mannix with a smile.

"Kevin, you're sure about this?" asked Bartlett in a serious tone.

Unfolding his call sheets, Mannix replied, "Kristin, look at this. He called each intelligence organization on successive days. He's shopping something. He has to be. And we'll know next week from the call patterns who the buyer is. That's why I want the God Box— for those calls," said Mannix, cementing his argument to Bartlett.

Bartlett knew Mannix had what was considered the most important talent when it came to intelligence: the gift of "gut feel," and it was why one day he too would be DDI of the NSA.

After a moment to think it over, Bartlett called to her assistant, "Beth, get me on the director's schedule. Also get me on Lisa Collins's schedule too."

Later that afternoon, Lisa Collins's administrative assistant buzzed to let Collins know that Kristin Bartlett had arrived.

Collins considered Bartlett a friend and a mentor. After all, there weren't that many women in their field, let alone women who had advanced to their levels of responsibility.

"Kristin, nice to see you. How's Mike doing?"

"Good afternoon, Director," said Bartlett, addressing her by her title, according to protocol. "He's fine. I spoke with him last night. Between talking to him and his emails, it isn't too bad, but he has been away only three months now."

Bartlett was referring to her husband, who was now deployed in the Indian Ocean and the CO of a Navy amphibious landing ship.

"So, what brings you to Langley in such a rush?" asked the CIA director.

"Lisa, it's Salman Rahman. He's resurfaced."

"I thought we sent a message to the Saudis that they needed to control him or else we would. I thought that would have been enough to keep him quiet," said Collins.

"I did as well, but apparently it wasn't. Over the past week Salman has been in contact with the Russian, Chinese, North Korean, and Iranian intelligence agencies," Bartlett informed her.

"He's got something to sell," said the savvy CIA director.

Kristin Bartlett was once again impressed by Collins's ability to quickly process information to the correct conclusion. "That's what our people think as well. But the other reason for my coming is La Rue."

Collins nodded. "She's in Copenhagen with Ed Holland starting the negotiations with Denmark."

"Yes, I'm aware, but with Salman back on the radar she's at risk," said Bartlett.

"I agree," said Collins, "but I put her on Holland's team myself. I really want to keep her there. Frankly, I trust her more than Holland."

"Lisa, it's a risk—a big risk. If Salman were to get her, he'd have her tortured."

"Let's move her into the US embassy. We can protect her there. It'll mean that all negotiations with the Danes will need to take place there, which isn't optimal, but it will have to do," said Collins.

"There's another thing. My lead analyst, Kevin Mannix, wants to deploy the God Box on all of Salman's communications," requested Bartlett.

"He's right. One, we need to know what Salman's doing in order to protect La Rue, and two, we need to know who he's working with," said Collins. "If Gordon agrees, you have my support," said Collins, referring to the NSA director, who also had to approve the use of the top secret cybertechnology.

"I have a meeting with him this afternoon, but I'm confident he'll support the request, especially now that I have you on board," said Bartlett.

Having addressed the pressing business, Bartlett and Collins spent a few minutes on personal talk. Kristin confided in Collins that she was pregnant, which was both a joy and a concern, with her husband away on deployment.

CHAPTER ELEVEN

Beware of Greeks Bearing Gifts

Sergey Latsanych had discovered that Lars Larsen, son of Maersk's CEO, worked at a Danish tech start-up, but more important, he was a liberal user of cannabis.

While illegal in Denmark, cannabis and cannabidiol (CBD) gels, gummies, and extracts were readily available. And today's cannabis was much more potent than in the past. Cannabis and CBD products now contained much higher concentrations of tetrahydrocannabinol (THC), the natural compound found in cannabis plants.

Sergey knew that if he could get close to Lars, and he expected he could do so, he could provide the son with increasingly potent and addicting drugs. He had done it many times in the past, and with Lars already a recreational drug user, it would be a very achievable task.

In this case Latsanych would employ a female SVR agent to get close to the young man in order to get him hooked.

Sergey determined that in a matter of a month he would have control over the Maersk CEO's son, along with a collection of videos that would give Sergey the leverage he needed over the chief executive. Things were coming together.

Next on Latsanych's target list was Magnus Nielsen, the Danish minister of defense. In his case the opening was driven by ambition. Nielsen wanted to become prime minister of Denmark, and Latsanych could dangle some incentives that could assist in that goal. Russia was particularly effective at using labor unions to generate political support. Plus, as it had demonstrated over the previous two presidential elections in the United States, the SVR and its cyberteams were expert in misinformation campaigns that could be used to embarrass the current prime minister.

Like Zlovna, Latsanych knew his business was an immoral one, preying on human frailties. But it was also a business driven by adrenaline and power, making it an addictive profession. In that way, it was no different from what his counterparts did in Washington, Beijing, or Moscow.

Latsanych smiled, thinking how they were all caught up in the race. It was "Life in the Fast Lane."

■

On Lisa Collins's directive, Ed Holland and Lauren La Rue had now been moved into the US embassy in Denmark, which was located in central Copenhagen on the main street, Dag Hammarskjölds Allé.

Looking out the window, La Rue said, "Interesting view," referring to the fact that the US embassy backed onto Garnison Cemetery.

Ed Holland nodded and said, "That building over there is the Russian embassy, and that one"—he pointed straight across the cemetery—"is the British embassy."

La Rue noted that the Russian embassy was only about one hundred yards away.

La Rue and Holland then made their way to the embassy's secure interior conference room. It was a stated practice at US embassies around the world that all important meetings took place in hardened conference rooms. That meant no windows, and walls that were impervious to eavesdropping devices.

Also attending the meeting were three staff members from Holland's team and the US ambassador, James McGinley, as well as his deputy and chief of staff.

"The minister of defense and his coterie will be arriving in an hour," said Holland. "Let's go over the presentation one last time."

After flipping through the slides, La Rue said, "Ed, setting the tone during this first meeting will be key. We need to ensure we don't come off as 'too American.'"

"The problem with that, Lauren"—Holland smirked—"is that I am American."

"As am I," she responded. "But one of the things I learned while doing business in the Middle East is a little humility goes a long way."

"I can confirm Lauren's approach is a better way to deal with the Danes," chimed in Ambassador McGinley.

"Just to be clear, we're not here to make friends with the Danes. We're here to get a deal done," said an increasingly exasperated Holland. It was somewhat puzzling La Rue thought as it was Holland who coached her earlier about not coming off too brash. La Rue thought to herself, "This Holland is unpredictable."

The ambassador replied, "Ed, no one's saying that. It's just important that we don't come off as arrogant."

"Guys, this isn't my first rodeo," retorted Holland.

La Rue said, "Let's hope this doesn't turn into a rodeo."

With those words, it was now time for the meeting to start. The Danish contingent had already passed through the US embassy's metal detectors. In addition, due to the sensitive nature of the meeting, both sides had agreed that no smartphones would be allowed in the meeting. It had become common practice in diplomatic circles to always exclude technology from meetings to avoid the leaking of classified information.

After the formal introductions and greetings were out of the way, Holland began. "Minister Nielsen, the United States has long considered Denmark to be an important ally and NATO member. Our diplomatic relationship has witnessed many successes. Mutual successes. Today, we come to you with a proposal for another mutual success."

After a few slides that summarized the relationship between the two countries, Holland advanced to the next slide.

"Mr. Minister, Greenland represents a great opportunity for the Danish government to advance the quality of life for both Danes and Greenlanders to a level not seen before."

"Mr. Holland, we are quite proud of our quality of life already," said Magnus Nielsen. "Our Agency for Higher Education and Science has just published its 2020 Social Progress Index. Denmark ranked second in the world across fifty dimensions of well-being, social justice, and quality of life. It's worth pointing out, Mr. Holland, that the United States was one of three countries in the world that showed a decline in social progress over the past decade, along with Brazil and Hungary."

It was time for La Rue to enter the discussion. "Minister Nielsen, you are correct. Denmark has done an amazing job creating a society that places a high importance on quality of life. But what we're talking about is taking it to an entirely different level. For example, today we estimate there are approximately 2.6 million passenger cars in Denmark. Imagine over the next five years if 90 percent of those cars were converted to EVs.

"Imagine at the same time being able to make all your colleges and universities no-cost. Imagine opening an additional one hundred new healthcare clinics—with all services free to Danes," added La Rue. "And you could do all this while you halve your tax rate from today's level of forty-six percent to twenty-three percent."

Nielsen was impressed but knew better than to react to La Rue's vision.

Instead, he paused for effect, looking at Holland, McGinley, and La Rue before retorting, "Are you familiar with the Latin phrase *Timeo Danaos et dona ferentes*? It was written by Virgil. It means, *I fear the Greeks, even those bearing gifts*."

It was a powerful and well-delivered reply.

CHAPTER TWELVE

The God Box

Having gained the support of the directors of the CIA and NSA, Kevin Mannix was now authorized to employ the God Box technology on all communications from Salman Rahman.

Mannix knew that current Internet communications employed a technology known as hypertext transfer protocol secure, or https, which is the primary protocol used to send data between a web browser and a website.

What is important about https is that it is encrypted in order to increase the security of data transfer. This is particularly critical when users transmit sensitive data, such as banking information or emails, or when using the Internet for Voice over Internet Protocol, or VoIP, calls.

All https relies on the network's Transport Layer Security, or TLS, protocol keys. TLS uses two different keys to encrypt communications between parties. First is the private key, which is controlled by the owner of a website. The second key is the public one, which is available to everyone who wants to interact with a particular server.

The God Box intercepted all TLS communications to and from certain IP addresses by a process known as deep packet inspection, or DPI.

This intercepting of packets is what is known in cybersecurity circles as a man-in-the-middle technique. By inserting itself in the middle of communications, the NSA's God Box was able to collect both the private and public keys and thereby decrypt all the packets from a targeted source.

All Mannix had to do to engage the God Box was to input a list of IP addresses that he wanted to trace. These IP addresses tended to change all the time, so the NSA also had technology that would dynamically track IP addresses for certain locations.

Once that was completed, Mannix was ready to intercept all of Salman's communications.

It didn't take long.

Mannix's screen soon lit up, notifying him that Rahman was initiating a call. Pressing a few buttons, Mannix was able to listen to the call as well as see a real-time text stream of the conversation. The technology used for this was not unlike what most people know on their TVs as closed-captioning.

The director of the Russian SVR, Svetlana Ivanovna Zlovna, was speaking to Salman Rahman. "Salman, my people have agreed and we wish to purchase your photos."

Salman responded, "We haven't discussed a price, but I am glad to know my property is of interest to you."

"We will pay you €25 million for the exclusive rights to your material. That means we will want your assurance that you will not copy and sell the items to anyone else. Our technical people have a process that will allow us to convert your files so that we will be the only ones who can decrypt them."

"And what about my other demands?" asked the sheik's son.

"We will use our best efforts to capture your person of interest.

We do not guarantee it, but we know where she is and it does not represent an especially difficult challenge to us," said Zlovna.

"And embarrassing the president?"

"Salman, given the nature of your material, it is quite certain that it will greatly embarrass the American president."

Salman flipped through the images of Kennedy Russell again, as he had done many times, while listening to Zlovna.

Kevin Mannix watched as six images of a naked woman appeared on his screen. He was capturing the data so he would be able to perform image recognition later to determine who the person was. But he wouldn't need the image-recognition software.

He already knew who the person was.

Kevin Mannix quickly pulled the files from when the president's family was kidnapped in 2017. The report told of how the Islamic Front, led by Sheik Abdul Er Rahman, funded and masterminded the plot to kidnap the president's wife and children.

Reading through the notes, Mannix noted that the first lady had been released separately from her captors after she had been infected with a highly contagious virus that they hoped she would pass on to the president. To a certain extent the plot worked. The first lady wound up infecting several people involved with the case, but not the president. One of the people infected was Massachusetts State Trooper William Herbert, who was the person who rescued Kennedy Russell.

Next Mannix pulled the report from State Trooper Herbert.

It was early evening on Saturday, August 12th. My duty station was the traffic circle at the nexus of Milestone Road, Orange Street, and Old South Road on Nantucket. While on station, I glanced up and saw a figure emerge from the wooded area off Milestone Road.

It appeared to be a middle-aged woman. She was calling for help and she was completely naked.

I instinctively drew my weapon and scanned the surrounding area to make sure this lady wasn't a decoy for someone else sneaking up on us.

I then called my two partners for assistance. We all stood as the woman approached us.

To our surprise, the woman said, "My name is Kennedy Russell. My husband is the president of the United States."

She had to say it again for us to fully comprehend.

We got the blanket from the trunk of our cruiser and wrapped her in it and then helped her into the back of the cruiser and shut the door carefully . . .

It was now after 7 p.m. and the rest of the people in his department had left for the day. That allowed Mannix to bring up the images he had captured from Salman's phone call on his larger, higher-resolution monitor. He zoomed in and out on each photo many times. At first Mannix thought the Massachusetts state troopers could have taken the pictures of the first lady. But he concluded these pictures must have been taken by Kennedy Russell's captors before they released her. In the photos she was unconscious and lying on the ground, which was covered by mostly pine needles.

Mannix next brought up the metadata for each image and confirmed his theory. The date and time stamp as well as the longitude and latitude matched exactly the date, time, and location of an area next to the traffic circle on Nantucket. To be extra sure, he matched the image lats and longs with Google Earth. It was an exact match for that area of Nantucket.

Mannix now believed the images were real and not some sort of photoshopped fakes.

The question was what to do with them.

NSA headquarters in Fort Meade, Maryland, wasn't your typical office environment. Mannix could not simply download the images to a thumb drive and take them home for safekeeping.

After the Edward Snowden breach, both the CIA and NSA got serious about data security. To that end, all servers and personal computers logged every keystroke. In addition, USB ports were disabled or removed on all systems. Plus, every day everyone went through metal detectors that would pick up if someone was trying to leave with a thumb drive.

Mannix thought over how to remove the jpeg files of the pictures of the first lady from his PC without being detected.

He knew of a way.

It was called image hexadecimalizing. It would allow him to convert the jpeg images into hexadecimal characters.

First, he needed to convert the images from color to grayscale using a special tool called Rec. 601 luma.

Then he needed to hexation each image. The formula for hexation was:

$$(Y = 0.2989R + 0.5870G + 0.1140BY = 0.2989R + 0.5870G + 0.1140B)$$

What he ended up with was a hexadecimal file for each image looking something like the following:

```
496620796f752061726520
72656164696e672074686
97320796f7520617265206
120737465656c792065796
5642d6d697373696c65206
d616e2e20436f6e6772617
4756c6174696f6e732c205
4686616420447570706572
```

Next Mannix printed the binary images using a seven-point font. It took about two hundred pages per image. Once the print-out was completed, he simply put the paper in his backpack.

No one at the NSA cared if Mannix carried work home on paper. They expected it. But just to be sure he inserted the pages into a report he was working on.

Next Mannix deleted the images from his PC and used a bit-wash program to ensure the disk tracks where the images were stored had been written over.

That was the easy part. What to do with the images was the harder part.

■

"Thank you, Minister, for taking my call," began the US ambassador. "I have a request from the director of the CIA to arrange a call with you at your earliest convenience."

"Can you give me an indication as to what the subject matter is?" asked Nielsen.

"I don't have any additional information other than the director emphasized that it was a matter of importance to Denmark."

Nielsen brought up his calendar. "Ambassador, I can do a call at three o'clock today. Will you arrange the secure link?"

"Yes, I will. And thank you, Minister." McGinley rang off.

■

At the same time, in a second-floor conference room of the US embassy in Copenhagen, Lauren La Rue was welcoming Søren Larsen, the CEO of shipping giant A.P. Moller-Maersk.

"Mr. Larsen, thank you for coming and I apologize for not being able to meet at your offices," began La Rue.

"No problem, Miss La Rue. It was a short drive from our head-quarters on the Esplanade," replied Larsen. "But I am curious as to what this meeting is about."

"Mr. Larsen, before joining the CIA I worked in finance in the Middle East," said La Rue.

Nodding, Larsen said, "Please call me Søren. We're not so formal here in Denmark."

"Thank you, Søren. And likewise, please call me Lauren. To get right to the point. Your company is under attack."

"How's that, Lauren?"

La Rue opened her folder and spread five sheets of paper across the conference table. "Each one of these groups owns somewhere between four and a half and eight percent of Maersk stock. No doubt you've witnessed the strength in your stock over the past weeks."

Larsen looked over each sheet. "You're sure about this?" he asked.

"One hundred percent. Søren, Maersk is under attack by a wolf pack led by a Russian-based hedge fund. We believe it's being done to exert influence on Maersk regarding the ongoing negotiations over the mineral rights of Greenland," said La Rue, showing her entire hand.

Larsen replied, "I am aware of those negotiations."

"And Russia is eager to secure them," said La Rue. "Søren, Maersk is perceived as having input, if not influence in those negotiations."

"Lauren, I appreciate this information. I'll return the favor by sharing that we are advocating that any agreement will require a stipulation that all minerals must be transported exclusively on A.P. Moller-Maersk ships."

La Rue noted the new information Larsen had just shared with her. "Søren, you will no doubt be informing your board regarding these new investors," she said.

Larsen simply nodded.

"You should also inform them that at the open of trading tomorrow, a collection of US-based investment banks will start accumulating positions in your company. They will continue acquiring shares until they too have amassed a 30 percent ownership position. This buying will naturally drive up the price of your stock from today's open price of 13,980 kroner to well over 25,000," La Rue informed him. "The US is committed to not allowing Russia to have a controlling position in Maersk."

Larsen sat processing the information. He pondered the impact of his stock doubling not only for his investors but on his own net worth.

"My advice to you is that no insiders, officers, or board members sell any Maersk stock for the next thirty days. If anyone has any 10b-5 plans in place, they should pause them today," said La Rue, referring to stock plans that insiders put in place that allow them to trade a company's stock even during blackout periods.

Given the new information, Larsen agreed with La Rue on the insider trading.

"Is that it?" asked Larsen.

"No," said La Rue, "there's something else."

■

With the conference call established, Lisa Collins began, "Thank you, Minister, for agreeing to this conversation on such notice."

"Of course, Director," responded Magnus Nielsen.

"Minister, given the negotiations underway between our governments regarding Greenland's mineral rights, we have information on officials and citizens of Denmark who, we believe, are being targeted by other countries also interested in securing those rights," said Collins.

"Targeted in what way?" asked Nielsen.

"In a series of ways, but all with the goal of wielding influence to sway the negotiations," said Collins. "We know of an investor group based in Russia that is amassing an ownership position in A.P. Moller-Maersk. And we believe this group of prominent people"— Collins brought up a slide of business leaders, military flag-rank officers, and public officials—"are also targets."

Magnus Nielsen looked over the list, somewhat surprised that his name wasn't on it.

Truth be told, his name was on the list, but Lisa Collins had deleted it just for the call.

"Director Collins, how am I to trust that this is not a ploy by the US government to sway us to favor your proposal?" asked the Dane.

"I'm sure your intelligence organization will be able to confirm our allegations about the people on this list," she replied. "And regarding Maersk, you just need to look at their trading volumes and movement in their stock along with recent SEC filings. We've seen this behavior before, most recently in Indonesia and Brazil when they were also negotiating government deals," finished Collins.

"I thank you for providing me with this information, Director Collins. Any additional supporting information you can provide will also be welcomed," replied Nielsen.

And with that the call concluded.

Nielsen immediately instructed his secretary to arrange a dinner meeting with Sergey Latsanych for that evening.

CHAPTER THIRTEEN

Xaverian

Now back in Copenhagen, Dr. Alma Thomsen was in her third-floor apartment at 33 Vestergade Street, which was only three blocks from the University of Copenhagen's main campus.

Sipping a cup of tea, Thomsen reflected on her whirlwind last two weeks. She went from conducting research in the Arctic on an American icebreaker to crashing in a helicopter, then becoming part of the Russian research project. Only to have it canceled prematurely due to a mechanical issue. Then finally being flown back to Copenhagen via Canada.

Upon her return she had just been contacted by the minister of defense's office for a meeting later this week. No reason was given, nor did they provide an agenda for the meeting. She was simply asked to appear at 10 a.m. on Friday at the ministry.

If she had to bet on the topic for the meeting, she would guess it was regarding the Greenland mineral negotiations. But for the moment, she set aside any ideas about the meeting as she started to gather her things to meet her friends for dinner.

Thomsen walked to the top of her block and entered Boghallen, her favorite bookstore just across the street from campus. She browsed mindlessly, savoring the luxury of being able to peruse the shelves. It was one of her favorite things to do. She came across one of her favorite authors, Karen Blixen, better known under her pen name of Isak Dinesen, and picked up a copy of *Babette's Feast*. She thought reading about nineteenth-century Paris would be good therapy for her.

Soon it was time to meet her friends for dinner. She walked a few blocks and entered another university landmark, Mamma's restaurant, where she met her three dearest friends.

"Alma, it's so great to see you," said each woman. They were all in their early thirties, each with colorful scarves wrapped around their necks, as was the style in Europe these days.

"Anna, Lily, Olivia, so good to see you all," said Alma, tightly squeezing each one as they hugged.

"Have you warmed up after all that time in the Arctic?" asked Anna.

"Barely." Alma smiled. "So, what's new in Copenhagen? Olivia are you still seeing Lars?"

When drinks arrived, Lily announced, "I'm headed to Colorado for a ski vacation with Carl."

Anna replied, "Carl, really? I didn't know that was back on."

Lily replied, "Well, it is, and we're going."

Alma said rather aggressively, "Don't you get tired of the Americans?"

"I'm not moving there, Alma; I'm just going on holiday," retorted her friend.

"They always have to win; they're so arrogant. And I'll tell you another thing, they're going to ruin this planet," said Alma, her voice getting louder as she spoke.

What was unusual was that Thomsen didn't even realize what she was saying. It was like the words just came out of their own volition.

Olivia smiled. "Alma, did someone have a bad breakup while in the Arctic?"

Catching herself this time, she replied, "Something like that." Changing the topic, Alma said, "Anna, tell us about the Klee Exhibition. I'm dying to see it. You must be so proud."

The small talk continued, as it does with friends, until it was eventually time to say good night.

■

Kevin Mannix fed the hexadecimal pages into the scanner of his home printer and reconstituted the jpeg images of the first lady. He then loaded them onto a thumb drive and placed the thumb drive in an old shoe in his closet for safekeeping.

He then shredded the bitmap pages and dropped them in garbage cans around his town—at a 7-Eleven, a Home Depot, and a Starbucks.

The next morning, he met with his boss, Kristin Bartlett, to give her a status report on his work on Salman Rahman.

"Kristin, I have the God Box in place and we are collecting all of Rahman's communications. He's continuing to talk with the intelligence agencies of Russia and China but no longer with North Korea or Iran. His communications with Russia are the most substantive."

"Do we know what he's selling?" asked Bartlett.

"Yes, I think I do," replied Mannix.

"What is it?"

"That's just it, I can't tell you."

"What?" asked an incredulous Bartlett.

"I can't tell you. Or rather, in this case, I won't tell you," Mannix replied.

"Kevin, what are you talking about.? Have you lost your mind?" said Bartlett raising her voice.

"Kristin, I know what Salman is selling. It's something highly personal and it involves President Russell. I'll share that information with him and him alone," said Mannix to a stunned Bartlett.

"Kevin, I don't care how personal it is. You need to tell me what it is," demanded Bartlett.

"No, ma'am. I will not," Mannix said.

For the next couple of minutes, they just sat there in a standoff, staring at each other.

"Kristin, I need to get a one-on-one meeting with the president."

"Oh, okay, sure, no problem," replied Bartlett. "Would you like us to request that he come here or are you willing to go to the Oval Office?"

"Kristin, I'm convinced what I'm doing is the right thing. I have something that only the president can see. I think he'll appreciate my discretion. And I think you will respect my decision—eventually," said Mannix.

"Kevin, you need to think this through carefully. I want you to go back to your desk and think this over. Then I want you to come back and brief me on what you have," ordered Bartlett.

"I will," said Mannix, "but, Kristin, I'm not going to change my mind."

After Mannix left Bartlett's office, she called one of her team leaders. "Jim, I want you to pull Kevin Mannix's keystroke logs for the last week and let me know what he's been up to."

Two hours later the team leader entered Bartlett's office and gave his debrief. "Kristin, Mannix has a three-hour gap in his logs on Tuesday. They have been wiped."

Bartlett had expected something like that. She knew Mannix was smart enough to cover his tracks, especially on something that was clearly so important to him. On the one hand, she admired Mannix's position based on loyalty to the president. On the other hand, there was a chain of command that he was violating. Mannix was putting his entire career on the line.

After more thought, Bartlett called Mannix into her office. "Kevin, just so you know, I don't agree with any of this. If I shared this with the director, he'd dismiss you immediately. But I know you wouldn't be so stubborn unless it was of immense importance, something that you're willing to bet your career on."

Mannix just nodded.

"I'll try to get you a meeting with the president. I'm not sure Sterling Spencer will agree to it, though," said Bartlett. "And, Kevin, if the director catches wind of this, you'll be on your own."

"Kristin, thank you. You know I wouldn't be asking if it weren't of great importance," replied Mannix, who now was visibly sweating.

Bartlett's next call was to Spencer Sterling, and she knew it would be a difficult one.

■

The president, Spencer, and Collins were wrapping up a briefing on China when the president's secretary came in and announced that the CNO and Coast Guard commandant were waiting.

Collins and Spencer acknowledged the two flag-rank officers as they entered the Oval Office and saluted the president.

They were there to provide an update on the project to convert mothballed Ticonderoga cruisers to icebreakers. They were ahead of plan.

"Sir, we should have the first Ticonderoga icebreaker operational within twelve months," the US Coast Guard admiral began.

"Ahead of plan. That's remarkable. Why the improvement?" asked the president.

"The engines were in better shape than we anticipated, so we were able to shave a few months off the schedule, sir," responded the CNO.

"I'm not sure all the cruisers will follow the same timeline, however," added Admiral Parrish, the Coast Guard commandant.

"We'll take them as soon as we can get them," replied the president.

Having completed the briefing, the CNO, Admiral Brian Jacobsen, exited the Oval Office and ran into the CEO of American Airlines, Doug Paulsen, whom he knew from their time in the Navy. Paulsen, an academy grad, had been the air boss on the USS *John C. Stennis* when Jacobsen and the president were young lieutenants on their second deployment.

"Doug, nice to see you. What brings you to the White House?" asked the CNO.

"Brian, good to see you. The boss wants to talk to me," said Paulsen, referring to the president. "How are Ann and the children?" he asked.

"Everyone's good," replied the CNO. "Getting accustomed to Washington after Hampton Roads," his previous billet as commander fleet forces in Newport News, Virginia. "Are you in town long?"

"Just for the night," replied Paulsen.

"Are you free for dinner tonight, at the Army Navy Club?"

"I am now, Admiral," Paulsen replied, knowing time with the CNO was always time well spent.

"Say seven. See you then," said the CNO.

"Aye, aye, sir," replied Paulsen with a smile.

Jacobsen had two reasons for suggesting dinner. First, he was friends with Paulsen and it would be good to hear what it was like running American Airlines. But second, he was curious about why he was meeting with the president.

It was five thirty and the day was drawing to a close.

"What's left?" the president asked his private secretary.

"Sir, you have the NSA analyst Kevin Mannix," she replied.

The president was puzzled. "Remind me, why am I meeting with him?"

"Sir, I'm not sure but the meeting was scheduled by Kristin Bartlett and she indicated it was important," replied Ahern.

"Well then, send him in."

A minute later NSA lead analyst Kevin Mannix wearing his best (and only) suit entered the Oval Office.

The president was sitting behind the Resolute desk and looked up.

Mannix took a deep breath, taking in the full magnitude of the Oval Office. It was a common reaction for anyone visiting the Oval Office for the first time.

Recognizing Mannix's reaction, the president stood, walked around the desk, and made his way to his chair.

"Kevin Mannix of the NSA. I'm told you did some good work on the Nantucket operation."

"Yes, sir, Mr. President," was all Mannix could get out.

"Kevin, sit down, and it would be good if you breathed." The president spoke the words he often used for first-time visitors.

Mannix nodded. "Yes, Mr. President, I did work the Nantucket operation. And that's why I'm here, sir."

The president just listened as Mannix spoke.

Twenty minutes later the president said, "Kevin, I appreciate you bringing this to my attention. You're certain you are the only one who has seen these photos?"

"Mr. President, I am absolutely sure that I'm the only person in the US who has seen them. I erased all files at the NSA myself. But, sir, Salman Rahman has these, and I know he's shopping them to the Russians. I suspect he's probably shown them to the Chinese, Iranian, and North Korean intelligence organizations as well."

"Son, you did the right thing," said the president. "And I realize you likely incurred some career risk seeking this meeting," he added.

Mannix was relieved to hear the president's words.

"Kevin, we have a code word around here we use with my secretary that can get you on my calendar, no questions asked," said the president. "I want to you to continue to work on this and report back to me—and to me only," he instructed.

"I understand, Mr. President."

"*Xaverian*. It's the name of my high school. That's the code word. If you call Alice Ahern and use that word, you'll immediately be placed on my calendar. You understand?"

Mannix repeated, "*Xaverian*, sir, your high school."

The president nodded. "That's correct Kevin, *Xaverian*."

With that, Mannix was escorted out of the Oval Office by Alice Ahern.

That left the president alone to ponder how, when, or even if he was going to share this information with his wife, Kennedy.

■

It was now Holland and La Rue's third session with the Danish minister of defense on the topic of Greenland.

"Mr. Minister, we have listened to your comments from our last meeting and have an updated proposal for your consideration," began Holland.

The minister nodded.

"Our new proposal is for a fifty-year lease. There'll be an option at year twenty-five for Denmark to renegotiate the terms or exit the agreement. However, the US will retain the right of first refusal should you elect to go with another partner," Holland explained.

La Rue covered the financials. "Mr. Minister, the US will pay Denmark US$39.5 billion per year for the Greenland lease rights. That would be split $38 billion for Denmark and $1.5 billion for Greenland. To put that in perspective, today Denmark's GDP is approximately $350 billion. It really hasn't increased since 2008. You have a population of 5.8 million people. At $38 billion that would equate to an annual stipend of $6,550 per person. For a family of four that would be $26,000 per year. And for the people of Greenland, they would receive almost $25,000 per person per year."

"Miss La Rue," responded Nielsen, "Our unemployment rate is only 5.1 percent. I can see that influx of funds creating runaway inflation for us."

He wasn't wrong about that, but La Rue had anticipated the objection.

"Correct, Mr. Minister, but my figures were simply for illustrative purposes. We don't suggest Denmark should pay the $39.5 billion out in stipends. We think you should take some of the funds and use them to cut your tax rate by approximately 10 percent. That would account for $17.5 billion. Then take the remaining $22.5 billion and use it for social causes, environmental programs, childcare, and higher education. And keep in mind, this $39.5 billion is paid every year—at least for the first twenty-five years of the lease," added La Rue.

Nielsen listened to La Rue and had to admit she was convincing. In addition, the US proposal was more than twice the amount the Russians were offering (even with China's contribution). Nielsen knew Latsanych would not be happy to hear that.

Nielsen pivoted. "Tell me about your plans to develop Greenland."

Again, La Rue was prepared.

"Minister, today Greenland's population stands at fifty-six thousand, with eighteen thousand in its capital, Nuuk. Our priority will be to build infrastructure." She advanced her slides. "We plan to hire the firm that built the Denver airport in Colorado. It is our most advanced airport in the United States. It comprises fifty-four square miles and has six active runways, with space to add another six. That will be our model for a new Nuuk airport. That way Greenland can handle wide-body, long-range aircraft. In addition, we will build a state-of-the-art port that can handle the largest container ships and tankers. We plan to consult with Maersk on its design. At the same time, we'll build power plants, wind farms, and roads. We'll employ the Army Corps of Engineers to oversee the projects." La Rue gave Nielsen and his team a moment to absorb the data.

After a minute she continued. "Housing will be needed and we have a plan for that." La Rue advanced to another slide. "Here we plan to use a prebuilt modular design."

"What will be the environmental impact of all this development? And I haven't yet heard one word about the mining operations, which after all is your reason for wanting Greenland," Nielsen said.

"Your environmental experts from Copenhagen University will be invited to work alongside our experts to develop an environmental plan that is acceptable to the people of Greenland. The real benefit, Mr. Nielsen, is we can take advantage of today's innovations across all this development. The cities and roads we build will use twenty-first-century technology. For example, we propose using only EV passenger cars in Greenland, as well as EV trucks, too, once they're available. We plan to leverage wind and solar as much as we can," added La Rue.

"Solar?" asked Nielsen. "You realize during the winter the sun doesn't shine there for four months."

"That's why we will use natural gas as well," said Holland.

Holland added, "Mr. Minister, I would like to suggest you and your staff take a few days to review our latest proposal, and then we can reconvene. Say, in a week's time?"

Nielsen replied, "Yes, that sounds agreeable. At our next meeting I will be expanding our team. I have asked Dr. Alma Thomsen, one of our leading geologists and experts on Greenland, and Søren Larsen, the CEO of A.P. Moller-Maersk, to join us."

La Rue and Holland knew their proposal had been well received. In addition, the information they had collected indicated they were well ahead of Russia and China.

Their next move was to update the president and his chief of staff.

■

For Lisa Collins, the day had finally arrived. Her car pulled up to the North Drive of the White House, where she and her husband were met by Andrew and Kennedy Russell. It was a good photo op for all four of them.

A few minutes later the two couples, along with their key staff members, made their way into the White House briefing room, where the press was in attendance.

The president began, "Today, I have the distinct honor and pleasure to nominate Lisa Collins to become the fiftieth vice president of the United States. As you know, my friend and our current vice president, Jack McMasters, has stepped down in order to deal with a serious health issue. I know all Americans join Kennedy and me in keeping Jack, his wife Helen, and his family in our prayers as we extend our best wishes for his speedy recovery."

The president then went on to summarize Collins's qualifications for the position before introducing her.

"Thank you, Mr. President, and I gratefully accept your nomination for vice president," said Collins with a smile. "As director of the CIA for the last two and a half years, which was the culmination of my twenty-five years at the CIA, I have always worked tirelessly to put the safety of the American people first and foremost. Today, we live in an increasingly interconnected world. And while that has provided great innovations and improvements in productivity, not to mention advances in healthcare, education, and overall quality of life, at the same time, our interconnectivity represents an area of vulnerability that we must always be on guard to protect. I believe my time at the CIA has given me a unique perspective in the areas of cybersecurity as well as intelligence that I can leverage and bring to the administration and the American people now in the position of vice president."

It was a message that had been vetted and agreed upon by the president and his chief of staff. Its emphasis on cyber was meant to be a clear message to the world—to US allies and adversaries alike.

Sterling Spencer was pleased with Collins's presentation. He would now focus on the next phase of the process, which would have her meet with the key members of Congress so that her nomination would be overwhelmingly approved three weeks from today.

The clock was ticking, Spencer thought. It was always a risk for the country to be without an acting VP. And there were those who would recognize that risk. With that in mind, the Secret Service had implemented an enhanced protection plan for the president. Until Collins's nomination was approved, the president would be on virtual lockdown. There would be no travel outside the White House during that time, with one exception.

The president's son had the lead role of Professor Harold Hill in his high school's performance of *The Music Man*, and the president was adamant that he would attend all three performances.

The head of the president's Secret Service detail told his team, "That's trouble with a capital *T*, that rhymes with *P* and that stands for POTUS."

CHAPTER FOURTEEN

A Heart of Darkness

Magnus Nielsen was shown to the private dining room at Noma, one of Copenhagen's toniest restaurants.

Sitting at the lone table was Sergey Latsanych. "I got your message," he said.

Nodding, Nielsen sat down. "Apparently so."

Latsanych had already ordered a bottle of Merlot, which they both enjoyed before getting down to business.

"The Americans have come in with an updated and very strong proposal," said Nielsen, handing Latsanych a thumb drive.

"We expected they would," replied Latsanych, putting the USB drive into his jacket pocket.

"Not like this, you didn't," replied Nielsen. "Their proposal is easily double yours and it favors Maersk to the point where they will no doubt support it."

"Magnus, we've been anticipating this move by the Americans. It's predictable, no?" said Latsanych with a smile as he waved to the waiter through the glass door to bring another bottle of Merlot. "Your prime minister," said Latsanych, "is supportive of the Americans. That much is clear to us."

"Yes, she is. As you know she is pro-globalization and sees Greenland as an opportunity to put Denmark on a larger international stage. That is part of her reason for going to the White House next month," Nielsen said.

"We're going to start the social media campaign against her that states she is selling out Denmark to the Americans. It will be subtle at first, and then it will grow in aggressiveness and tone. Next, we're going to work to turn the trade unions against her," Latsanych said matter-of-factly as he cut into his filet mignon.

"She's popular as our first female prime minister," warned Nielsen.

"No, she's naïve, inexperienced, and much too close to the Americans," replied Latsanych with a smile. "At the same time as we start attacking her, we're going to start raising your digital profile as the person who has Denmark's identity and best interests at heart. Let us do the work. You should remain neutral in all your public comments," lectured Latsanych.

"The social media campaign is all fine and good, but the American proposal will be well received by our people," returned Nielsen.

That is when Latsanych dropped the bomb.

"We have plans underway that, we are certain, will result in the Americans withdrawing their proposal," said Latsanych.

"Withdraw their proposal?" said Nielsen in an incredulous tone.

"That is correct. This will, no doubt, cause your prime minister great embarrassment and will feed into the narrative that she is too inexperienced on the world stage," added Latsanych.

Nielsen nodded as he took in Latsanych's words.

"That will open the door for a more practical and experienced person to become prime minister. Do you know someone who would fit that profile?" said Latsanych, smiling.

Returning the smile, Nielsen said, "As a matter of fact, I do."

■

Salman Rahman settled into his chair and established his secure link. "Good afternoon, Madam Director."

"I have spoken to our president, and he has approved the transfer of funds for your photos."

"That's good news, but, Director, as you know, I'm already a wealthy person. The money is nice, but what motivates me is justice," said Rahman.

"Yes, I know. You're a true patriot, Salman," said Zlovna.

Salman, not knowing how to take her comment, let it go.

Zlovna continued, "We know where La Rue is. It will not be difficult for us to deliver her to you."

"Excellent."

"As for Andrew Russell," said Zlovna, "we have a plan for how we can use your photos to maximum benefit."

"And that is plan is?"

"That, Salman, is for us, not for you, and besides, your not knowing will be an advantage to you. Should the photos ever become public, you will want to be able to tell your government that you had nothing to do with it."

"Should they become public? What do you mean? Are you suggesting they might not be released?" asked a more animated Rahman.

"Salman, if we posted them on the Internet tonight, they would greatly embarrass the president. Our plan is much more potent than that. I need you to trust us. We'll wire the funds to your account tomorrow. Our cyberpeople will be in contact with you to add a blockchain to the photos so we'll have singular control over the images," said Zlovna.

"And when do I get La Rue?" demanded Rahman.

"We'll coordinate that with you. It will take a week to ten days," said Zlovna.

With that, a pleased Rahman terminated the call.

■

Sitting at his desk five thousand miles away, Kevin Mannix was deciphering the communications he had just intercepted between Zlovna and Rahman.

After a couple of hours of work, he was able to summarize the situation as follows:

1. The young Saudi had decided to sell his photos to the Russians—meaning all other bidders were now out. And that was supported by the falloff in call volumes with the other countries.
2. Lauren La Rue was part of the deal, and as such her safety was now at great risk. Action would need to be taken to return her to the US.
3. Clearly the Russians planned to embarrass—or threaten to embarrass—the US president with the release of these photos.

Mannix thought through the permutations of how the photos could be used. Yes, they could be posted on the Internet to great effect. But more likely, the SVR would use them more specifically to gain leverage or to even blackmail the US president.

Mannix knew that analysis of information this important needed to be vetted carefully. To that end, he wanted to sleep on it to ensure he hadn't jumped to conclusions.

It was the next day at noon when Mannix picked up the phone and placed a call to the president's private secretary. After identifying himself on the call, he said the code word, "Xaverian."

■

Søren Larsen began, "Tim, thank you for taking my call."

"Not at all," said Tim Cook, the CEO of Apple.

"Tim, this is something of a personal matter," said Larsen.

Cook was well aware that Maersk was one of the largest shippers of Apple products. Plus, Cook was keen to reinforce Apple's relationship with the highly influential Danish magnate.

"It's my son, Tim," said Larsen. "He wants to move to California. My wife isn't thrilled about it, but he feels, and I agree with him, an assignment in the US would be a good next step for his career."

"I understand," said Cook, having taken many calls like this before. "What is his field?"

"He's a techie," said Larsen. "A software engineer. He programs in Python, C++, and OpenStack."

"Well, we can always use more software engineering talent," said Cook. "Søren, I'm going to have our SVP of engineering reach out to you to arrange an interview for your son."

"Thank you, Tim. I owe you," said Larsen.

Who Larsen really owed was Lauren La Rue. She had given Larsen the heads-up that the Russian SVR was going to try to compromise his son in order to gain influence over Larsen in the Greenland negotiations. He, in turn, was doing an end run around the Russians to ensure their blackmail effort would fail.

■

Mannix had just enough time to go home and change into his suit before heading to the White House for his 5:45 p.m. meeting.

At 5:45 p.m. on the dot, Alice Ahern escorted Kevin Mannix into the Oval Office.

Mannix was surprised. In addition to the president were Lisa Collins and Sterling Spencer.

The president said, "Kevin, I've asked my chief of staff and newly nominated VP to join us."

Mannix took a deep breath as he sat on the couch opposite the two senior members of the Russell administration.

"Kevin, I've briefed Sterl and Lisa on what you shared with me a few days ago," said the president.

"Thank you, Mr. President," said Mannix. "Yesterday, I intercepted a call between Salman Rahman and the Russian director of the SVR. Sir, it's clear that Russia will be the ones obtaining the material. During the call, the SVR director, Svetlana Ivanovna Zlovna, agreed they would be able to deliver Lauren La Rue to Rahman as part of their agreement."

"Sir," said Lisa Collins to the president, "we have La Rue and Ed Holland staying at the US embassy in Copenhagen with orders that La Rue not leave the compound."

"Given this new information," said the president, "I would say we're going to have to augment her security or bring her home."

"Quite right, sir," replied Collins.

"Sir," continued Mannix, "it was clear from the conversation that the SVR plans to use the material to either embarrass you or to blackmail you."

The president smiled as Mannix used the term "material" rather than "photos" or "images." He was showing a loyalty to him that Russell appreciated.

However, having been briefed by the president, both Spencer and Collins knew what the material was that Mannix was referencing. That said, neither had seen the photos.

"Mr. President, we can look to invoke revenge-porn laws that have been passed in forty-six of the fifty states plus in Washington, D.C., and the US military," said Spencer.

"Sterl, I don't think accusing the Russians of violating our revenge-porn laws will do much," the president replied.

"There's another approach, sir," added Collins. "We can assert these photos are deepfakes, and as such, are prohibited under American law. Plus, it will call into question the authenticity of the photos."

The president thought it over for a minute. He did like the idea of claiming the photos were fakes, whether it was true or not.

Spencer, who had been researching the matter since the president brought it to his attention, was prepared. "But there still is a problem with that approach. It's *US v. Alvarez*, decided in 2012, where the Supreme Court held that the First Amendment prohibits the government from regulating speech simply because it's a lie.

"What it means, sir," said Spencer, "is that if we claimed the pictures were deepfakes—and certainly we can—we can't count on the Supreme Court to help us. They'll no doubt tell us even false claims are protected by the First Amendment."

"Lisa, with your intelligence background, I'm going to ask you to work this issue. As a country, we're going to have to have a legal and technical way to protect our citizens from these kinds of deepfakes," said the president.

"I'll get on it, sir," said Collins. "At the CIA we've already done some work on this. Yes, they can be used to show someone doing some awful things, usually something sexual, but they can be used other ways too. Deepfakes can show someone doing something they never did. Sir, it could be something as inconsequential as you bench-pressing two hundred pounds or dunking a basketball. But they could also be used maliciously regarding a police shooting or a protest. To your point, sir, very soon deepfakes are going to be a very big deal. Authenticity is going to be critical. We're going to need to involve Silicon Valley in this as we look to set standards, and it will most likely involve the blockchain."

"Wonderful," said the president. "But if the first lady were here, I don't think she'd care too much about *US v. Alvarez* or the blockchain."

"Sir, the Russians will no doubt try to threaten you with the release of this material. They'll want something in return for not releasing it, and that's where the blackmail comes in," said Mannix.

"Well, they won't get anywhere trying to blackmail me," said the president in a tone that no one dared challenge.

"What about mitigation?" said Spencer. "If the images were released, can we limit their distribution?"

Collins answered, "It would be very difficult. Not impossible, but very difficult. Sir, we could talk to the social media companies and they could filter out the images from their platforms. Going further, we could talk to all the network carriers as well as the cable companies. We could put in place a regulation via Congress and the FCC that any site that posted these images would be inaccessible from their networks. Technically, it's a relatively easy thing to do. However, getting buy-in from all parties will be the challenge."

"Sir, we could use technology the NSA has to sift through thousands of web servers. If we find a server that has one of the images on it, we could send that IP address to all the carriers and they could block access to that site by putting it on their blacklists," said Mannix.

"What's a 'blacklist'?" asked the president.

"Sir, cybersecurity companies are constantly scanning the web looking for malicious sites. These are sites that propagate malware, viruses, or have bots that try to steal personal information. These cybersecurity firms produce a list of these bad sites, collecting their IP addresses twenty-four hours a day. The list of these bad sites is known as a blacklist. Once compiled, the blacklist is then sent to carriers that subscribe to the service. Blacklists are updated and distributed on a regular basis—usually every hour or so. So, the mechanism to distribute a blacklist already exists. The NSA could create its own blacklist, which as a matter of fact we already do. But in this case, the NSA backlist would include sites that have the material posted on them," said Mannix.

"Let me summarize," said the president. "We know the Russians are going to get these photos. And they'll try to blackmail me with them. We'll assert the images are deepfakes. Then by working with Silicon Valley and the telecom carriers, we'll work to put a process in place to block the distribution of these images as best we can. Going further, Lisa, you'll head up a task force to put together a policy and propose regulations for how the US will deal with deepfakes in the future."

The president turned to Mannix. "Kevin, thank you again. Continue to keep me apprised of all new developments."

With Mannix gone, Russell turned to Spencer and Collins. "They may have shot down one of our helicopters, and now they're getting these photos to try and leverage or embarrass me. What are their reasons for taking these provocative actions?"

Spencer said, "It's almost like they're trying to provoke us, sir."

"Provoke us? I think they are trying to provoke me," replied the president.

Collins sat silently. She wasn't so sure.

■

Until she was confirmed by the Senate as vice president, Lisa Collins was still the director of the CIA. Which was why this morning found her on a video conference with Lauren La Rue.

"Lauren, our old friend the sheik's son, Salman Rahman, has resurfaced," said Collins.

"I thought that might be the reason behind our being moved into the embassy," replied La Rue.

"It was," said Collins. "But, Lauren, with Salman active again, I want to give you the option to return home."

"Just how active are we talking about?" asked La Rue.

"We've picked up chatter that he's negotiating with the Russians about abducting you."

"Lisa, if you were me, would you return home?"

"I might, but you are in a very secure location and the embassy Marines have already been briefed about the threat," answered Collins.

"I have to tell you, I think my participation in these negotiations is critical. I have my doubts about Holland being able to cross the goal line for us on this," La Rue replied.

"That's exactly why I wanted you on the assignment," said Collins, adding, "The president has more faith in Holland than I do."

"Lisa, if I were to stay, what would be the security plan?"

"Do you remember Chris Dunbar?"

"Yes, of course."

Dunbar was the CIA agent who had worked with La Rue on the Dubrovnik assignment a year and a half earlier. What La Rue wasn't sure about was whether Collins knew La Rue and Dunbar had had a brief romantic relationship afterward. It was over now, but they were still friendly.

"Dunbar is now a team leader, and you know firsthand how capable he is," said Collins. "Our plan is to send Dunbar and his team to Copenhagen as your protective detail for the duration. We can have the team there by morning."

"Well, all right, then, I'll stay. But, if you hear things are getting worse with Salman, let me know and I'll come home," replied La Rue.

"Very well. There's another topic I need to discuss with you," said Collins. "We think the Russians may have compromised Magnus Nielsen."

"It doesn't surprise me. He seems to have a bias for them."

"Lauren, my father was an SVP at Dun & Bradstreet. He used to tell me whenever they licensed their marketing file, they would always add a few fake records to the file. The fake records were unique to each client. That way D&B could always identify and track where their files went. If those fake records ever showed up at another client, D&B would know where the file had originated. It was a simple but effective way to track file versions," said Collins.

La Rue anticipated where Collins was headed. "We're going to set Nielsen up," said La Rue.

"Not just Nielsen but his whole team," said Collins. "For our next proposal, each copy will have just the slightest of changes— only a word or two—or some punctuation alterations. You'll note who gets each copy. If one of those copies winds up in Moscow, we'll know where the leak originated."

La Rue understood that Collins had a source in Moscow able to access the proposal if it got there.

"Lauren, this is for our eyes only. No need to bring Holland in on this," said the director of the CIA.

"Understood," was La Rue's reply.

■

Director Zlovna had her weekly status call with Latsanych.

"How are you progressing, Sergey?" she asked.

"Madam Director, we're making good progress. We are ready for the social media campaigns to begin against the Danish prime minister," he said.

"They can begin this weekend," stated Zlovna.

"Madam Director, the Americans are presenting a very compelling financial proposal."

"We've got to continue to drive home that our plan is less disruptive to the Greenland ecosystem. We know we won't be able to compete against the Americans on financial incentives, so we need to rely on an eco-friendly plan," said Zlovna.

"Madam Director, I had another idea I want to run by you. We know all the negotiating meetings between the Danes and Americans are occurring at the American embassy. I'd like your permission to deploy a sonic weapon," said Latsanych referring to a technology that Russia had successfully used in Cuba against the US Embassy.

Zlovna reflected on Latsanych's plan, which highlighted how the Russian Federation had outdistanced the US in terms of psyops. While the Americans built their aircraft carriers and submarines, the

Russians were investing in psyops and cyberwarfare. From that perspective, both Collins and Zlovna—two extremely powerful women and quite likely the future leaders of their countries—were correct. The future would be centered on offensive and defensive weapons based on cyber and psyops rather than metal decks and missiles. Going further, from an economic stance, the return on investment for psyops and cyber was much more favorable than that for building new physical weapons systems.

Zlovna asked, "Sergey, what's your goal for the sonic weapon?"

"At a low setting the sonic weapon can cause irritability and headaches. I suggest we deploy it to impact the US meetings with the Danes."

"Is there any risk the weapon can do more damage than that?" asked Zlovna.

"At a higher setting, yes, it can cause more damage, but we would only use it on a low setting. Just enough to affect the US personnel and to impact their meetings."

"Sergey, I approve the use of the sonic weapon, but no mistakes. Is that clear?"

"Crystal clear, Madam Director. No mistakes," committed Latsanych.

CHAPTER FIFTEEN

Man's Best Friend

Chris Dunbar and his CIA security team landed their C-130J in Denmark on a rather sunny morning. The C-130J would remain in Copenhagen until Dunbar's mission was completed. Gathering their gear, they were transported to the US embassy, located in the heart of Copenhagen.

The Marine captain in charge of the embassy's security detail welcomed Dunbar and his team. The embassy Marine detachment numbered twelve. That plus Dunbar's team of five was deemed to be an adequate-sized force to support the Greenland negotiations and provided added protection for La Rue while still covering the standard embassy security needs.

In addition to the twelve Marines, there were also three German shepherds as part of the detachment's K-9 team, trained to detect explosives. A dog lover, Chris Dunbar spent a few minutes petting the dogs and getting acquainted.

He was crouched down with the dogs when he heard a woman's voice say, "I was told the best of the best were going to be here."

Looking up, Dunbar saw Lauren La Rue coming down the embassy's main staircase.

For a moment neither said another word. Then Dunbar turned

to his team and said, "Team, this is our protectee: Miss Lauren La Rue. She's with the Agency's Cyber & Financial Analytics Team."

La Rue approached Dunbar, saying, "Chris, I'm glad you're here. You look well."

"Yes, ma'am," said an embarrassed Dunbar.

La Rue could obviously sense Dunbar's discomfort and pivoted. "Introduce me to your team, Agent Dunbar."

"Moorhead, Macklem, Maubach, and Dinkel," said Dunbar with each agent nodding as they acknowledged La Rue.

La Rue replied with a lighthearted, "It sounds more like the name of a law firm."

Unlike the business attire the embassy personnel wore or the US Marines in their camouflage uniforms, Dunbar's team was clad in black tactical suits complete with bulletproof vests and helmets.

"Chris, I'm sure you and your team need to get settled. Once that's out of the way, come see me. I have a meeting this morning, but I'll be free this afternoon," said La Rue with a smile.

■

At 10 a.m. Magnus Nielsen and his delegation arrived for their next session with Holland and La Rue's team.

As promised, along with Nielsen was Denmark's leading geologist and expert on Greenland's rare-earth minerals, Dr. Alma Thomsen, and A.P. Moller-Maersk's CEO, Søren Larsen.

Holland and La Rue stood as Nielsen's team entered the conference room.

Holland held out his hand to Dr. Thomsen and simply said, "Dr. Thomsen, I've heard many good things about you. It is a pleasure to meet you. I'm Ed Holland, the president's senior economic adviser."

Thomsen simply said, "Hello," and shook Holland's hand.

La Rue got a similar greeting from Thomsen, but when it came to the Maersk CEO, he gave La Rue a rather warm hello, which surprised Magnus Nielsen, as he did not know the two were acquainted.

"Lauren, it is good to see you again," said Larsen.

"Søren, good to see you too. I trust your family is well?" asked La Rue.

"Quite well, thank you," said Larsen with a smile.

Pleasantries exchanged, the meeting began in earnest, with La Rue's team handing out updated proposals to Nielsen and each member of his team.

Holland began, "To recap, our proposal is for a fifty-year lease with a twenty-five-year out for the exclusive rights to all of Greenland's minerals and natural resources. The US will compensate Denmark at the rate of US$38 billion per annum and $1.5 billion per annum for Greenland."

Thomsen interrupted. "You Americans. I'm continually amazed by your arrogance. You think you can come to Denmark and buy our consent?"

The American team was at a loss at Thomsen's remarks and aggressiveness.

For all Holland yielded to La Rue in terms of financial savvy, he did possess the greater experience with diplomacy and responded, "I'm sorry, Doctor, if my approach struck you as abrupt, but we've been working on this proposal for some time now and I thought in the spirit of brevity I could be direct."

Holland paused to gauge Thomsen's body language, which was still hostile, before adding, "But clearly, I was mistaken. My apologizes. For the record, the United States recognizes—and values dearly—our relationship with Denmark as it does with Greenland."

Thomsen didn't respond.

Lauren entered the conversation. "From our last proposal we have agreed to increase the percentage of materials transported from Greenland on Maersk ships from 35 percent to 50 percent."

"Ms. La Rue, my board and I are expecting that 75 percent of all shipping will occur on Maersk ships," Larsen interjected.

La Rue, an experienced negotiator from her deals with the sheik, countered, "I understand, and we'll take that point under consideration." She knew they weren't going to lose this deal over the percentage of Maersk shipping.

Holland added, "Minister Nielsen, you'll notice in our latest proposal that the US will provide a 25 percent discount to any Dane purchasing a Tesla or any other EV vehicle. We believe this will be a strong incentive and will be a big step to improving the air quality and climate of Denmark."

President Russell himself had suggested the Tesla discount in their last call.

With Nielsen and his staff reviewing the latest proposal, Thomsen said, "And while you are 'improving' the quality of our air, what about the people of Greenland?"

Holland responded, "Doctor, in our earlier meetings we already agreed that all new passenger cars on Greenland will be EVs, and as soon as commercial EV trucks are available, we will transition to them as well."

Thomsen asked, "Just where will all the electricity come from to power all these EVs in Nuuk?"

La Rue took that one. "We have plans to build an electric plant in Nuuk that is powered by geothermal energy."

"I'd like to see those plans, Miss La Rue," added Thomsen, not giving an inch.

La Rue, one not to be talked down to, added, "We're also enhancing our payments to Greenland's pro-environment Inuit Ataqatigiit government from $1.5 billion to $2 billion per year."

The meeting continued for the next two hours, with Thomsen continuing to voice her objections to the American proposal.

At the end, Holland summarized: "We believe our latest proposal addresses all of your previous concerns. Minister Nielsen, as you know, your prime minister will be visiting the White House next month. It is our hope that we can turn that meeting into a signing ceremony."

"There is another matter that is critical to us," replied Nielsen.

"And what is that?" asked a surprised Holland.

"We need the US to drop its opposition to the Nord Stream 2 project," Nielsen replied.

That was a curveball neither Holland nor La Rue had anticipated.

"We'll need to pass this by Washington, of course," said Holland smoothly.

"Nord Stream 2 is important not only for Denmark but for our European allies," added Nielsen. "And as mentioned, we'll need a larger incentive for our people to purchase EVs. In addition, Mr. Larsen's request for more of the shipping to take place on his company's ships is critical to us."

La Rue knew Nielsen's points on additional EV incentives and more Maersk shipping were both easy to agree to, and, in the big picture, immaterial.

Again, Thomsen spoke up. "Just for the record, I am opposed to this entire agreement. I see this proposal by the Americans as causing irreparable damage to the fragile ecosystem of Greenland. I will make these opinions known to Prime Minister Henriksen directly."

The American delegation was caught off guard by Thomsen's recurring opposition to their proposal. But, as it was time for the meeting to adjourn, La Rue and Holland thanked the attendees for their time. La Rue took note that everyone placed their copies of the proposal in their briefcases.

Thomsen's objections aside, Nielsen was not surprised by the updated American proposal. It was clear the Americans would agree to almost anything the Danes requested in order to secure this agreement. But the new angle from the meeting to be explored was whether Thomsen's objections could be leveraged by the Russians.

Nielsen expected that Latsanych would soon be launching an aggressive social media campaign to persuade the Danish people to oppose the American proposal.

Thinking politically, Nielsen could see how he could use Thomsen as an ally in his attempts to inflict political damage on Prime Minister Henriksen.

CHAPTER SIXTEEN

Havana Syndrome

Latsanych badgered Nielsen into getting a copy of the American's latest proposal. With that in hand, Latsanych forwarded a copy to Zlovna. Zlovna would communicate with the Chinese that they would have to improve their offer if they wished to be considered competitive with the Americans.

But it was clear that even with an improved economic offer, the Russian and Chinese proposal would not compare favorably with the American proposal, which was clearly superior. That meant the SVR would have to use every asset at its disposal to gain an advantage. That included the photos of Kennedy Russell as well as deploying a microwave weapon that would disrupt the American negotiations. The sonic weapon would impart severe vertigo and debilitating headaches on the American negotiating team.

Russia had perfected this new class of sonic weapons, which would use directed energy to cause traumatic brain injury, or TBI, now termed "Havana syndrome."

With the sonic transponder aimed through the windows of the Russian embassy and targeting the US embassy, which was a short one hundred yards away, the SVR technician entered a few commands at Latsanych's direction, and the amplifiers started to broadcast the invisible and inaudible-to-the-human-ear signals over the air toward the three-story US embassy.

Chris Dunbar had just come back from his afternoon run and was playing with the embassy dogs when, for no apparent reason, they started to yelp and bark. It was strange behavior because there was no one around other than Dunbar and the dogs' handlers. And there were no packages nearby that could set the dogs off to alert.

Dunbar shook his head in puzzlement, but had to get cleaned up to meet with his team and then prepare for his status call with Langley and Fort Meade.

An hour and a half later, as Dunbar made his way to the embassy conference room, he noted the dogs were still acting oddly, but he had no time to stop and check things out.

As he settled into the conference room chair, Lauren La Rue entered.

"I've been asked to join the call," she said.

"That's fine," replied Dunbar, adding, "Lauren, sorry I was so businesslike before."

"Yeah, I wasn't sure what was going on there," she replied.

"How have you been?"

"Fine, but hip-deep in this Greenland negotiation."

"Well, you look well," said Dunbar.

Just then images started to appear on the flat-screen.

On the call from the NSA were Kristin Bartlett and Kevin Mannix. From the CIA was Lisa Collins and two of her direct reports.

As everyone for the call was assembling, La Rue asked Dunbar, "What's with the dogs?"

Dunbar replied, "I don't know. They've been acting like that all day."

With that Lisa Collins began, "Well, if we are done talking about the dogs, maybe we can get to the business at hand."

"Yes, Director," said La Rue, who covertly rolled her eyes at Dunbar.

The first part of the meeting involved an update on the Greenland negotiations. Holland wasn't present since this call did not involve the White House.

La Rue provided the updates along with sharing Dr. Thomsen's objections. She added, "Nielsen brought up Nord Stream 2. They want us to drop our sanctions and opposition to the project."

Collins noted La Rue's comments. She was vaguely familiar with the Nord Stream project but would have to do more research on it before she could give La Rue any direction.

They then discussed the distribution of the unique copies of the proposals and how Collins would be following up with her sources in Moscow to determine which copy, if any, wound up there.

Chris Dunbar gave a report on the security plan they had in place for La Rue.

After another thirty minutes the call concluded.

■

The next morning, before meeting with Sterling Spencer, Lisa Collins familiarized herself with the Nord Stream project.

Back in 2011, the Russians and Germans came to an agreement whereby the Russians would sell natural gas to the Germans. That led to the development of a controversial gas line between Russia and Germany known as the Nord Stream project.

The United States, as well as several European countries, objected to the project because of concerns the pipeline would increase Russia's influence over the region. Nevertheless, and over the objections of the US, the first line, Nord Stream 1, went live in November 2011, delivering a capacity of 1.9 trillion cubic feet of gas per year to the German population.

However, the second line, known as Nord Stream 2, which was intended to go live in 2020, had been delayed due to the imposition of US sanctions. Part of the resistance to Nord Stream 2 was due to the US's increased production of natural gas from its own expanded shale and fracking activities. As a new power player in energy, the US sought to become the supplier of natural gas to Western Europe, and as a result saw Nord Stream as a competitor.

So, there was not just an economic and security concern interest but also a political one, realized Collins, mindful of her new position.

In her meeting in Sterling Spencer's office, Collins relayed, "Our negotiations have progressed nicely on the Greenland project. But they did add a new condition. The Danes want us to drop our opposition to Nord Stream 2."

"That will take some doing. And you say it just came up? Hmm, I'll need to talk to the president about it, but I doubt we will let it stand in the way of signing the Greenland deal," he said.

Spencer knew that Nord Stream was critically important to Germany and now with the first pipeline already in place, the American objections to a second pipeline was more window dressing than hard policy.

■

The Marine on duty at the Copenhagen embassy noticed a flashing light on his security panel. It was an alarm he was not familiar with. He called his supervisor and they determined that one of the embassy's rooftop sensors had detected a signal indicating some sort of sonic event was taking place.

As protocol, they called in to Langley to report the incident. That caused a series of activities to take place back in the US.

One was to page the NSA's acoustic expert, Alex Zucker.

Alex Zucker was called by the duty center to investigate why the acoustic sensor had triggered an alarm at the Copenhagen embassy.

Calling the embassy, Zucker spoke with the Marine on duty and gave him some commands to run on the sensor to first ensure it was not malfunctioning.

With the diagnostics passed, Zucker asked if anything was out of the ordinary at the embassy.

The Marine on duty replied, "No, everything is quiet here. Except our dogs are barking and acting kind of strange."

"Your dogs were barking?" asked Zucker.

"Yes, sir," replied the Marine.

Zucker started tilting his head back and forth before asking, "When did that start?"

"Sometime this morning, I think. I can ask the sergeant who handles the dogs if you need a more specific time," added the Marine.

"Yes, please do. I want to speak with him," said Zucker.

It took a few minutes, but Alex Zucker finally got through to the Marine sergeant in charge of the canines.

After speaking with the sergeant, Zucker had a lead he wanted to pursue, but in order to do that he needed to enlist the help of the CIA team leader, Chris Dunbar.

Speaking to him on the phone a few minutes later, he said, "Agent Dunbar, I'm Alex Zucker. I work for Kristin Bartlett and Kevin Mannix at the Fort," shorthand for NSA headquarters.

"How can I help you?" asked Dunbar.

"Agent Dunbar, I'm an acoustic expert. We had a rooftop sensor go off and I am following up on that."

"I don't know anything about a sensor going off," replied Dunbar.

"I spoke with the Marine sergeant in charge of the canines over there. He said his dogs started to act up this morning."

"Listen, Mr. Zucker, I really don't think I can help you," said an increasingly impatient Dunbar.

"Agent Dunbar, I've been studying ultrasonic weapons that use various types of sound to injure, incapacitate, or kill a target. By employing a focused ultrasonic beam one can create cavitations and tissue shearing, which can cause a disorder of the brain called encephalopathy," stated Zucker.

Dunbar didn't follow much of what Zucker said, but he did lock on to the phrase "kill a target."

Zucker said, "Do you remember what happened at our embassy in Cuba back in 2016? We believe the Russians executed a micro-wave strike, or directed-energy attack, that resulted in sonic delusions and lasting brain damage among our embassy staff and their family members. It led to what is now referred to as 'Havana syndrome.'"

Dunbar replied, "You've piqued my interest, Mr. Zucker. Is there any easy way to know if we're being hit by sonic signals?"

"Are you familiar with parabolic microphones, the type you see on the sidelines at football games?" asked Zucker.

"The big plastic dishes?"

"Exactly. I need you to get one. We then have to hook it up to a laptop to capture some wave files. Send the files to me and I'll process them against my algorithms, and we'll know if you're under sonic attack or not," said Zucker.

"Where do I get one of these microphones?" asked Dunbar.

Zucker knew the names of manufacturers of the microphones, but they didn't have time to order one. Thinking for a minute, Zucker came up with an idea.

"Go to a local television station, one that broadcasts soccer matches over there. They should have one," said Zucker.

"Mr. Zucker, are there any symptoms from one of these sonic weapons?" asked Dunbar.

"It depends on the power setting. At a low setting it would cause people to become irritable and short-tempered. At a high setting it could cause brain damage, but that usually takes a couple days of exposure. If this is a sonic attack and it's been going on for most of the day, you should already start seeing symptoms in people's behavior," continued Zucker.

"Okay, I'm going to look into getting one of these parabolic mics as soon as we can. Once I have it, I'll get back in touch with you."

"I'll be here. Just call me when you have the mic. You'll want to set it up on the roof and tune it in until we find the signal. One last thing, Agent. I could be completely wrong on this. The dogs might be reacting to something completely unrelated," said Zucker.

"You may be wrong, but we need to find out for sure," said Dunbar, who was already pinging his men via his radio.

Chris Dunbar's next move was to inform James McGinley, the US ambassador.

In turn, McGinley correctly brought Ed Holland and Lauren La Rue into the conversation.

"Now that you mention it, I've noticed some short tempers from my staff today," commented the ambassador.

Holland and La Rue both wondered if this could explain some of Dr. Thomsen's behavior in their meeting, but then they returned to the matter at hand.

"TV 2 is the Danish television channel that broadcasts the Danish soccer matches. They'll be the ones most likely to have one of these parabolic microphones," said the ambassador. He buzzed his attaché to get the CEO of TV 2 on the phone.

A few minutes later McGinley was speaking with the TV 2 CEO, Anna Stig Christensen.

After he explained what he was looking for and why, Christensen replied, "Ambassador, let me check with my VP of operations to determine if we have the device you're looking for and, if so, where it is. I will get back to you shortly."

In the meantime, McGinley told his chief of staff to alert all embassy employees to go home and plan to work remotely the following day. It was going on 5:00 p.m. in Copenhagen.

A few minutes later the TV 2 CEO rang back. "We have one of those microphones at our facility at Parken Stadium. I am sending one of our people there now to find it and get it ready for your people to pick it up."

McGinley said, "That is wonderful news. Thank you, Ms. Christensen; we are grateful for your help."

McGinley turned to Dunbar, saying, "The soccer stadium isn't far from here."

Dunbar replied, "I know where it is. I run by it every morning. Sir, my team and I will head there now. Once we have the device, we have technicians standing by at the NSA to help us set it up."

"Very well," said McGinley. "Let me know once you have the equipment, and then I would appreciate regular updates."

"Yes, Ambassador, I'll keep you apprised of our progress."

In a matter of minutes Dunbar and his team pulled into the stadium parking lot. Waiting for them was a TV 2 engineer holding a parabolic microphone.

"I've been told to provide any assistance you may require."

Because of the urgency of the situation, Dunbar decided to accept the technician's offer to help set up the equipment.

Twenty minutes later Dunbar and his team, along with the TV 2 technician, Sven, were on the roof of the embassy setting up the parabolic microphone on its tripod.

Dunbar got Zucker on the line, connecting him with Sven so they could talk technically.

It took more than an hour to correctly align the microphone. Then the hard work started. Using software scripts, Alex Zucker started to tune the parabolic microphone to pick up wavelengths in the 19–20 kHz range.

Dunbar asked, "Alex, how long will this take?"

"It will take as long as it takes," replied Zucker, who was not known for his people skills within the NSA. Zucker added, "I think it will take an hour or so more to recalibrate the microphone. Once that's done, I'll be able to start collecting the wave files. But, Chris, running the wave files against my algorithms—that will take all night."

By daybreak in Copenhagen, Zucker had collected enough wave files to start feeding his algorithms.

It didn't take him long.

"Bingo," said Zucker. His algorithms had detected and decrypted the signals. But knowing the shit storm this would create, Zucker took another hour to process three more files to ensure his assessment was correct.

A little after 9:00 a.m. in Copenhagen, Zucker was ready to share his information. That meant a conference call had to be hastily arranged.

It was a few minutes after 2:00 a.m. in Washington when the conference bridge was opened. On the call were Lisa Collins, Kristin Bartlett, Kevin Mannix, and, of course, Alex Zucker. The Copenhagen team was comprised of McGinley, Holland, La Rue, Dunbar, and the Marine captain.

Zucker jumped right into the technical explanation. "By using my algorithms I have detected that a long-range acoustic device, or LRAD, is bombarding our embassy in Copenhagen with an ultrasonic weapon, or USW. We should think of this device as showering our embassy with what amounts to sonic bullets or sonic grenades."

Collins asked, "What's the risk to our people?"

"Right now, because of the wide spread of the beam, the effect has been irritability and headaches. But if the power settings were increased or the beam columnated, our people would start feeling intense pain, with brain damage to follow if the exposure was long enough, Director."

Collins questioned, "Alex, are you certain the beam is originating from the Russian embassy?"

"I'm as certain of this as I am lithium is the number three element on the periodic table," said Zucker.

Kristin Bartlett, who was well aware of Zucker's brilliance but also his quirkiness, interjected before anyone else could and asked, "Alex, in English, are you sure this is coming from the Russian embassy?"

Zucker replied, "Yes, ma'am, one hundred percent."

Collins was already thinking about next steps. "Ambassador, what is the status of your staff?"

McGinley replied, "All nonessential personnel are working from home today. That leaves only my staff of five plus the Marine contingent of twelve along with Mr. Holland's CIA team."

"Alex, can we jam this signal?" asked Collins.

"In time we could, but it would take days to set up. At the current power setting, this beam does not represent a lethal dose, but there is nothing to say the Russians won't increase the power of the beam in the next five minutes," replied Zucker.

Bartlett asked, "If we can't jam it, can we take it out?"

"It will take me some work, but yes, I'm sure I could determine which window the beam is coming from," said Zucker.

"If you can determine which window the beam is coming from, how hard of a shot would that be?" next asked Collins.

Dunbar said, "The Russian embassy is only about a hundred yards from us. It is an easy target for any member of my team. We can shoot out the window and have another sniper ready to take out the transponder once the glass is cleared."

"When we shoot through the window, what assurances do we have we won't hit a Russian?" asked Collins.

The ambassador responded, "Why do we care? They're attacking us. We're just defending ourselves." Collins wasn't sure if this was McGinley's real advice or an example of the irritability caused by the sonic weapon. Either way she decided not to respond to him.

"Chris, can you take the shot and minimize the likelihood of hitting someone at the Russian embassy?" asked Collins.

"Ma'am, I think we could shoot out the corners of the window and that would minimize the chances of hitting someone," replied Dunbar.

"Lisa, I'm sure President Russell would prefer us defending ourselves rather than running from the danger," said McGinley.

Collins paused, then said, "Alex, work with Agent Dunbar and the Marines and identify the location of the beam. Once we have the window identified, deploy your sharpshooters but do not fire until we give you a green light. Is that understood? You have a weapons HOLD until we speak again."

"Yes, Director. Understood," replied Dunbar.

With that, Dunbar, the Marine captain, Zucker, and Mannix were asked to drop off the call to work the problem.

That left Collins, Bartlett, McGinley, Holland, and La Rue on the call.

La Rue now joined the conversation. "The bigger question is why are the Russians doing this?"

"They want to disrupt our negotiations?" Holland questioned.

It made sense. At the lower power setting this would just cause aggravation, which could cause the negotiation meetings to become testy.

Collins was already thinking through the permutations of this suggestion. The negotiations were important—but important enough for the Russians to take this provocative step? But then she realized there could be another reason.

Using the confidential chat line, Collins sent a message just to Bartlett. It was only one word—La Rue.

Bartlett typed a reply, "They want our team to evacuate the embassy so they can abduct La Rue?"

"Maybe," replied Collins.

Collins spoke aloud, "Ambassador, let us know as soon as the snipers are in place. If there is any delay in determining the exact location of the sonic weapon, you need to be prepared to evacuate the embassy."

∎

Meanwhile, not a quarter mile away in the Russian embassy, Sergey Latsanych was with his team monitoring the situation.

"Should we increase the power of the beam?" asked the technician.

"No, just keep it as it is," were Latsanych's orders.

Latsanych initiated a call with Director Zlovna.

"Madam Director, we are ready to commence the next phase of the mission," said Latsanych.

"Are you sure the Americans have detected our sonic weapon?" asked Zlovna.

"We noticed they have placed a parabolic microphone on the roof and most of the embassy staff did not come into work this morning. So, I think it is very likely they have detected our beam," replied Latsanych.

"Good, then terminate the beam and move on to phase two of the operation. Make sure your people are in place," said Zlovna.

"Understood, Madam Director," Latsanych said, terminating the call so he could get on with his other tasks.

It only took a few minutes for Latsanych to tell his team to terminate the sonic weapon and to begin to disassemble the equipment.

∎

Alex Zucker said, "Wait a minute. I've lost the signal."

"What do you mean we've lost the signal?" asked Dunbar.

"Hold on a second," said Zucker, wanting to check a few things before responding to the CIA agent. "No, it's gone," said Zucker with certainty.

"What does that mean?" asked Dunbar.

"It means they are no longer broadcasting. They've turned off their device," answered a still puzzled Zucker.

"Do we at least know which window it was coming from?" asked Dunbar.

"We know it was from their fifth floor, but we haven't located the exact window yet. It could be one of four, I would say," replied Zucker.

Dunbar went to brief the ambassador, Holland, and La Rue.

∎

Latsanych texted his team who were standing by in a white van parked in the alley across the street from the American embassy. "The breakfast will be ready in ten minutes."

Next Latsanych ordered the technician in the Russian embassy, "Initiate pressure increase."

The Russians had replaced the gas regulators' pressure sensors that the local gas company, Ørsted, had on the lines that fed the US embassy. The Ørsted main line fed gas from a high-pressure (75 psi, or pounds per square inch) main pipeline via regulators controlled by sensors that typically would reduce the pressure to 0.5 psi.

With this change, the Russians could, on command, send the main pipeline's full pressure into the embassy.

The procedure caused natural gas to build up in the embassy's kitchen, where, with no personnel on duty, no one detected the smell of gas.

Within a matter of minutes, the kitchen filled with natural gas, which exploded at 9:27 a.m., igniting a major fire at the rear of the first floor of the embassy.

With fire alarms blaring, the Marines initiated their evacuation plan.

Dunbar said to the US ambassador, Holland, and La Rue, "With the embassy no longer secure, I'm making the call that we leave Denmark. I've got the C-130 spinning up at the airport."

Dunbar was sharing the escape plan that had been put in place in case the need arose for a quick exit from Copenhagen. Dunbar decided that time had come, and it was his call and his alone.

"Is it really necessary that we leave? Our work here is critical," said Ed Holland.

"Your safety is my responsibility—first the sonic attack and now the fire. Someone wants us out of this building," said Dunbar.

He addressed his team of CIA agents. "Dan, you take Wade and Holland in your vehicle. I'll take Rick, Amanda, and La Rue in my vehicle. We depart in three minutes. We'll take Route 1 to the airport," said Dunbar.

Looking at the Marine captain, Dunbar ordered, "Captain deploy your men out front in two teams on either side of our vehicles. Make sure the rescue and fire personnel and vehicles don't block our exit."

The Marine captain turned to his men, issuing commands as they each grabbed their M4/M4A1 5.56mm carbines, now the standard-issue firearm for most units in the US military.

"Copy that, sir. We're ready to rock," said the Marine captain, as he and his team exited the embassy with their rifles on full auto.

Everyone exited the embassy and got into the Suburbans as the Marines took their positions.

Dunbar said, "We don't stop for anything. Let's move out."

At the airport, the two US Air Force pilots along with their crew of three, who were staying at a motel across the street from

Copenhagen's Kastrup Airport, got the call to scramble. They quickly packed their bags, got into their rental vehicle, and made their way to their C-130J, which was parked off by itself on the apron of runway 22R.

Preflighting their Super Hercules and spinning up their engines, the Air Force pilots notified the tower that they planned to be departing shortly and asked for priority departure procedures. That meant they would be able to choose which of the three active runways they wanted to depart from—04L/22R (3,600m/11,811ft), 04R/22L (3,300m/10,827ft), or 12/30 (2,800m/9,186ft).

The scene at the US embassy was increasingly hectic, with Copenhagen Emergency Services arriving. Based on that activity Latsanych's team decided it would be better to engage Dunbar's team at the airport. As a result, the white van with its five commandos departed for Kastrup Airport five minutes before Dunbar's Suburbans pulled out of the embassy driveway.

It was a well-informed decision, as the Marine complement of twelve, all armed with M4s, as well as Dunbar's team of five would have no doubt outgunned Latsanych's team of five.

Dunbar yelled, "Let's go," as the two black SUVs made an abrupt left turn out of the embassy driveway. The ten-kilometer drive to Copenhagen's Kastrup Airport would normally take about twenty minutes. But Dunbar didn't care about traffic or speed limits this morning. With grill lights flashing, the two black Suburbans wove in and out of traffic, arriving at the airport just a few minutes after 10 a.m.

The C-130J already had its engines turned up and the rear cargo ramp was down, anticipating the arrival of Dunbar and his charges.

Dunbar's team surrounded La Rue and Holland as they started to make their way to the cargo ramp.

No one heard the shot when it rang out, but they could see one of the engines on the C-130J start to smoke.

A Russian sniper was firing silenced rounds into engines 1 and 2 on the aircraft's left wing. It was clear that the C-130J wouldn't be able to fly.

Surveying the situation, Dunbar shouted, "Back to the cars."

As they made their way to the Suburbans, they started to take fire. Quickly Dunbar moved his team behind the lead SUV, which provided a shield from the gunfire that was originating from the hangar some fifty feet away from them.

Dunbar looked over and saw that Macklem was hit in the leg. Dinkel helped Macklem to the rear of the first Suburban and tried to administer some basic field dressing to his wound.

Dunbar and his team carried HK416 assault rifles manufactured by the German company Heckler & Koch. With a design based on the AR-15, the HK416 relied on its proprietary short-stroke gas piston system, which provided a faster rate of fire with less chance of jamming. The HK416 was the standard assault rifle for the Navy SEALs as well as many foreign forces.

The automatic fire quickly turned the lead SUV into a wreck, but it had served its purpose of providing cover for Dunbar and his team. Fire was now coming from three shooters in the hangar as well as two shooters on the roof.

Dunbar sent Moorhead and Macklem behind the first Suburban as the other laid down a hail of automatic fire. They were still pinned down, but at least now they had two fire points to return fire.

Dunbar was basically sitting on La Rue, using his body as a shield.

CIA Agent Dinkel had centered his sights on the rooftop just as one of the Russian commandos raised his head to fire. He never got the chance. Dinkel took him out with a 5.56x45mm bottlenecked rimless intermediate cartridge. It was no surprise. Dinkel was the best shot on the team.

But the fire being laid down by the three commandos from the hangar was keeping Dunbar and his charges from getting into the remaining SUV and fleeing—and that was a problem.

"Argh," came the sound from Maubach. She had been hit in the right arm. Dunbar rolled over to her position and helped place a sterile pad around her arm, taping it to contain the blood.

Two of Dunbar's team were now injured. They were still in the fight, but Dunbar knew they were losing the initiative, which was always key in any engagement.

Just then a torrent of machine-gun fire erupted into the hangar.

Two of the flight crew from the C-130J had opened up with their M240 7.62mm machine guns. With a rate of fire of 550 rounds per minute, the two Air Force sergeants were changing out their ammo boxes as fast as they could while keeping the Russian commandos pinned down.

The onslaught of fire from the M240s allowed Dunbar and his team to pile into the remaining SUV, with Dunbar yelling to the driver, "Just go. Go."

Dunbar wasn't sure where to head, knowing the embassy wouldn't be secure due to the fire. But he knew he needed to get medical treatment for his two injured agents.

"We need to find a hospital," yelled Dunbar. At his command, La Rue started to search for the nearest hospital on her phone. Finding one, she handed her phone to Dunbar, who directed the driver, "Here's our twenty"—the code word for "destination."

Next Dunbar called the embassy Marine captain, saying with urgency, "Captain, I have two injured agents. We're headed to Rigshospitalet University Hospital. I need you to send a five-man detail there to provide security. Also, we're low on ammo. We need you to bring us some mags."

"Copy. I'll send my team there now, sir," replied the Marine captain. "We'll bring some ammo for you too."

It didn't take long before the black SUV pulled into the emergency entrance of Rigshospitalet. Dunbar and his team of two uninjured got out, still carrying their automatic weapons as they burst into the lobby area.

"We need two gurneys now," yelled Dunbar to the shocked staff.

An emergency room orderly quickly grabbed a nearby gurney and started for the door.

At the same time, hospital security began to draw their pistols, when Dunbar yelled, "We're American CIA. Put your weapons down."

La Rue helped the injured agent Amanda Maubach into the emergency room and onto a vacant bed in one of the treatment rooms.

Doctors quickly circled Maubach and Macklem, administering treatment.

Just then the US Marines arrived, adding to the chaos of the situation.

The Marine captain started moving three boxes of 5.56 mags into the back of Dunbar's SUV.

"Sir, we've got this," said the Marine captain to Dunbar.

Dunbar spoke to Maubach and Macklem, telling them the Marines would stay at the hospital until they were both released back to the embassy.

"Copy that," said Macklem, who was already feeling better.

Nodding, Dunbar said, "We need to go. Dan, Rick, get La Rue and Holland back into the SUV. We're leaving."

"We need to get out of here, but I don't know exactly where we should go. Maybe the British embassy," said Dunbar, thinking out loud.

With everyone now in the SUV, Dunbar demanded, "Give me your cell phones."

Taking them one by one, he threw the phones out the window of the SUV as it sped away from the hospital.

"We're now EMCOM," said Dunbar, which meant they were going radio silent and wouldn't be using any of their cell phones or radios.

"Where to, sir?" asked Moorhead, who was driving.

"I'm not sure. We need to find a place to lay low for a while," Dunbar responded.

Just then he saw a parking garage. "There," Dunbar yelled. "The parking garage."

Moorhead turned into the garage, navigated the SUV to the third floor, and then parked.

For a moment no one spoke. They just let the adrenaline discharge from their bodies.

"What's the plan, sir?" asked Dinkel.

"I'm not sure, but we need to get some new phones," Dunbar replied.

Dunbar looked at Moorhead and Dinkel in their black tactical outfits and knew he couldn't send them to buy the phones.

He knew La Rue would volunteer, but she was the last person he wanted out of his sight, suspecting some of this chaos might have been because of her.

Dunbar then looked at Holland, who was wearing a button-down shirt and jacket.

"Mr. Holland, we need your assistance," said Dunbar in a calm tone.

A few minutes later Agent Dinkel, wearing Holland's shirt and jacket, ventured out on the streets of downtown Copenhagen to procure several prepaid cell phones.

No one noticed Dinkel's tactical pants or boots, and they fit in with what many of the young men in Copenhagen wore. Especially as they were black, which was the common color for most of the clothing in the urban city.

While Dinkel was out getting the phones, La Rue spoke up. "I have an idea."

After a few minutes of discussion, Dunbar agreed with La Rue's plan.

■

Latsanych was taking stock of his situation and he wasn't happy. He had lost three men in the Kastrup Airport attack and failed to accomplish his mission's goal, which was to capture Lauren La Rue.

He knew the Americans had not returned to their embassy, which meant they were still at large somewhere in Copenhagen. Plus, with their plane disabled, they would need to look for an alternative way to leave Copenhagen.

Latsanych thought about what he would do if he were the Americans. They might seek protection from the Danish authorities, which Latsanych hoped for, as his relationship with Nielsen would come into play.

Beyond seeking help from the Danes, it was possible the Americans could ask for help from the Brits. Considering the choices, Latsanych decided the British option was the most likely. There was a benefit in that too, since the British embassy was basically right next door to the Russian embassy. Recalling his commando team, or what was left of them, Latsanych had them monitor the British embassy for any trace of the Americans.

■

Meanwhile, at the parking garage, La Rue was expanding on her idea.

The first step was for La Rue to call the Maersk CEO, with whom she had developed a good working relationship, to explain their situation.

Using one of their prepaid phones, it took a few minutes for La Rue to navigate her way through the Maersk administrative hierarchy before she finally was connected to Søren Larsen.

After absorbing La Rue's situation, Søren Larsen, the Maersk CEO, brought up the traffic-control screen from his executive management system. Scrolling through the data, Larsen said, "The *Mette Maersk*, Pier 11. That's our next departure. She leaves today at three o'clock."

After a short discussion with Dunbar and Holland, they agreed leaving Copenhagen on the *Mette Maersk* was their best and soonest option.

It was already a little after noon, so they only had a couple of hours before the ship would depart.

Larsen told La Rue, "I'll alert the captain and let him know that you'll be boarding. When do you think you will be ready?"

La Rue talked it over with Dunbar and said, "Søren, we can be there in an hour. Will that work for your people?"

"I'll make it work, Lauren."

La Rue said, "Thank you so much, Søren."

Larsen acknowledged her gratitude and wished Lauren and the team well.

Dunbar then used another one of their prepaid phones to inform Ambassador McGinley of their plans.

McGinley asked Dunbar what he thought the Russians were up to given the sonic weapon, the fire, and the attack at the airport.

"I'm not sure other than it's clear the Russians wanted us out of the embassy. I know from recent intelligence reports that Lauren La Rue has been a target of the Islamic Front. It could be the Russians are also after La Rue. I'm not sure. But I know the sooner we leave Denmark, the better off we'll be," said Dunbar.

"We could ask the Brits to house you at their embassy," suggested McGinley.

"The British embassy that's right next to the Russian embassy?" asked Dunbar. "No, thank you. Our best option is to get out of Dodge and do it soon."

"And you don't want to ask the Danes for help?" asked McGinley.

"We don't know who's our friend and who isn't at this point. So, we need to assume everyone is compromised," clarified Dunbar.

Just before terminating the call, Dunbar told the ambassador he would not hear from them again that day.

The plan went exactly as expected, and forty-five minutes later Dunbar, La Rue, and Holland, along with Moorhead and Dinkel, drove their SUV to Pier 11 on the Copenhagen waterfront.

With La Rue and Holland surrounded by Dunbar and his two agents, they hurried up the *Mette Maersk*'s gangway.

Once on board, Dunbar stationed Moorhead and Dinkel at the top of the gangway, as the remaining three were escorted to the bridge of the *Mette Maersk* to meet its master, Captain Ted Holms, a Dane.

For the next few minutes Dunbar and Holms went over the details of their departure. With the details discussed, Holland thanked Holms for his assistance.

Captain Holms hadn't been expecting an additional five travelers, but his ship was massive, and he had a few empty staterooms. He allocated two staterooms to La Rue and Holland and then set up Dunbar's team in one of the crew dayrooms on E Deck.

At 1,309 feet in length and more than 210,000 tons, the *Mette Maersk* was one of the newer container ships and the pride of the Maersk fleet. Known as a Triple E-Class, the *Mette Maersk* could carry more than eighteen thousand twenty-foot equivalent units, or TEUs.

Holms told Dunbar, "Agent, our current destination is the port of Salalah, Oman."

"That's fine, Captain. We won't interfere with your destination or schedule," replied Dunbar.

It was now almost 8 a.m. in Washington and time for McGinley to share Dunbar's plan with the folks back in DC over his secure line.

After McGinley explained what was happening, a conference call was arranged with the CIA, NSA, and Navy so they could create and coordinate their plan to get Dunbar and his people off the *Mette Maersk* at the earliest opportunity.

The news regarding Dunbar's escape reached CNO Admiral Brian Jacobsen.

After arriving in the Pentagon's Operations Center, Jacobsen briefed the watch commander on the situation.

"Sir, the *Mette Maersk* will need to transit the Skagerrak, the passage between Sweden, Norway, and Denmark, which leads directly to the North Sea. After that she'll be in the North Atlantic," summarized the Navy commander in charge of the ops center.

Jacobsen asked, "What do we have in the area?"

Bringing up the plot, the commander zoomed in on the North Sea.

"Sir, we have two attack subs, the *Vermont* and *North Dakota*, a boomer, *Alaska Blue*, and the *Michael Monsoor*."

Jacobsen then organized a conference call with the commander of the Atlantic Fleet, COMFORFLT, who had responsibility for US Navy ships operating in that Area of Responsibility (AOR), along with COMSUBLANT, the admiral in charge of the Atlantic who deployed submarines.

Jacobsen then called the lieutenant general in charge of the Joint Special Operations Command (JSOC) in Fort Bragg.

"Scott, it's Brian. We need to deploy a SEAL team to the North Sea just east of Gothenburg. Priority One."

"Copy that. SEAL Team 2 is the ready alert team. I'll have my operations people interface with your team. Will we be putting them on land or sea?" asked the three-star Air Force general in charge of JSOC.

"We'll have them rendezvous with the USS *Vermont*. They'll have plenty of time to be briefed in transit. For now, though, we need to get them airborne," said the CNO.

The Pentagon team and JSOC worked out the details of how SEAL Team 2 would come aboard the fast-attack submarine USS *Vermont*. It took the better part of three hours before the brass had arrived at a plan. But Jacobsen knew that if the shit hit the fan on the *Mette Maersk*, he wanted to have some assets on station.

With the admirals and generals now in agreement, the following orders were issued:

From: COMSUBLANT
To: USS Vermont (SSN-792)
Subject: Priority Action Message

Remarks:

1. SEAL Team 2 en route to rendezvous with you at 57.625, 5.355 via parachute drop at 20:00 Zulu.
2. Once SEAL Team on board, make best possible speed to 57.553, 7.950, where you will stand by to lend assistance to USS Michael Monsoor, who will effect transfer of US personnel from Danish-flagged merchantman Mette Maersk.
3. Believe Russian Federation Akula-class submarine in your AOR.

From: COMFORFLT
To: USS Michael Monsoor (DDG-1001)
Subject: Priority Action Message

Remarks:1. Make best possible speed to 57.553, 7.950, where you will intercept Danish-flagged merchantman Mette Maersk and effect transfer of US personnel.
2. Coordinate with USS Vermont, who will be on station.
3. Believe Russian Federation Akula-class submarine in your AOR.

The next step was to communicate their plan to Dunbar on the *Mette Maersk* via the most secure channel available. That involved a discussion with the Maersk headquarters security team, which suggested they use Maersk's encrypted email, which employed the firewall on board the *Mette*.

Captain Mark Zeller was on the bridge of the USS *Michael Monsoor* (DDG-1001), the second ship of the Zumwalt class of guided missile destroyers, when the flash message was handed to him.

"Have the XO join me, if you would please," said Captain Zeller to his officer of the deck (OOD).

"XO to the bridge," called the OOD over his walkie-talkie.

In less than five minutes the XO entered the bridge, with the watch stander announcing, "XO's on the bridge."

"Tom, take a look at this," said Zeller, who was hunched over the navigation station as he handed the message to his XO.

After reading the note and looking at the plot, the XO said, "The CNO is ordering us to make best possible speed and head here?" He pointed to the longitude and latitude from the message.

"That's the order," said Zeller. After a few minutes of studying the plot, Captain Zeller called, "Navigator, plot a speed course to this location."

"Aye, aye, Captain," replied the navigator as he started to work out the course and speed calculations.

A few minutes later the navigator called out, "Sir, I recommend a heading of 037 degrees to point Zulu." He used his cursor to lay out the course for the CO and XO on his electronic chart.

After a quick review came the order. "OOD, come to 037 degrees, increase speed to all ahead full," ordered the captain.

"Aye, aye, sir, coming to course 037 degrees, making turns for one hundred rpms, increasing speed to thirty knots," repeated the OOD, as the six-hundred-foot, sixteen-thousand-ton guided missile destroyer started to vibrate as the rpms from her engines increased.

The *Michael Monsoor* was the second ship of the controversial Zumwalt class of guided missile destroyers. The original cost of these ships was budgeted at $3 billion each, but the costs swelled to over $7.5 billion each. Due to these budgetary overruns, the Navy canceled their plans to build thirty-two Zumwalt-class destroyers and cut the number to only three.

Controversy aside, the Zumwalts were a very advanced class of ships. Their unique hull design, known as a "tumblehome design," was what gave the ships their futuristic appearance and dramatically reduced radar cross section, making them exceedingly hard to detect on radar. In fact, these six-hundred-foot warships would look no larger than a fishing boat on an enemy's radar—an advantage that was about to pay off for the crew of the USS *Michael Monsoor.*

From a firepower perspective, these destroyers were armed with an array of missiles as well as two Mk 46 Mod 2 gun weapon systems (GWS), each containing a single 30mm Mk 44 Bushmaster II automatic cannon, which was mounted over the helicopter hangar near the stern of the ship. These guns were controlled by the weapons officer, whose station was in the ship's combat information center, or CIC.

Intended primarily for close-in defense against smaller surface threats, this gun system operated via a state-of-the-art set of control consoles that aimed the cannons by way of visual, low-light-level, and infrared video cameras, as well as built-in laser range finders.

Of course, that wasn't the original armament plan for the Zumwalts. They were intended to have a main battery consisting of two electromagnetic 155mm railguns that fired what was called a Long Range Land Attack Projectile or LRLAP hypervelocity projectile. But the Navy canceled their plans for these guns after the cost of an LRLAP round inflated to a mind-boggling $800,000 each.

■

On board the USS *Vermont* (SSN-792), Captain Mike Lanam read the flash message that had just been handed to him.

After conferring with his XO, Lanam ordered, "Officer of the Watch, plot a speed course to this point." He handed the longitude and latitude readings to the OOW.

"Sir, I recommend we come to 088 degrees," relayed the OOW, who had worked out the course with the *Vermont*'s navigator.

"Come to 088 degrees, all ahead flank, maintain depth two hundred," ordered Lanam.

Both the OOW and the chief of the boat (COB) repeated the captain's orders as the newest Virginia-class attack submarine in the fleet accelerated to thirty-five knots.

The USS *Vermont* was what was known as a Block IV Virginia-class attack submarine. In plain language, that meant it was the newest, most advanced Virginia-class submarine in the fleet.

At 377 feet and almost eight thousand tons, the *Vermont* carried an impressive array of missiles and torpedoes and was powered by the S9G nuclear reactor, which delivered forty thousand shaft horse-power that could propel the submarine at over thirty-five knots with a test depth reported to exceed sixteen hundred feet.

Shipping a crew of 120 enlisted sailors and fourteen officers, the *Vermont* relied on an array of state-of-the-art weapons and sensors featuring a revised bow, which housed the Large Aperture Bow (LAB) sonar array. This horseshoe-shaped LAB sonar array consisted of both passive and medium-frequency active arrays and was water-backed, as opposed to earlier sonar arrays, which were air-backed.

And even more modern, the *Vermont* employed the new Hybrid Multi-Material Rotor (HMMR) system, which offered an improved propeller design that reduced weight and costs while at the same time improving overall acoustic performance.

When it came to sonar, the later-model Virginias employed a modernized integrated combat system known as the AN/BYG-1, which was integrated with the submarine's tactical control system (TCS) and weapons control system (WCS).

The TCS operating in conjunction with the AN/BYG-1 combat system provided Captain Lanam with sensor data fusion, target motion analysis, tactical situational awareness, and command decision tools, which enabled his watch standers and officers to execute their mission.

The *Vermont* was well armed, with twelve vertical launching systems (VLS) and four torpedo tubes capable of launching the Advanced Capability (ADCAP) Mark 48 Mod 7 torpedoes, UGM-109 Tactical Tomahawks, and Harpoon anti-ship missiles, as well as the new advanced mobile mines.

From a defensive perspective, the *Vermont* relied on the Mk 2 Mod 7 and Mk 3 Mod 1 Acoustic Device Countermeasures (ADC) as defenses against incoming adversarial torpedoes.

However, all this capability came at a cost. The cost of the newer Virginia-class attack submarine now exceeds US$2 billion, which is remarkable, as the Virginias were to be the budget alternative to the Seawolf attack submarines, whose final cost exceeded $4 billion per copy (which explains why there are only three in the fleet).

And now it was time to find out if all that money had paid off.

CHAPTER SEVENTEEN

Mette Maersk Departing

With his lines now singled up, the *Mette Maersk* captain completed his last checks before the massive thirteen-hundred-foot container ship started to slowly pirouette away from Pier 11.

Employing the bow thrusters, the ship slowly and carefully swung away from the quay under the supervision of the Copenhagen Harbor pilot. The pilot would be in command of the *Mette Maersk* for the next eighty miles or until they passed the Skagen Peninsula, which was the northern headland of Denmark. The pilot would be staying on board longer than usual, due to the fact that this time of year it got dark early, and the waters of Denmark and Norway were treacherous.

Entering the bridge, Dunbar said, "Captain, when you have a moment, I'd like to discuss our extraction plan with you."

"Mr. Dunbar, it will have to wait until we clear the harbor, in about two hours," said the master of the *Mette Maersk*, who was close behind the harbor pilot on the starboard wing of the massive ship.

His response surprised Dunbar, but he was in no position to disagree with the captain, nor did he wish to come across as ungrateful for his assistance.

Dunbar simply replied, "Copy that, Captain." And with that he left the bridge to update his men and lay out a watch plan.

With a tugboat on either side, the *Mette Maersk* made a slow 180-degree turn to put her on a northern heading up the channel that separated Denmark from Sweden.

■

Sergey Latsanych had just been briefed about the two American CIA agents who were being treated at the Copenhagen University Hospital. Latsanych speculated about whether the CIA team, along with La Rue, remained in Denmark.

We know they're not at the US embassy. We also know they haven't contacted the Danish Defense Ministry, thought Latsanych.

Latsanych knew he'd have to provide an update to Moscow soon, but at the moment, he had more questions than answers.

It was about then that Latsanych received a call from Magnus Nielsen.

"Sergey, I'm getting reports of an attack on the American aircraft at the airport and a fire at the American embassy."

"An attack on an American plane you say? I don't know anything about that. We noted the fire from our embassy this morning," responded Latsanych, without tipping his hand in the slightest.

"Sergey, this is serious. We have three unidentified bodies at the airport and two wounded Americans in the hospital," said Nielsen.

"Any suspects?" asked Latsanych.

"Right now, we're saying this was a gang-related action by an Armenian mob," said Nielsen.

Latsanych wasn't sure if Nielsen was telling him the truth or if this was a cover story that he and his team had concocted for Danish public consumption and to placate the Americans.

Latsanych's need for more information drove his next question. "Minister Nielsen, do you have information concerning the whereabouts of the American negotiating team?"

Nielsen was surprised by Latsanych's directness to ask such a pointed question of him.

"Sergey, I can share with you what I know. They're not at the US or British embassies, nor are they at any of our locations. We know they haven't departed from any of our airports, nor have they transited any of the border crossings into Germany or Sweden. Furthermore, we don't know of any safe houses the Americans have in Denmark either," Nielsen told him.

As Latsanych listened to the Danish defense minister, he started to construct a binary tree in his head of true and false answers. No, the Americans hadn't flown out of Denmark. No, the Americans weren't at any of their allies' embassies. Thinking it through, that just left two options. Either they were still in Denmark or they had departed by sea.

"Magnus," said Latsanych, "can you get me a list of all the ships—large or small—that have departed from Denmark today?"

Thinking through Latsanych's request, Nielsen responded, "I believe I can obtain that information."

"Also, I am not sure of what surveillance capabilities you have, but any chatter you pick up about the whereabouts of the Americans would be greatly appreciated," added Latsanych.

"Of course," replied Nielsen. "I'll call you back once I have the shipping data."

Then Nielsen rung off to gather the requested data.

Latsanych's next call would be with his boss, Zlovna, who didn't react well to disappointment.

■

Captain Holms of the *Mette Maersk* sent for Dunbar now that he was clear of Helsingborg. "Mr. Dunbar, what is it you wished to discuss with me?" he asked.

"Captain, we have arranged for a US Navy destroyer to rendezvous with you at this location: 57.553, 7.950," said Dunbar.

Holms immediately typed the coordinates into his navigation screen, which brought up the plot.

"Captain, how long will it take us to reach that position?" asked Dunbar.

Entering a few commands, Holm responded, "At our present course and speed we will reach the designated location at 9:38 tonight."

"Thank you, Captain, that was the information I was looking for. I'll pass it along to the Navy," said Dunbar. "And, Captain, if you ask your crew to avoid the deck that we are staying on, I think that would be all for the best—security-wise."

"I'll pass that along to my men," replied Holms. "In the meantime, I'll have our ship's cook prepare some food you can bring to your team, seeing you must be hungry," said the captain, showing the level of professionalism and courtesy that the Maersk Line was known for.

"That would be greatly appreciated, Captain," said a grateful Dunbar.

With that, Dunbar left the bridge to relay the logistic information on the secure line back to Maersk headquarters, which would in turn forward it on to Washington.

■

An hour later Magnus Nielsen was back on the phone with Sergey Latsanych.

"We have compiled a list of all ships that have departed at least one hour after the American CIA agents were admitted into Rigshospitalet. We have five container ships and thirteen fishing boats. But seven of those fishing boats departed from the northern port of Frederikshavn, which is three hundred miles away from Copenhagen and too far to be considered. Plus, we certainly would have captured a closed-circuit picture of them from one of our highway video cameras."

Continuing, Nielsen said, "Four of the container ships departed from Aarhus, only one from Copenhagen. Of the remaining fishing boats, two departed Copenhagen and three from Aarhus."

Latsanych's next question was key. "Were any of the container ships Maersk ships?"

Scanning down the list, Nielsen answered, "Two Maersk ships departed during that time frame. The *Emma Maersk* from Aarhus at 5:00 p.m. and the *Mette Maersk* from Copenhagen at 1:40 p.m."

"And the other ships?" asked Latsanych.

"The three container ships from Aarhus were from the Lauritzen, Baltic, and Niels Winther Lines. They left at 12:45 p.m., 2:15 p.m., and 4:45 p.m., respectively," added Nielsen.

Latsanych smiled as he wrote down the information. "Magnus, do you recall telling me how you noticed how friendly Søren Larsen and Lauren La Rue were at your last meeting?"

Nielsen now understood Latsanych's logic. "Yes, I do."

"I think the Americans are on a Maersk ship. And if I had to place a bet, I'd pick the one that departed Copenhagen earlier—the

Mette Maersk. Let's see if we can confirm my hunch," said Latsanych. "Call the Maersk CEO and tell him you've been contacted by the Americans about the transfer of La Rue and her party from his ship to a US Navy ship. Tell him there was some confusion whether it is the *Mette* or *Emma Maersk.* See how he reacts to that."

■

At the Pentagon, CNO Jacobsen was in the ops center checking on the progress of his plan for the *Monsoor* and *Vermont.*

"Bring up the plot of the *Monsoor,*" requested the CNO of the duty commander.

The duty commander moved his cursor and then zoomed in on the area where the *Monsoor* was currently located.

"Sir, the *Michael Monsoor* is approaching the prescribed coordinates. They should be on station by 20:40 Zulu," said the commander.

"What about the *Vermont?*" asked the CNO.

"They're almost to the location to pick up SEAL Team 2. It should happen within the hour," answered the commander.

"Now bring up the *Mette Maersk,*" ordered the CNO.

On the large screen three dots appeared, representing the ships and submarine, which were now only two hundred miles apart.

"Good, good," said the CNO. The two ships were scheduled to rendezvous in six hours.

■

Nielsen called Latsanych. "You were correct. They're on the *Mette Maersk.*"

It took only a few minutes before Latsanych was on a priority call with Svetlana Ivanovna Zlovna. "The Americans are on the *Mette Maersk*, which is headed to Oman."

"They will be put on a sub long before they get to Oman," Zlovna replied. "Sergey, let us work on some options here. I'll get back to you shortly."

∎

Alice Ahern entered the Oval Office and announced,"Mr. President, the Prime Minister of the United Kingdom is on line one."

James King, the UK Prime Minister, was as close a friend as President Andrew Russell had. Their friendship was formed when as a Congressman from Brooklyn Andrew Russell went to the UK to work on an Intelligence sharing agreement. James King then a member of the House of Lords was a leading member of his Conservative Party.

Later with their ascension to leadership positions Andrew Russell and James King relied on each other's counsel on a wide range of issues involving politics, security and trade.

James King, who spent two years in America while in his twenties, was immensely popular with his constituents as his time in the United States gave him just the slightest touch of bravado which was exactly what was needed in the Post Brexit United Kingdom. Make no mistake King was British in the best sense of the word but he was more forceful and self-confident then the typical Brit and as such he commanded the attention of every room he entered. Not since Winston had the UK had such a charismatic leader. And as a result, he and Andrew Russell got along extremely well.

"Mr. Prime Minister, good to hear from you. How are Emily and the children? " asked the president.

"Very well, Mr. President and thank you for asking," said the PM.

"Of course, James," replied the President. The two had settled on the practice of referring to each other by their formal titles for the salutation but there after using their first names.

"Andrew, I've just been briefed on the happenings in Copenhagen," said the PM.

"Yes, we have on-going operation there. We are in the process of extracting our trade team that was negotiating the rights to Greenland's minerals," replied the president.

"I'm sure you're aware it was the Russians. And MI-6 believes they are dispatching a Spetsnaz team to intercept your people on the container ship," added King.

The President was surprised just how accurate and up-to-the-minute the British information was.

"We have the *HMS Astute* in the North Sea ready to lend assistance," offered the British Prime Minister referring to the United Kingdom's class leading nuclear powered attack submarine.

"In addition, we will make our RAF bases at Lossiemouth and Leuchars in Scotland available to you should you need them," offered the eager-to-help PM.

"I will pass that information along to our Special Forces Operations Team," said the president.

"I can't imagine what motivated the Russians to be some confrontational. It's as if they're trying to draw you into a fight," opined the PM.

"It appears so, but we think they are doing this at China's behest," added the president.

"Very interesting," was all King said in reply.

"Mr. President the United Kingdom stands by to lend any assistance we can," closed the PM.

"Thank you, James. I can always rely on the UK to help," and with that, the called ended.

■

After conferring with her staff and plotting the exact location of the *Mette Maersk* as well as the Russian assets in the area, Zlovna had the makings of a plan.

The first step was to fly a Special Forces team from Moscow to a point just east of Gothenburg, Sweden. There they would be picked up by the newest Akula attack submarine in the Russian Federation's fleet—the *Gepard*.

Known in NATO circles as an Akula III, the *Gepard* (K-335) was 372 feet long and displaced 13,800 tons submerged. With her seven-blade single propellor, she was capable of in excess of thirty-five knots when submerged.

The Akula III boasted improved sound deadening as well as an advanced towed array. From an armament perspective, her sixty-two-person crew had access to twelve torpedoes she could launch from her four torpedo tubes. In addition, she carried Kalibr cruise missiles capable of attacking air-, surface-, or land-based targets.

A few hours later the eight-man Russian Special Forces team was safely on board the *Gepard*.

With the Special Forces team now on the *Gepard*, they initiated the next part of their plan. The Akula's Russian radio operator broadcast, "Mayday, Mayday. This is the fishing boat *Grimskar*. Mayday,

Mayday. We are issuing an SOS. Our position is 57.734, 8.793. Repeat 57.734, 8.793."

"This is Gothenburg Coast Guard, *Grimskar*. What is your emergency?"

"This is the *Grimskar*. Our engines have failed and we are taking on water. Our position is 57.734, 8.793. We are preparing to abandon ship."

"Copy that, *Grimskar*. Please stand by."

The Swedish Coast Guard plotted the location of the *Grimskar*. They had a cutter ninety miles away, which could be on station in three hours, which would be too long to survive in the frigid North Sea waters. However, the *Mette Maersk* was barely ten miles away from the fishing boat's location.

On board the *Mette Maersk*, they, too, picked up the *Grimskar*'s distress call. The first mate immediately notified Captain Holms, who minutes later entered the bridge asking, "What's their location?"

"Sir, we have them eleven miles off our starboard quarter," said the first mate, as both he and the captain lifted their night-vision binoculars to try to find the sinking fishing vessel.

"I don't see anything," called the captain.

The first mate scanned the dark waters and called, "I have a life raft."

Holms narrowed his area of focus to where the first mate was looking and could also make out the life raft drifting about ten miles from them.

"Flare," reported the first mate as the survivors in the raft launched a rescue flare.

"Helm, come right to course 290. Continue at present speed but prepare to slow," called the captain, knowing it took his ship three miles to come to a stop.

The massive container ship continued to approach at a speed of 13.3 knots, which meant they would be on station in less than forty minutes.

"Fire off a flare to let them know we see them," next ordered Holms. "Radio the Swedish Coast Guard and inform them of our position and our intention to lend assistance and pick up survivors.

"Ready the port-side accommodation ladder as we get closer," ordered Holms.

"*Mette Maersk*, this is Gothenburg Coast Guard acknowledging you will be lending assistance to fishing vessel *Grimskar*. We will be scrambling one of our rescue helicopters to provide additional assistance," called the Gothenburg station.

One of Dunbar's men noticed the flare launched from the *Mette Maersk*, which caused Dunbar to make his way to the bridge. His first thought was that Holms had spotted the US Navy destroyer.

"Captain, what was that flare for?" asked Dunbar.

"We're responding to a distress call. A Swedish fishing boat has gone down a few miles off our starboard quarter," said Holms, pointing in the direction of the survivors.

Dunbar asked to borrow the first mate's binoculars to make his own assessment.

Gazing into the dark waters of the North Sea, Dunbar could make out a single life raft with what looked to be six to eight survivors. The raft was low in the water, but he could make out various colored parkas and foul-weather gear.

"Is there no one else in the vicinity who could lend assistance?" asked Dunbar.

"Agent Dunbar, the United Nations Convention on the Law of the Sea clearly states," said Captain Holms reading Article 98 from his copy 'Every State shall require the master of a ship flying its flag, in so far as he can do so without serious danger to the ship, the crew or the passengers:

(a) to render assistance to any person found at sea in danger of being lost;

(b) to proceed with all possible speed to the rescue of persons in distress, if informed of their need of assistance, in so far as such action may reasonably be expected of him;

(c) after a collision, to render assistance to the other ship, its crew and its passengers and, where possible, to inform the other ship of the name of his own ship, its port of registry and the nearest port at which it will call.'

Continuing Holms added, "The Maersk Line adheres to these conventions, as do I, as the master of this ship."

As the *Mette Maersk* approached, Holms ordered, "Turn on the floodlights. Sound the whistle. All stop."

Talking into his walkie-talkie he ordered his second mate, "Brin, get ready to pick up survivors."

With that, Dunbar quickly exited the bridge to alert his men and to take up tactical positions to protect La Rue and Holland.

The massive container ship glided to a stop as it closed the one-mile distance to the raft with the men waving.

The *Mette Maersk* sounded its ship's horn with three blasts, letting the men in the raft know they saw them. Next the *Mette Maersk* illuminated the life raft with its powerful bridge spotlights.

The second mate of the *Mette Maersk* lowered a rope ladder from his position on the bottom of the accommodation ladder. A few seconds later the life raft reached the side of the giant ship.

The first survivor made his way up the ladder and then turned and helped the next man up. Soon four of the eight men were on board.

It was then that the first survivor drew his pistol and told the second mate to take them to the bridge.

Eager to check on the progress, Captain Holms called to his second mate but got no reply. Calling again, he still got no response.

Puzzled, Captain Holms told his first mate to go below and see what was going on, but before he could leave, four Russian commandos entered the bridge with automatic weapons drawn.

The bridge crew on the *Mette Maersk* only numbered four. That included Holms, his first mate, the navigator, and a seaman.

The Russian leader demanded, "Where are the Americans?"

Instinctively Holms raised his hands as he tried to absorb what was happening. The ship had a procedure to handle being boarded by unfriendlies, but he didn't expect to need that training in the North Sea.

Again, the leader demanded, "Where are the Americans?"

Holms replied, "What Americans?"

The Russian raised his assault rifle and pointed it at Holms. "I will not ask again."

"This is a Danish merchantman vessel. We do not carry passengers," said Holms.

The Special Forces commandos zip-tied the crew by their wrists and ankles and placed duct tape over their mouths. For the captain they only zip tied his hands.

"Show us a map of the ship," demanded the leader. After surveying the ship schematic, the Russian dispatched two of his men to join up with the four commandos below and begin searching the giant container ship starting at the lower levels.

■

As planned, the *Gepard* was submerged a mile off the bow of the *Mette Maersk* with its periscope raised. Its captain noted the raft tied up to the *Mette Maersk*'s port access ladder.

The captain ordered, "Bring us alongside the merchantman. I want to be a hundred yards off his port side. Once there, full stop."

■

On board the USS *Michael Monsoor*, they had been monitoring the communications from the *Grimskar*, the Norwegian Coast Guard, and the *Mette Maersk* so they were prepared for what they saw off their starboard quarter.

"Bridge, CIC. I have Sierra One at eleven miles, bearing 175 degrees off our starboard quarter. Sir, she's stopped."

On the bridge Captain Mark Zeller switched his screen to the CIC video-camera screen, where he could clearly make out the life raft tied up to the access ladder of the *Mette Maersk* on one of the high-def screens that employed a low-light camera.

Turning to his XO, Zeller asked, "Ben, what do you make of that?"

"It looks like the merchantman stopped to pick up the survivors from the fishing boat."

"It does, but at the same time we were supposed to rendezvous with them. Is it a coincidence? Seems awfully suspicious," said Zeller, with the hairs on the back of his neck sticking up.

Something wasn't right.

The *Monsoor* was supposed to make contact with the Danish merchantman about now, but with the *Mette Maersk* stopped and lit up like Luna Park, Zeller decided on another action.

"Stream the array," ordered the captain. "I want to know if there are any submerged contacts out there."

"Aye, aye, sir. Streaming the towed array," replied the CIC watch officer as he deployed the AN/SQR-20 multifunction towed array, which would aid in prosecuting any submerged targets.

Sitting in front of an array of screens, the *Monsoor*'s sonar operator controlled three highly advanced sonar systems, which he used to detect mines and submarines.

Superior to the systems on the Navy's other destroyers in the Arleigh Burke class, the *Monsoor* relied on a hull-mounted midfrequency sonar (AN/SQS-60) and a hull-mounted high-frequency sonar (AN/SQS-61), as well as a multifunction towed array sonar system (AN/SQR-20).

"Con, Sonar. I am picking up a submerged target close aboard Sierra One," called the sonar operator. "I'm starting a track on Sierra Two. Come on, baby, tell me who that is," muttered the operator as he adjusted the controls on his systems.

A few seconds later the screen flashed—it was a Russian Akula-class attack submarine.

"Bridge, Sonar. It's an Akula, sir. Bearing 005 degrees," called the excited sonarman.

Zeller ordered, "Come left to 185 degrees, all ahead one-third."

"Sonar, Bridge. Do you think he sees us?" asked Zeller.

"Negative, sir," replied the sonarman.

One of the advantages of the Zumwalt guided-missile destroyers was their stealthiness. The *Monsoor* had an acoustic signature comparable to that of the Los Angeles–class submarines, which few, if any, Akulas could detect.

■

On board the USS *Vermont*, Captain Lanam was also monitoring the radio broadcast to and from the Maersk containership.

The *Vermont* was only about ten miles from the *Mette Maersk* when they, too, picked up the presence of the Russian Akula.

Using his photonic mast, Lanam was also able to detect the life raft bobbing up and down attached to the starboard access ladder on the *Mette Maersk*.

Lanam called for the SEAL Team 2 commander, a lieutenant from Texas.

"What do you make of that?" asked the submarine commander of the SEAL leader.

Looking over the radio transmission log, the SEAL team leader said, "There are two options. First, the containership picked up legitimate survivors of a fishing boat. Or they picked up someone else. Judging from the action report I received en route, I would say there is a good chance this was a Russian Spetsnaz Special Forces Team. Have we heard anything from the CIA agents on board the ship?"

"Not yet," replied Lanam. "The communication link is not direct. The CIA agents can contact Maersk Operations or the Pentagon. Then any information is relayed to us. So there is going to be a delay."

"Captain, I think we need to assume those survivors are Special Forces. Let's work out a plan to get my team aboard the container ship. And since she's stopped, it will be a lot easier to do now than if she starts moving."

"Keep in mind, there's an Akula off the port beam of the Maersk ship," added Lanam.

"How about you bring us up on his starboard side. It's plenty dark, so I don't think my team will have too much trouble getting on board," said the SEAL team leader.

"I have a better idea," replied Lanam.

■

Standing on the bridge, with his hands zip-tied, Holms surveyed his three men who were on the floor leaning on the back wall of the bridge. One of the Russian commandos remained on the bridge to stand guard over Holms and his three restrained crewmen.

It was then an alarm went off, startling the Russian leader, who yelled, "What is that?"

Captain Holms replied, "It's the Deadman. When the ship is at sea, if the system detects no one has touched the wheel for ten minutes, an alarm goes off. It protects against overly relying on the autopilot."

The Russian ordered, "Turn it off."

Holms looked at the Russian and raised his zip-tied hands. "I will, but you need to cut these off."

With the alarm blaring at regular intervals, the Russian pulled his KA-BAR knife from his belt and sliced the ties off Holms's hands.

Pointing his assault rifle at Holms, he said, "Turn it off now."

Moving to the control panel, Holms entered a few keystrokes. First, he entered "ZX99@#" on the command line of his console, which was the distress code to alert the Maersk Operations Center that his ship was under attack or otherwise in peril. Then he entered the actual commands that silenced the alarm.

"There. Done," said Holms.

The Russian nodded as he placed a new set of zip ties on Holms's wrists.

A few seconds later, in the Maersk ops center in Copenhagen, one of the operators called out to the shift supervisor, "I'm getting a 99 code from the *Mette Maersk*."

The ops center manager replied, "Bring up the *Mette Maersk*."

Modern-day merchantman ships have black boxes similar to those the airlines use. They allow a remote operator to see all the real-time data from the ship's systems.

"She's stopped at the mouth of the North Sea. Engines are operating but idle," said the operator.

"Bring up the bridge cam," said the shift supervisor.

There they could clearly see the Russian commando with an automatic weapon on the bridge of the *Mette Maersk*.

That was all the shift supervisor needed. He entered a code into his system that immediately texted three executives at Maersk. Their chief security officer (CSO), their VP of operations, and the CEO all received the 99 emergency code.

As per protocol, a teleconference bridge was opened from the operations center with all the participants bridging in. It only took a few minutes before all members of the Maersk crisis team were on the call.

Assessing the situation, the crisis team radioed to the engine-room crew of the *Mette Maersk* and told them to execute their Intruder Alert Plan, which called for most of the crew to head to the engine room, where they would barricade the hatches and doors from incursions.

Given the *Maersk*'s location, the closest nation's Coast Guard was also notified of the attack, which in this case was Denmark.

In addition, due to the sensitive nature of the passengers on the *Mette Maersk*, Søren Larsen contacted the US ambassador, James McGinley, who immediately alerted the Pentagon, CIA, and NSA.

■

It took only a few minutes for word to get passed to the *Michael Monsoor* and the *Vermont*.

Chris Dunbar reviewed the plan with Tom Mahoney of SEAL Team 2.

"I'm not sure how long this link will remain up," said Dunbar, who was briefing Mahoney via a VoIP link they had arranged through the Maersk Ops Center.

Dunbar correctly suspected the Russians would shortly defeat all communications on the *Mette Maersk*.

"We'll be coming aboard via the engineering spaces. I'll then station two of my men near the bow on top of the containers to have eyes on the bridge," briefed Mahoney. "I need you to try and make your way to the engine room with your people."

"Negative," replied Dunbar. "The Russians are going to be expecting that. There are two emergency containers that are empty. We're going to try and get to them and wait for you there."

Just then the connection went dead. The Russians had destroyed the communications room, which knocked out all communications to and from the *Mette Maersk*. It also disabled all the video cameras on the ship.

The Russians had only been on the *Mette Maersk* for eight minutes.

■

"Captain, time to get us on the *Maersk*," said Mahoney to Lanam.

Mahoney opened their copies of the plans for the *Mette Maersk* and reviewed their mission for the umpteenth time.

Despite its enormous size, there weren't a lot of cabins and spaces on the ship. First, located amidships was the beige-painted, nine-deck structure known as the cabin tower, which housed the bridge, offices, accommodations, and all non-engineering functions. The second area was aft and was noteworthy for housing the ship's twin black funnels, which bore the blue riband with the Maersk star affixed to them. It was below the funnels where the engineering spaces were located. Besides these two structures there were two main passageways that ran the length of the ship: Passageway A to starboard and Passageway B to port.

The *Vermont* would approach the *Maersk*'s starboard side, just aft, so that Mahoney and his men could enter the engine room via one of the external doors on the hull.

"XO, bring us up slow and quiet," ordered Lanam.

That meant the *Vermont* would not be sounding its normal surface klaxon. Almost imperceptibly the eight-thousand-ton attack submarine rose from its depth of 150 feet to the surface of the pitch-black North Sea.

Mahoney had his men assembled in the main passageway of the *Vermont*, having double-checked their gear. He performed a radio check with the comm officer on the *Vermont* to ensure they would have communications. With the check completed, Mahoney looked at his men and asked, "Good to go?"

Each of the seven members of SEAL Team 2 answered with the traditional SEAL response, "Good to go!"

The *Vermont*, now on the surface with its deck awash, was positioned at a forty-five-degree angle only a couple of hundred feet from the *Mette Maersk* starboard side.

With SEAL Team 2 in their raft, they made their way to the engineering hatch. Once alongside the massive ship, one of the SEALs swung a line toward the hatch, hitting it with the grappling hook. That was the signal for the *Maersk* engineers to open the hatch.

In a matter of only a few minutes SEAL Team 2 was on board the *Mette Maersk*.

■

Dunbar and his team of two agents, La Rue, and Holland had made their way to the lower levels of the cabin tower. There they went to one of the emergency containers known as the "panic room." All Maersk ships went to sea with two empty containers on the lowest level, which were to be used as hiding places in case the ship was boarded by pirates. The "panic rooms" looked like every other container on the ship, measuring eight and a half feet high, eight feet wide, and twenty feet in length. These containers were identical to all the others, with the exception that the panic rooms had double-thick walls and emergency provisions stored inside—food, water, medical supplies, and the standard rescue equipment. These containers also had ventilation systems that provided fresh air from fans located at the rear of the containers that generated an imperceptible noise.

"We're going to leave you both in here. You'll be safe here. We need to set up a perimeter back on E Deck to lead the Russians away from here," said Dunbar.

"Chris, give me your pistol," said La Rue.

Taken aback by the request, Dunbar looked at her.

"Chris, I know the kinds of things the sheik's people are capable of. I won't let them take me," said La Rue with steel in her voice.

Dunbar thought about it for a moment and then handed his Sig Sauer P228 to La Rue.

"It has thirteen rounds, Lauren," said Dunbar, showing her how to disengage the safety.

Looking at La Rue and Holland, he added, "Don't open this door for anyone other than one of us by name or the SEALs—its SEAL Team 2."

With that, Dunbar closed the door, tapping twice on it so Holland and La Rue could set the lock from the inside.

Dunbar and his men made their way to the starboard stairwell on E Deck, where they planned to engage the Russians as they descended from the bridge. Dunbar knew he would be joined there by the majority of SEAL Team 2, who would be coming up the same stairway.

On the bridge the Spetsnaz team of eight assembled to begin their search for La Rue.

"Fly the drone," ordered the Spetsnaz commander. One of his men went out to the port wing of the bridge, opened his backpack, and began to unfold the wings of a drone the size of a garbage can cover. Powering up the drone, the pilot flew it to the stern of the *Mette* and started to call out readings to the commander.

"Sir, we have eighteen targets in the engineering space," called the drone pilot as he analyzed the screen on his controller. The Russian drone was equipped with a FLIR, or forward-looking infrared sensor, that could pick up body temperature through standard-thickness walls.

The commander replied, "That is the crew. Where are the Americans, Yuri?"

Flying the drone along the hull of the *Mette*, he called out, "We have a team of six advancing along the starboard side of the ship."

"That will no doubt be a SEAL team dispatched from the American Navy ship," said the Spetsnaz leader to his men, telling them to prepare to descend the starboard stairwell.

"Sir, I have another three figures on E Deck."

The commander processed the data. He knew from reports that three CIA agents accompanied La Rue and the American diplomat aboard the *Mette*.

Now the Spetsnaz leader turned to Holms and said, "What is the location of your panic room?"

Holms just responded with a look of puzzlement.

"I have no time for this," said the commander, and taking out his pistol, he shot one of the zip-tied crew members in the thigh.

"The next one will be to his head," said the commander.

Holms saw the look of panic on his men's faces. His responsibility was to his crew, not the Americans.

Holms said, "There are two panic-room containers on the lower level of the ship. One on the port side, the other to starboard: 133153 and 429454."

∎

"Sir, I'm tracking a small target on the Annie Square 61," called the CIC petty officer on board the *Monsoor* who was manning the AN/SQS-61 high-frequency sonar control panel.

Bringing up the *Monsoor*'s low-light-level and infrared video cameras, Zeller and the team in the CIC could make out a small drone hovering off the starboard side of the *Mette*.

"Is that one of ours?" asked the *Monsoor's* captain.

"Negative, sir, neither we nor the *Vermont* have anything up," said the CIC tactical action officer (TAO).

"That means it's Russian," concluded Zeller. "TAO, target that drone with our Bushmasters," he ordered.

The TAO, who oversaw the CIC, said, "Aye, aye, sir. Weps, lock on to that target with the 30mm."

The weapons petty officer directed his joystick-controlled automatic cannon and locked onto the target.

"Target acquired, sir. I have a lock."

Captain Zeller coolly ordered, "Take it out."

"Copy that," responded the TAO, and turning to his weapons operator he ordered, "Kill, kill, kill."

With the press of a button a stream of automatic firepower burst from one of the *Monsoor's* two Mk 46 Mod 2 GWS, which housed the 30mm Mk 44 Bushmaster II automatic cannons.

Zeller, the TAO, and the rest of the CIC crew watched on the camera screen as the drone exploded into a cloud of dust.

The Spetsnaz operator informed his commander of the destruction of his drone.

The Spetsnaz commander got on the radio to the Akula, which was standing off the port side of the *Mette*. "Darkstar, this is Lion One. We need you to chase off the American destroyer. Copy."

"Copy that, Lion One," was all that came back.

The Russian Akula dove to a 150-foot depth and turned toward the *Michael Monsoor*, which was stopped dead ahead of the *Mette* at a distance of less than a half mile.

Onboard the *Monsoor* came the call, "Con, Sonar. Sierra Two is stirring. She's diving and making turns."

With Zeller still in the CIC he asked, "What's her course?"

"Sir, she's bearing 167 degrees. She's headed right toward us," called the excited sonar operator.

"Bridge, CIC, come to course 045, make turns for twenty knots," ordered Zeller.

The *Gepard* captain ordered, "Ping the American." This meant his active sonar would send out a pulse of energy toward the *Monsoor*, an unnecessary but provocative move that would give the *Gepard* the exact position of the American destroyer.

Everyone in the CIC saw the display brighten as the active energy pulse from the Akula was detected on the *Monsoor*.

"Sir, Sierra Two's opening his torpedo tube doors," came back the sonar operator's report.

Zeller looked at his XO and said, "He's full of shit."

"Increase speed to twenty-five knots. Sound general quarters," ordered Zeller.

"Aye, aye, sir," responded the XO.

"CIC to Bridge. This is the XO. Sound general quarters."

At this the bosun mate on the bridge of the *Monsoor* hit the switch on the general quarters alarm. The officer of the deck then got on the 1MC and commanded, "*General quarters. General quarters. Man your battle stations.*"

Part of manning battle stations on the *Monsoor* called for the immediate launch of one of the destroyer's antisubmarine warfare (ASW) helicopters.

"Once *Bullet One* is airborne, have them begin ASW prosecution," added Zeller, referring to one of the two Seahawk MH-60R helicopters that sat on the stern of the *Monsoor*, part of Helicopter Sea Combat (HSC) Squadron 23, the Wildcards.

■

The Spetsnaz commander turned to his men and ordered, "Masks on."

On the lower decks of the *Mette*, Russian commandos had deployed canisters of a nerve gas that was a derivative of the nerve gas used during the 2002 hostage crisis when Chechen rebels took 850 hostages at a Moscow theater. One hundred seventy people died in the attack, some, it was speculated, as a result of the use of narcotic gas by the Russian security forces.

More potent than the gas used in the Moscow theater, Kolokol-5 was a nerve gas based on mefentanyl dissolved in a halothane base.

With everyone wearing their masks, the commander ordered, "Release the gas."

The commando specialist entered a few commands on his control device, which caused the valves on the canisters to start venting their noxious contents.

A sensor on SEAL Team 2 Commander Tom Mahoney's vest started to go off.

"Mask up," yelled Mahoney to his team.

Chris Dunbar and his two men were at a disadvantage, not having gas masks. In a matter of minutes, the three CIA agents crumpled to the metal floors on E Deck.

That changed the number of the American forces on the *Mette*. There were two SEAL snipers on the bow stationed on the highest container, affording them a clear line of sight to the bridge of the

Mette. Mahoney and his team of five were unaffected by the gas. But Dunbar and his team were out cold.

On the lowest level of the *Mette*, some of the gas was beginning to seep into the container where La Rue and Holland were hiding.

The Spetsnaz commander now ordered his men down the port stairs to find the "panic room" containers, 133153 and 429454.

■

On board the *Vermont*, which was now submerged and stationed off the *Mette*'s starboard amidships, the sonar operator called out, "Con, Sonar. Sierra Two is bearing 010. She's increasing speed and headed toward the *Monsoor*."

Captain Lanam in the *Vermont*'s control room closed his eyes to visualize the tactical plot that was happening around him.

He had the *Monsoor* turning on a west-northwest heading into the North Sea with her speed increasing to twenty-five knots. Not far behind was the Akula, which was pursuing the *Monsoor*. To what end, it was not clear.

Lanam's boat sat in silence, stopped and submerged just off the *Mette*'s starboard beam.

"Sir, should we pursue the Akula?" asked Lanam's XO.

"No, not yet. Let's let them play cat and mouse with the *Monsoor*. I'd rather keep our presence unknown until we get the SEALs and their packages on board," replied Lanam.

"Con, Sonar. The Akula's opening his torpedo doors," called the excited sonar operator.

The XO looked at Lanam, waiting for a reaction. "Bill, they're bluffing. They aren't going to fire. Plus, the *Monsoor* has her helo, so they'll start dipping soon." He was referring to how the *Monsoor*'s helicopter would be hunting for the Akula using its Magnetic Anomaly Detection-Extended Role (MAD-XR) system, which was deployed on the Navy's latest MH-60R Seahawk helicopters. The MAD-XR was a highly sensitive magnetometer designed to sense changes in the earth's magnetic field in order to detect submarines.

Lanam was correct. On board HSC-23 *Bullet One*, the MAD operator called out, "MAD, MAD, MAD," as he lowered his magnetometer on a cable into the dark ocean below.

Once underwater, the MAD sensor started to collect detection and discrimination data and data-link it back to the ASW operators on the *Monsoor*.

On board the Akula they detected the MAD entering the water and knew at such close range the *Monsoor* would have no trouble tracking their exact location and plot.

■

The Spetsnaz team hurried down the *Mette*'s port stairway to the lowest level of the ship to find the panic-room containers, where they believed they would find La Rue.

Advancing up the starboard passageway were the six members of SEAL Team 2—both teams were wearing their gas masks, which protected them from the effects of the Kolokol-5.

The masks obscured their vision, making it harder to see in the lower levels of the ship, which only had emergency lighting on as a result of the Russians taking out the *Mette*'s communications, command, and control room.

The Russians came across container 133153 first, located closer to the port side of the *Mette*. They planted small charges on the four corners of the container and the front panel of the container blew off from the concussion of the targeted charges.

Peering into the container, they could see that there was no one inside.

"Go find the other one," yelled the Spetsnaz commander.

Just then a shadow appeared down the passageway. A second later automatic fire erupted as both Special Forces teams came upon each other in the darkened corridors of the *Mette*'s lowest level.

Flash-bangs were thrown by either side, causing a momentary lull in the firing.

The Spetsnaz commander ordered three of his men to double-time down Passageway A on the starboard side of the *Mette*, hoping to outflank the SEALs and come in behind them.

The only problem with that tactic was that it was exactly what SEAL Team 2 was also attempting. So now the SEALs were separated into two teams of three, as were the Spetsnaz.

The byproduct of the division of the teams was that it allowed the Russians to reach container 429454 first.

Again, small charges were placed and the front of the container exploded off the main section. Looking inside, they could see both La Rue and Holland passed out as a result of the Kolokol-5.

Interested only in La Rue, one of the Spetsnaz threw her over his shoulder and the commander gave the order to retreat to the bridge of the *Mette*.

The entire operation, which was still ongoing, had taken only ten minutes.

The tactical situation showed the Americans holding the lower decks and the starboard stairwell on the *Mette*, while the Russians held the port-side stairwell and the bridge.

The Russian escape plan involved rappelling down ropes from the bridge on the port side to the *Gepard*, which was now on its way back to the *Mette*, having driven off the *Monsoor*.

The SEALs now had Holland in their protection, as well as Dunbar and his two agents, who were still lightheaded from the Russian nerve-gas cocktail. Their mission was to prevent the Russians from leaving the *Mette* with La Rue.

Two Spetsnaz commandos were positioned at the top of the starboard staircase to prevent the Americans from advancing up that entryway to the bridge.

SEAL Commander Tom Mahoney called on the radio, "*Bullet Two*, commence Dragonfly."

With that, the pilot of the *Monsoor*'s second Seahawk MH-60R helicopter lifted off from the stern of the guided-missile destroyer.

"*Bullet Two* copies. We'll be in position in two minutes."

The Americans had the tactical advantage. They had command of the air, they had superior naval assets on station, and they were on par with the personnel on the *Mette*. But the Russians had La Rue and commanded the bridge of the *Mette*, giving them a better perspective of the battlefield.

As planned, *Bullet Two* approached the bridge of the *Mette*. *Bullet Two* was specifically armed with the pylon-mounted GAU-21 .50-caliber machine gun and four AGM-114 Hellfire missiles for this mission.

The Spetsnaz leader just glared out the bridge windows as *Bullet Two* hovered barely fifty feet in front of the *Mette*'s bridge.

The Russian could easily see the machine guns and Hellfire missiles and knew at the press of a button the Seahawk could destroy the entire bridge of the Maersk liner. But that would come with the deaths of La Rue and the *Maersk*'s master.

To emphasize the point, the Spetsnaz leader grabbed La Rue and pointed his pistol at her head. Likewise, the other commando pointed his pistol at the head of Holms.

It represented an odd standoff: one of the most advanced military helicopters with all the latest technology facing off with two men holding 9mm pistols.

Mahoney called, "Alpha, Bravo, what is your status?"

"Winds calm, clear shot. Alpha's green," came back the first call.

"Bravo's red, I do not have a shot. I need them to move for a clean shot."

"*Bullet Two*, jig to the right some," called Mahoney.

"Copy," came the response from the pilot of the MH-60R as he slewed the cyclical that controlled his Seahawk, causing the helo to slide toward the right some fifteen feet.

"Bravo's green," came the call.

"Alpha's green."

"*Bullet Two*, break now," called Mahoney.

The Seahawk pilot pulled back hard on his cyclical, causing the helo to lift, and then he shifted hard right, exiting the airspace in front of the *Mette Maersk*.

Believing he had successfully stared down the Seahawk, the Spetsnaz commander and his partner lowered their pistols.

"Execute," Mahoney called to his two SEAL snipers, who were lying prone on the top container on the front of the *Mette Maersk*.

In an explosion of red, both the Spetsnaz commander and his partner were taken out, their brain matter splattering La Rue and Holms in the process.

"Charlie Team, advance now," called Mahoney as the starboard-side SEALs advanced up the stairwell.

By plan, the SEALs had left the port staircase unguarded as an escape route for the remaining Spetsnaz commandos.

Mahoney's men quickly dispatched the two Russian commandos in the starboard stairwell.

"*Bullet Two*, cover fire," called Mahoney.

The Seahawk that was now loitering off the port side of the *Maersk* fired a brief burst from its .50-caliber machine guns, preventing any of the remaining Spetsnaz commandos from reentering the bridge.

Just then the *Gepard* surfaced off the *Mette's* port quarter, expecting to pick up their commando team along with La Rue.

Mahoney and his team now entered the bridge, grabbed La Rue and Holms, and then descended back down the starboard stairwell.

"Alpha, Bravo, cover us," called Mahoney as he and his team exited the *Maersk's* bridge.

Between the SEAL snipers and the Seahawk loitering off the *Maersk*, the Spetsnaz team knew they couldn't get back to the bridge. Plus, now they weren't getting any orders from the now-dead commander.

The second-in-command, assessing the situation, called for an evacuation to the *Gepard*.

Bullet One now joined *Bullet Two*, both hovering on either side of the now-surfaced Akula.

The *Gepard* captain had a choice—he could take out either or both of the Seahawks, but he knew that would escalate the situation. The *Monsoor* would no doubt fire on him, and being surfaced, the *Gepard* would be a sitting duck.

"Captain, I'm leaving two SEALs with you as well as two SEALs on the bow of the *Mette* until we are one hundred percent certain all the Russians are off your ship. Once we're assured the ship is back under your control, we'll chop the SEALs off the *Mette*. Thank you for your help, sir," said Mahoney to a still shaken Holms.

With that, Mahoney ushered Dunbar and his team along with La Rue and Holland on board the surfaced USS *Vermont*, which lay just off the *Mette*'s starboard beam.

A few minutes later, with everyone on board the *Vermont*, Captain Lanam ordered, "OOW, dive the boat, bring us to 150 feet, five-degree down bubble, course 352 degrees, ultraquiet, dead slow."

In darkness the US Navy's most modern Virginia-class attack submarine slipped silently into the depths of the North Sea and crept away from the scene of the rescue.

On board the *Monsoor*, Captain Zeller kept his Seahawks airborne in a racetrack pattern from the *Mette* to the *Monsoor* until he was satisfied the Akula had departed the area.

Onboard the *Mette*, Captain Holms used the backup radio in the engine room to communicate with the Maersk Crisis Response Team. They agreed the *Mette* would put back into port at Aarhus to effect repairs and to change out the crew that had been through the ordeal.

CHAPTER EIGHTEEN

The Photos

Sergey Latsanych was on the phone with Svetlana Ivanovna Zlovna, debriefing from the operation.

"Madam Director, we were outgunned, outmanned, and at a disadvantage right from the start of this operation," relayed Latsanych.

"It was your operation, Latsanych," replied Zlovna.

"And I take full responsibility for it."

"Well, I will brief the president. He will not be pleased. Then I'll have to deal with that Saudi idiot," replied Zlovna, referring to Salman Rahman. "In order to avoid making this entire mission a failure, make sure the Danes gain the Americans' agreement to eliminate their objection over Nord Stream 2. Sergey, that's the very least we need to restore some semblance of balance from this debacle," said Zlovna.

From his experience, Latsanych knew he was in for it, as Zlovna only used "debacle" when she was furious. His career was now in the balance. "I'm sure the Americans will end their objections to Nord Stream 2," said Latsanych, trying to end on a positive note.

The only response Latsanych got was a click on the other end of the line.

∎

Lisa Collins, Sterling Spencer, and the president were receiving a briefing on the *Maersk* mission from the newly nominated CIA director, Dan McCauley, and the CNO.

"Sir, I have to give the credit to the Navy and the SEALs," said Collins.

"Yes, the Navy came through. Especially considering the mission was planned on the fly," added Spencer.

"Now to deal with the Russians," said the president, who was not going to let these hostile actions go without a response.

"Sir, we still have the issue of those photos hanging over our heads," added Collins.

"Over *our* heads?" asked the president. "More like hanging over my and my wife's heads."

"Sorry, sir, no doubt," was all Collins could come back with.

"Plus, we need to get word to the Danish prime minister that her minister of defense is compromised, and we need to do it covertly since that minister will most likely be monitoring all of the prime minister's calls," said the CIA chief.

"I have a way to do that," said the president, though he didn't provide any details.

n

In the White House residence, Andrew Russell was relaxing in the family room with his wife over an after-dinner glass of Johnnie Walker Blue.

"Ken, I know you don't like to talk about what happened on Nantucket," the president said.

"It's not so much that I don't want to talk about it. But what's there to talk about? It isn't a happy memory for me or our family," said Kennedy as they sat together on the couch.

"Well, I have something else that you're not going to like," said the president. "Do you recall when and in what state the state troopers found you?" he asked.

"Of course," replied Kennedy.

"Apparently, before your captors let you go, they took some pictures."

"Pictures? What are you talking about?"

"Pictures of you naked," said the president.

Kennedy just sat there processing the words.

"These photos made their way to Saudi Arabia, and now the Russians have them."

"I don't remember any photos," said Kennedy.

"You were unconscious. They must have taken the photos when you were lying in the woods."

"You've seen them?" she asked.

The president picked up a folder marked with "PEO" (President's Eyes Only) and handed it to his wife.

She looked at the six photos of herself lying naked and unconscious on a backdrop of pine needles. Her blond hair fell haphazardly across her face; nevertheless, you could easily tell it was her.

"I wondered why I was naked when I was found," said Kennedy. "Now I understand. And you say the Russians and Saudis have these?"

"That's what we understand," replied the president.

"Are they going to put them on the Internet?" she asked.

"That's a distinct possibility," said the president. "I'm more confident the Russians won't post them. It's the Saudis that are the problem. And to be specific—it's the sheik's son who has them."

"The sheik's son? The son of the sheik who organized the kidnapping? If he had these all this time, why are they coming out only now? It's been over two years."

"I can't answer that. I suspect they were holding them until they thought they could get the maximum leverage out of them," replied the president.

"Andy, the kids," said Kennedy thinking about their sixteen and fourteen-year-old son and daughter. "You know how awful high school kids can be."

"We're working on some options," said the president.

"Andrew, first they kidnap our family and now they want to violate my dignity. Just how much do I have to give?"

"I totally understand. If anyone releases them, they'll come to regret it. I can promise you that," said the most powerful man in the world.

Kennedy continued to look at the photos.

The president tried to lighten the mood. "For what's it's worth, I think you look pretty damn good."

"Andy, how would you feel if someone released nude photos of you?"

"Me? I think they would be disappointed. I'm just saying, you look good."

The first lady looked at the photos again, shaking her head, and said, "I'm going to bed."

■

"How do I refer to you now? As Your Excellency or Your Eminence-designate?" asked the president as George Deas entered the Oval Office.

"Mr. President, how about a simple Father George?" suggested the prelate.

"All right, then, Father. I did want to see you before you left for Rome."

"Thank you, Mr. President; it's very kind of you."

"Personally, Kennedy and I would have loved to attend your installation," said the president.

"Perhaps you can attend my first Mass at the cathedral," replied Bishop Deas.

"We'll look forward to that," said the president. "In the meantime, George, there's something else I want to discuss with you."

■

La Rue, Holland, and Dunbar were transferred from the USS *Vermont* to the USS *Monsoor* after putting about one hundred miles between them and the Russian Akula. Once on board the *Monsoor*, their party was flown via helicopter to RAF base Lossiemouth, Scotland, where they hopped a Navy transport back to the States.

Now back in Washington, Lauren La Rue, now under strict security, took a call from Søren Larsen. "Good afternoon, Søren," said La Rue.

"Lauren, I hope you are well," said Larsen.

"I am and so is our entire team, in a large part due your help. Søren, I'm indebted to you for your assistance," said La Rue.

"You're very welcome. In addition to checking on how you are, there's a matter of importance that I am calling about," said Larsen.

"You're concerned that Russia is going to start dumping their shares of your company's stock," La Rue responded.

Larsen, once again, was impressed by La Rue's intellect. "Exactly."

"The US will carry you," said La Rue. "We already have investors lined up to start buying your common shares should any excess selling occur in your stock."

"Thank you. That's what I was hoping you would say," said Larsen.

"Søren, the US takes care of its allies, and, even more importantly, we take care of our friends. And we consider Maersk a friend. You'll also note that in our final proposal as to the Maersk shipping percentage regarding Greenland," said La Rue.

"Thank you very much. By the way, Lauren, what did you think of the *Mette*?" asked Larsen.

"It was a colossus. Of course, I would have preferred my visit to have been under less stressful circumstances," said La Rue. "And let me add a special word of gratitude for Captain Holms. Under extremely difficult and risky conditions he and the entire crew performed admirably."

■

Lisa Collins entered the Oval Office, where Sterling Spencer and the president were already seated.

"Good afternoon, Lisa," said the president. "Sterl tells me that your confirmation is proceeding as planned."

Sterling Spencer nodded and added, "The votes are tracking to our projections and we are set to have you take the oath next Thursday."

Changing the topic, the president said, "I spoke with the first lady last night about the photos."

No one said anything.

"She took it about as well as you could expect, considering the subject," said the president. "Lisa, given your background in intelligence, I want to know what options we have to block the spread of these pictures."

"We have several options. As Kevin Mannix mentioned at our last meeting, the NSA can distribute a blacklist several times a day to block the IP address of any web server that hosts them. That said, there are a lot of websites out there. It's unlikely we'll be able to block all of the sites," said Collins.

Spencer added, "Sir, we can also approach the tech giants. I'm sure Apple, Google, Facebook, Twitter, and others will be very aggressive in blocking the distribution of the photos. They already have technology in place that prevents nude photos from being posted on their sites."

"Proactively, what steps can we take to block these photos?"

Collins replied, "Mr. President, we can target any building in Russia or Saudi Arabia with an e-pulse weapon and fry every chip in the building, but that would be very aggressive."

"I'm less worried about Russia doing anything. Any foreign government would know there would be hell to pay if they released them. Not to mention the precedent it would be setting. My bigger concern is the sheik's son—he's the problem."

"We've already talked to the Saudis in the past about having him stand down, but that obviously only worked temporarily," said Collins. "As long as he's around, he represents a risk regarding the release of the photos, as well as to La Rue. She's become an important asset to us."

"Lisa, I want you to contact Prince Alwaleed bin Saud. Explain to him that I want his personal guarantee that no one there will release the photos. I know you have your swearing-in next week, but this is a top priority," said the president.

"I understand, sir. I'll contact him immediately."

The president called to his secretary, "Alice, will you get Doug Paulsen on the phone for me?" He needed to discuss a matter with the CEO of American Airlines and his old Navy friend.

"Mr. President," said the President's secretary, "the British Prime Minister is on line one."

"Mr. Prime Minister, good to hear from you," said the president as he picked up the handset.

"Likewise, Mr. President and thank you for taking my call," said the PM.

"Of course, James," replied the President.

"Andrew, I received a briefing yesterday from MI-6 that I wanted to bring to your attention," opened King.

The President had a foreshadowing of what the topic would be.

"It involves the Saudi Salman Rahman," added King.

The President had guessed correctly and responded, "I believe I know what you are referring to."

"It goes back to the incident in Nantucket and involves the First Lady," added King in the typical British polite and indirect manner.

"Yes, I am aware of that matter," replied the President with a frankness that was reserved for those only his most trusted circle.

"Andrew, I didn't want this information communicated to you via our intelligence channels," said King.

"I appreciate that James," said the President in earnest.

"Andrew, if you don't mind me saying. You should have dealt with this issue years ago," added King.

There were only a very few people who could speak to Andrew Russell in this manner. James King was one of them.

Without any posturing or caution the President responded, " I wanted to give him a second chance. That was a mistake that my wife and I are now paying for."

Continuing James King asked," Does Kennedy know?"

"She does. As you can appreciate, at first, she was mortified. But after some reflection her feelings turned to indignation. Which is exactly what I expected. I think she will stay in the anger phase for a very long time. And from that anger will come strength."

There was a pause James King absorbed the president's words.

Then he closed with, "Quite right. Quite right. If we can be of any assistance, please do not hesitate to let me know."

"Thank you, James. I appreciate that. I think the best salve for this will be time. And on that other matter you are correct, and I intend to correct it shortly," closed the President.

Setting the phone into its cradle the President he knew he was right to give Rahman a second chance. It was a risk he was willing to take at the time not knowing what the implications would be for he and his wife.

The President would often counsel to his people, "It is alright to make a mistake – but what isn't alright is not to learn from it." President Russell was about to show that he had learned from his mistake.

■

"Salman, we weren't able to get La Rue in Copenhagen," said Zlovna.

He screamed, "Ayreh feek, ya sharmouta," which roughly translated into *Fuck you, you bitch*. He went on for another minute in Arabic, clearly expanding on his initial attack.

"Salman, calm yourself," instructed Zlovna.

"Easy for you to say. You failed. I knew I should've dealt with the Chinese instead of incompetents like you people," yelled Rahman.

"Salman, I'll only say it one more time. You need to calm down," said Zlovna.

Taking a breath, Salman regrouped. "Well then, what is your plan?"

"It's just a matter of time before we'll be able to get her," said Zlovna.

"I've already waited two years! I thought I had partnered with professionals," he spat back.

Zlovna knew she could have a bullet put in this insolent brat's head with one command, but she now shifted her messaging, saying, "Salman, you need to take steps to protect yourself. We know our move on La Rue will certainly be traced back to you. The Americans will no doubt retaliate."

"Those godless infidels. I welcome their wrath. I will gut them myself," said Rahman.

Zlovna recognized his father's vengeful temper in Salman. Unfortunately, he lacked the older man's perspective.

"Salman, go into hiding and do it today. That is the best advice I can give you," said Zlovna, and she hung up.

CHAPTER NINETEEN

The Red Hat

The day had arrived for the ordinary public consistory, or the formal meeting of the College of Cardinals.

Hanging above the altar in St. Peter's Basilica in Rome was the crucifix of Jesus Christ, below which sat the Holy Father Pope Francis.

His Excellency the Most Reverend George T. Deas, the bishop of Brooklyn, along with seven other prelates who were also to be elevated to the position of cardinal in the Catholic Church, processed down the main aisle.

The secretary of state for the Catholic Church, Cardinal Abruzzi, administered the oath in Latin to the honorees.

"I, [state your name], cardinal of the Holy Roman Church, promise and swear from this day forth and as long as I live, to remain faithful to Christ and his gospel. Constantly obedient to the Holy Apostolic Roman Church, to Blessed Peter and the person of the Supreme Pontiff and become members of the Roman Clergy and cooperate more directly with Francis and his canonically elected successors.

"Always to remain in communion with the Catholic Church in thy words and actions. Not to make known to anyone matters entrusted to me in confidence. The disclosure of which could bring damage and dishonor to the Holy Church. To carry out diligently and faithfully the duties to which I am called by my service to the church. According to the norms laid down by law. So help me God."

Next the Holy Father spoke. "To the Glory of Almighty God and honor of the Apostolic See receive the scarlet biretta as a sign of the dignity of the cardinalate. Signify your readiness to act with courage even to the shedding of your blood for the increase of the Christian faith for the peace and tranquility of the people of God. And for the freedom and growth of the Holy Roman Church."

The cardinals-elect now came forward to receive the biretta, also known as the red hat.

George Deas approached and knelt in front of the Holy Father. The assisting bishop placed a red skullcap on Deas's head, and then the Pope placed the biretta on his bowed head.

The Holy Father then said, "Receive this ring from the hands of St. Peter and know that your love for the church is strengthened by the love of the Prince of the Apostolic."

With deep solemnity, the now Cardinal Deas looked up to the Holy Father, who profoundly and compassionately said, "Wear them well, my brother."

With the ceremony completed, the Holy Father's vicar handed him his crozier as he administered the final blessing.

"May the blessing of Almighty God, Father, Son, and the Holy Spirit, descend upon you and remain with you forever."

The organ then played "Salve Regina" as the master, thurifer, and Holy Father took up positions. They bowed, turned, and recessed down the main aisle, followed by the newly elected cardinals, as the rest of the College of Cardinals applauded their newly elevated brothers.

It is said that only Britain's royal family can come close to matching the pageantry and pomp of the Catholic Church, and that was certainly true on this day.

After a few days of meetings in the Vatican, Cardinal Deas and his secretary, a priest from the Diocese of Brooklyn, prepared for their return to the United States.

The cardinal and his secretary boarded the American Airlines triple 7 airliner at Da Vinci Airport for their flight back to Washington, Dulles.

Due to strong winds, the American Airlines 777 took a northernly route up over Austria and Germany, then past Hamburg.

It was then the captain made an announcement.

"Ladies and gentlemen, we are experiencing a minor technical difficulty. There is no reason to be alarmed. Our port engine is registering a higher temperature than is normal. With safety in mind, we have decided to land in Copenhagen. Our customer service people have been informed of our situation and are already working on rebooking you on the next available flights to Dulles. We apologize for the inconvenience, but we always put safety first at American Airlines."

Cardinal Deas's secretary said, "Your Eminence, when we land, I'll take care of rebooking our flight."

"Jim," said the cardinal, "I know the bishop of the Diocese of Copenhagen, Bishop Kozon. We worked together on a Committee for the Perpetual Faith years ago. Let's contact him once we land and suggest we visit for a day or two. We can make something positive from this delay."

The secretary was surprised by the cardinal's suggestion but was certainly not going to object to it.

After landing and passing through Danish customs, the secretary contacted Bishop Kozon, who couldn't have been more welcoming and accommodating and immediately dispatched a car to pick up the Cardinal.

It was a short while later that Cardinal Deas and his secretary arrived at the bishop's residence at St. Ansgar's Cathedral.

It was over diner that Bishop Kozon said, "Your Eminence, I'm sure Prime Minister Henriksen would be delighted to meet with you. She's not a Catholic, but it is rare for us to have a prince of the church visit Copenhagen."

Cardinal Deas replied, "By all means, if she has the availability, I would enjoy meeting her."

The next morning after Mass, the bishop informed the cardinal's secretary that he had been successful in procuring a meeting for the cardinal with the prime minister for that afternoon.

■

As agreed, Lisa Collins spoke with Prince Alwaleed bin Saud about Salman Rahman.

"Prince Saud, the actions of Salman Rahman run a great risk of creating unrecoverable animosity between our two countries," said Collins, who was beginning to refine her political acumen.

"I understand completely. And let me clearly state that Salman's actions are in no way representative of the attitude or intentions of the government of Saudi Arabia," replied the prince.

"Prince, I don't doubt that, but there is only so much we can endure. There is only so much President Russell will endure. We will give you one week to address this issue. After that we'll have no other choice than to deal with the matter ourselves," said Collins forcefully.

"Thank you for bringing this to my attention. I assure you that I will deal with it. And congratulations on your nomination. I look forward to a long and productive relationship with you," said the prince as he ended the call.

Collins sat back and mulled over the conversation. She knew the distrust the president had for the Saudis in general. While the call had ostensibly achieved its goals, Collins still was in the Andrew Russell camp where the Saudis were concerned. They were ideologically opposed to everything the US stood for, and sooner or later it was going to reach a boiling point.

Collins's next call was to update Sterling Spencer.

"Do you trust him?" asked Spencer.

"I don't have any experience with him to gauge his sincerity," she replied.

"Well, I do," said Spencer. "You can always count on the prince to do whatever is in his best interest. There's a better-than-even chance that he'll take care of Salman himself just because he's complicating the prince's agenda with us."

There was a lot of truth to Spencer's comment. Not only had Salman created a problem for the Saudi government, but Saudi Arabia had a history of dealing with problems like Salman by simply eliminating the irritant. Sooner or later Salman was going to learn that it wasn't good to have the US, Russia, and the Saudis as your enemies.

And then, of course, there was Andrew Russell. It was never smart to make an enemy of him—especially where his family was concerned.

■

Cardinal Deas wore his black cassock trimmed in red, along with a red sash and, of course, his red zucchetto, or what is colloquially called a skullcap. Around his neck he wore a crucifix given to him personally by the Holy Father.

He was shown into the office of Freja Henriksen, Denmark's first female prime minister.

"Madam Prime Minister, it is an honor," said the cardinal as he extended his hand, not for his ring to be kissed but rather to shake the prime minister's hand.

Having been informed as to the proper way to address a cardinal, the prime minister replied, "Thank you, Your Eminence. We are happy to have you visit Copenhagen. Please have a seat."

"Thank you," said the cardinal, adding, "Along with showing me St. Ansgar's Cathedral, Bishop Kozon has given me a tour of Copenhagen. It is a lovely city, Prime Minister."

"I'm glad you liked it. It isn't often we get a prince of the Catholic Church to visit us in Denmark," said the prime minister.

"Prime Minister, as you may know, I am now the Archbishop of Washington, DC, and as a result I sometimes am entrusted with diplomatic matters. That, in addition to the fact that President Andrew Russell and I are well acquainted from our time together in Brooklyn, is the reason for my stop in Copenhagen."

The prime minister now understood this meeting wasn't simply a courtesy call. "I see," was all she said.

Opening his briefcase, the cardinal took out a briefing document bearing the Seal of the President of the United States.

"Madam Prime Minister, I was asked by President Russell to give this to you and you alone," said the cardinal, handing the folder to the prime minister. "I do not know its contents. But the president asked me to relay to you directly, in confidence, that the US has unequivocal proof that your minister of defense, Magnus Nielsen, has betrayed Denmark and is currently sharing top secret information with the Russians."

The prime minister was speechless. The meeting had certainly taken an unexpected turn.

"Due to the fact that this information implicates your minister of defense, the president was concerned that your communications may be monitored," said the cardinal.

The prime minister just listened.

"In addition," continued the cardinal, "the recent negative social media campaigns against you are being orchestrated by the Russians in an attempt to convince you to support their Greenland proposal."

Henriksen would have to verify it all to ensure that she wasn't being played by the Americans, but certainly everything the cardinal said made sense.

The meeting had reached its scheduled twenty minutes, and any longer would get the attention of her staff.

The cardinal said to the prime minister, within earshot of her staff, "I do hope that while you're in Washington we'll have time to meet again. I would enjoy showing you our Cathedral of St. Matthew the Apostle."

"Thank you, Your Eminence. I do hope we can meet when I'm in the US," said the prime minister.

And with that the meeting ended. Cardinal Deas had completed his first of what he expected would be many assignments for President Russell.

■

Prince Alwaleed bin Saud, who had a flair for the extravagant, as did many Saudi princes and sheiks, had invited twenty of the power brokers of Dubai to his palace for an evening's entertainment centered around a private showing of the epic movie *The Godfather*. Often the prince would send a message by his choice of films.

Also in attendance was young Salman Rahman. After the movie ended, the guests all were invited to one of the palace's many patio areas, where the evening's entertainment took on a more adult tone.

While everyone was enjoying themselves, Prince Saud asked Salman Rahman to join him in his private study.

"Salman, it was good of you to come," said the prince, knowing to decline his invitation would be a great insult and would finish any aspirations Salman may have had of rising in the Saudi power structure.

"Thank you, Your Highness, for inviting me. It is a great honor," said the young sheik.

"What did you think of the movie?" asked the prince.

"To be honest, it was typical American ideological trash."

Nodding, the prince said, "That may be, but I selected it especially for you, Salman."

Salman did not know how to take the prince's comment, nor what it meant.

"You see, Salman, you are Sonny from the movie," said the prince. "You act rather than think. You let your passions rule over you."

Salman was beginning to get angry but knew better than to show it and checked himself.

Continuing, the prince said, "Salman, you are bright and gifted, but you continually let your emotions get the better of you. Salman, I want you to be more like Michael and less like Sonny."

Salman remained quiet as he continued to listen.

"Salman, with the untimely passing of your father, I would like to assume the role of becoming your mentor," said one of the most powerful men in all of Saudi Arabia.

Salman was touched by the prince's offer.

"Learn from me, Salman, and you will grow in wisdom," added the prince.

"But, Your Highness. The Americans must pay for what they did to my father," replied Salman.

"Sonny, Sonny, Sonny. They will—in time," said the prince. "But not now. Do you understand? And that includes not releasing the photos of the first lady."

Salman grimaced at the prince's words as if he was being stabbed in his stomach.

"Now, Salman," said the prince, "tell me you understand. I need to hear you say it."

After a moment of resistance Salman relented. "I understand, Your Highness," said Salman. "But, Your Highness, I have no influence over the Russians or what they will do with the photos of the president's wife," he added.

"Don't worry about the Russians. I will take care of them. Just make sure the photos don't get posted here, Salman," said bin Saud. His tone was impossible to misunderstand.

■

Lisa Collins took an incoming call from Prince Saud. "Good evening, Prince."

"Thank you for accepting my call, Madam Vice President–nominee," said the prince. "I want to update you and give you my assurances that Salman Rahman will no longer be a problem to you."

"Prince, how should I interpret your words?" asked Collins.

"I spoke with him directly and will be taking on something of a mentoring role with him."

Somewhat relieved by his response, Collins asked, "And you're one hundred percent certain he will no longer be a problem for us?"

"One hundred percent," replied the prince. "However, there is another issue over which we no longer have control. The photos. Do you understand what I am referring to?" asked the prince.

"Yes, I do."

"These photos, the Russians have them."

"And what did the Russians promise to do in return for the photos?" asked Collins directly.

"There were some funds involved, but more importantly Salman wanted the Russians to abduct his father's finance person, who now works for you," said bin Saud.

Collins was surprised by how candid the prince was. He had just confirmed exactly what the Americans believed were Salman's motives. "Can you give us your assurance that any copies of the photos that Salman had have been destroyed?" she asked.

"Madam Vice President, I have talked to Salman directly and have his word that he has destroyed any copies he had," said the prince.

Collins mulled over the prince's words.

"Prince, can I give the president of the United States your personal guarantee that all photos outside of Russia have been destroyed? And that neither Salman, nor anyone else in Saudi Arabia, will release the photos?" asked Collins.

There was silence for a moment.

"Madam Vice President, you can tell the president that Salman has given me his word that he has destroyed his copies and he will not release the photos," said the prince.

"Yes, I heard you, but how do we know he hasn't given copies to his colleagues? Your words, Your Highness, are artful and nuanced and do not fill me with a great deal of confidence."

"Madam Vice President, interpret my words however you wish, but I have shared with you what I know," said the prince.

"I understand," replied Collins. "Now I want you to hear my words. If we detect Salman is in any way involved in any future operations against the US, we will hold you personally responsible. Is that clear?"

"Madam Vice President, threats are not appreciated," said the prince.

"Threat? That wasn't a threat, Prince Saud. It was a promise," said Collins.

At which point they both terminated the call.

CHAPTER TWENTY

We Got Trouble with
a Capital *T*

As the president, the first lady, and their daughter made their way to their seats in the school theater, the president acknowledged the growing round of applause.

After they were settled, with Secret Service agents sitting in the rows in front, behind, and next to the first family, the overture began.

A conductor walked onto the stage and proclaimed, "River City Junction—River City, next station stop!"

As so began the Sidwell Friends School's production of *The Music Man* featuring Andrew Russell Jr. as Professor Harold Hill.

The president, first lady, and their daughter all held their collective breaths as Andrew turned to the audience and delivered his opening line, "Gentlemen, you intrigue me. I think I'll have to give Iowa a try."

An irrepressible grin broke across the faces of the president and the first lady. Katie smiled too.

Before the start of the second act, Bryan Garman, the Sidwell Friends School head, took to the stage.

"It is indeed a great honor for the Sidwell Friends School to welcome the president and first lady to this evening's performance of *The Music Man*."

Again, applause broke out for the exceedingly popular forty-sixth president of the United States and the first lady.

"I would ask everyone, once the play has ended, that you remain seated until the president and first family have departed. That is unless our wonderful actors have moved you to give them a standing ovation. Thank you all again for attending, and now on with the show," finished the principal of the SFS.

And, of course, the students did get a standing ovation. This scene would be repeated the next two nights, with the first family attending all three performances of the play's run.

On closing night, the first family remained so all the actors and their families could take pictures with the president and first lady. That alone made the Sidwell Friends' $46,490 annual tuition worth it.

■

Back in Copenhagen Prime Minister Henriksen, having absorbed the report given to her by Cardinal Deas, was now ready to confront Magnus Nielsen.

"Minister Nielsen, thank you for coming," said Henriksen.

"Not at all, Prime Minister. How can I be of service, ma'am?" said Nielsen.

"Well, since you ask, you can start by resigning your post immediately," said the prime minister, not mincing any words.

"I beg your pardon?" was all the defense minister could get out.

"Mr. Nielsen, I have corroborated proof that you have not acted in the best interest of Denmark and, in fact, you've been sharing secret documents with agents of the Russian Federation."

"I don't know what proof you are citing. Of course, I've conversed with Russian personnel as part of our Greenland negotiations. But I've interacted equally with all participants. I have worked closely will all bidders including the Americans, the Russians, and to a lesser extent the Chinese. It is my remit to do that," Nielsen retorted.

"Was it part of your remit to share the proposals from the Americans with the Russians, Magnus? Was it also part of your remit to let the Russians know the Americans were on the *Mette Maersk*?" asked the prime minister.

"Again, I don't know what information you've been fed, Prime Minister, but I assure you all my interactions were for the benefit of Denmark. To suggest otherwise is a great insult and, I might add, most likely politically motivated."

The prime minister dryly stated, "You've always overrated yourself, Magnus. I put up with it because I thought you were reasonably effective. But now I see you are untrustworthy at best and a traitor at worst. I'll give you the courtesy of allowing you to resign by tomorrow morning. If you do not, you'll be removed from office tomorrow afternoon and charges will be brought against you."

"You're not going to do that, Prime Minister. I've anticipated this sort of action from you, and to that end, I have incriminating information about your husband and his business practices that I can make public," threatened Nielsen.

"Again, Magnus, you have overplayed your hand. We have proof that your copy of the American proposal found its way to Moscow within a day of your receiving it. The Americans inserted subtle text changes in each copy. It was your copy that wound up in Moscow. You have until tomorrow morning to resign. That's all. You're dismissed," said the prime minister, causing Nielsen to flush with anger.

■

"Mr. President, I want to bring to a conclusion our position on Nord Stream 2. We know how important this is to Denmark and Germany. Dropping our opposition will be an about-face on the issue, but since it is tied to the Greenland negotiations, the change would be justified," Spencer said.

"That shouldn't be a problem, but before we make the final decision, I want to mull it over a little longer," said the president, looking distracted.

Spencer knew that meant the president would be going on his Peloton for a workout.

A few minutes later the president clipped into his bike for a forty-five-minute '80s class with his favorite Peloton instructor, Denis Morton.

The Secret Service had set it up so the president's Peloton would connect using a double VPN that would mask the unit's IP address. They also disabled his camera by using the hi-tech method of placing a piece of tape over it.

The harder the president worked in the spin class, the clearer his thoughts became.

In addition to Nord Stream, the president needed to think through what his response would be if the photos of the first lady were released. And on top of all that, the president was getting troubling reports regarding China's actions on Taiwan. The president needed to wrap up the Greenland negotiations and put an end to these Russian distractions so he could turn his attention to his next challenge, which, without a doubt, would be China.

Yes, they would agree to waive their objections on Nord Stream 2, he concluded. Greenland was more important than the gas pipeline.

It only took a couple of days until work restarted on Nord Stream 2, highlighted by the Reuters report Spencer was handed by his staff.

MOSCOW (Reuters) - A pipe-laying vessel has entered Danish waters ahead of the resumption of construction of the Nord Stream 2 gas pipeline, the consortium behind the project said on Tuesday.

This week the pipe-laying vessel *Fortuna*, owned by the firm KVT-RUS, is ready to begin work in the construction Danish EEZ corridor.

"All work is being performed in line with relevant permits," said the Nord Stream 2 project manager.

The construction of the pipeline, which would double the capacity of the existing Nord Stream link from Russia to Germany, was suspended in December 2019 following the imposition of sanctions from the United States, but that resistance has now been waived, cited the Danish Maritime Authority.

After reading the article, Spencer said to his staff, "Well, that didn't take long."

■

It was Thursday morning, and an associate justice of the Supreme Court arrived at the White House to swear in Lisa Collins as the fiftieth vice president of the United States.

As a result of some arm twisting, Spencer had exceeded his projections regarding Collins's approval in the Senate and the House. Collins was approved by a wide margin, with just five senators and only twelve congresspersons casting either "no" or "abstain" votes against her.

The morning ceremony along with some speeches and photographs went as planned, as the United States swore in its first female vice president.

As the celebration continued, Sterling Spencer whispered to the president.

"Sir, the photos of the first lady were just released on a website in Yemen."

The president did not react, knowing he was in the glow of the cameras. Sterling Spencer now nodded to the White House press secretary as their prearranged signal letting her know she needed to exit the president from the Briefing Room posthaste.

On their way to the Sit Room, Spencer and the president were joined by newly appointed CIA director Dan McCauley, who added, "Sir, we have the IP address of the server in Yemen and we've already launched a DDoS attack on it. No one will be able to access the server while we have it under attack."

A DDoS, a distributed denial-of-service cyberattack, would incapacitate the targeted server by flooding it with an avalanche of spurious requests, effectively taking it off-line.

Entering the Sit Room, the NSA director added, "The Yemen server is connected to a Saudi company. We think the company is a front for Salman Rahman."

"What cyber offensive steps can we take against Saudi Arabia and Yemen right now?" asked the president.

Lisa Collins, who probably had the best knowledge in the room of the US's offensive cyber capabilities, responded, "Sir, depending on the level of response you wish to enact, we can disrupt their

Internet communications, take down all their voice and data networks, and we can even launch an e-pulse attack that can fry chips
in any series of buildings there."

"I am going to meet with my wife now. In two hours, I want
options that cover all the possibilities Lisa mentioned." With that the
president left the Sit Room to make his way to the first lady's office
in the East Wing.

It was rare for the president to enter the East Wing of the White
House, so it was quite a surprise when the president approached the
first lady's secretary and asked, "Is she in?"

Standing, the secretary said, "Yes, sir, she is."

Nodding, the president entered the office of the first lady.

Kennedy Russell looked up from her desk and could immediately read the look on her husband's face. "What is it, Andy?"

The president tightened his lips and said, "Ken, the photos
are out."

A look of powerlessness came over the first lady.

"I'm so sorry, Ken," the president added.

"Who released them? Can you block them?"

"We're working on that as we speak."

"The kids. I need to speak to them. I don't want them
hearing about this at school or from the press," said Kennedy,
who was thinking out loud and beginning to show the first
signs of panic.

"The Secret Service can get the kids and bring them home,"
added the president.

The first lady picked up her phone and told her secretary
to have Ed Jordan, who oversaw the president's Secret Service
detail, come to her office immediately.

"Once they're home, I want the Internet turned off. I don't want them seeing or reading about them," ordered Kennedy.

The president nodded, knowing his wife would need time to process what had happened, and he needed to get back to the Oval to work on his own public statement, not to mention determine his retaliatory actions.

The president's press secretary was already working on two possible drafts of press announcements to address the release of the photos. The two releases had markedly different tones. The first expressed a tone of indignation and outrage. The second was more in keeping with the president's style and took a much harder tone and included retaliation.

"Keep working on them," said the president.

Meanwhile, Collins couldn't believe the photos were posted just days after she had discussed the matter with Prince Saud.

■

In Moscow, Svetlana Ivanovna Zlovna was being briefed on the release of the photos.

"Did Salman release them?"

"We are not one hundred percent certain, Madam Director, but we believe so," said the head of the SVR's cyberunit.

"We know they are emanating from the Middle East. So far, we have servers in Yemen, Syria, Iran, and Lebanon posting them."

"I don't want any of our press outlets reporting on the photos. If a server in Russia posts the photos, take it down fast," ordered Zlovna. "I want one hundred percent deniability on these photos. Is that understood? Put a lock on them, hard."

Her next step was to try to reach Salman Rahman, who no doubt was now in hiding.

■

"Sir, we have response scenarios for your consideration," said Collins.

"Plus, sir, we have now detected servers in Syria, Lebanon, Iran, and Indonesia that are posting the photos," added the NSA director.

"Every time we detect a server posting the photos, we DDoS them. But we are playing catch-up, sir, not offense," said Director McCauley.

"Lisa, what are the scenarios?" asked the president.

"Sir, first we can blacklist every IP address from any country posting the photos. That will block all communications from a targeted country. But it is a massive action, as it will basically turn off all Internet traffic from the country. For example, it will block all e-commerce, all banking, and all email, VoIP, and social media posts. Second, we can bring down any network in any of the posting countries. And, of course, we can launch targeted e-pulse attacks."

She added, "We can target Iran, Yemen, Syria, Lebanon, and Indonesia right now, sir."

"What about Saudi Arabia? Don't we believe they originated there?" asked the president.

"We can target Saudi too, sir, but as an ally we thought you would prefer not to take that step," added Collins.

"Sterl, what do you think?" asked the president, knowing that he would act, as he always did, as a check on the president's temper.

"Sir, I think we disrupt all Internet communications for countries posting the photos. We also, via State and our intelligence agencies, warn all nations that if these photos wind up on any server in their country, they can expect the same action. I think most countries will act aggressively to self-police their networks and block the dissemination of the photos," said Spencer, his tone cool and rational.

"And Saudi Arabia?" asked the president.

"Sir, I think we take our time and decide how to deal with them," answered Spencer.

Thinking about for a few minutes, the president responded, "You have a go on taking down the networks in the countries listed. Also, I want a list of all commercial and government sites in Saudi and the UAE for possible e-pulse attacks."

The president, Collins, and Spencer departed the Sit Room to meet with the press secretary.

The president stopped at the door and turned back. "Admiral, who do we have in the Arabian Sea?"

Checking his ships-at-sea screen, Admiral Jacobsen replied, "Sir, the closest group we have is Carrier Group 8, the *Harry Truman* Strike Group."

"Move them to two hundred miles off the coast of Yemen. Priority," ordered the president.

"Aye, aye, sir," was all the CNO said, as the president was now already out of the room.

■

Prince Saud yelled at his staff, "Get me Salman Rahman on the phone now."

It took time to get ahold of Rahman, but with some effort the call was connected to Saud.

"What did you do?" asked the irate Saudi prince.

"I did what I had to do to defend my father's honor," replied Rahman.

"What did I tell you?" demanded Saud.

"Allah is smiling on me as I attack the infidels. That is who I serve," replied Rahman.

"Where are you?"

"I am far from your reach."

The prince put the call on hold, yelling, "I want a trace on this line."

Calmer now, the prince reopened his line with Rahman, "Salman, I tried. I really did. But you have sealed your own fate," said Saud.

Putting Rahman on mute, a member of his staff updated the prince. "Your Highness, this call is coming from a satellite phone. We cannot track it with a high degree of accuracy."

Returning to Rahman, all Saud added was, "Allah be with you."

With that Prince Saud, the second-most powerful person in Saudi Arabia, second only to the king, realized Rahman had become a terrible liability and one that could no longer be tolerated.

∎

"What do you think about a national address?" the president asked the team he had assembled in the Oval Office.

"It puts more focus on this matter and certainly would elevate it to the level of a national crisis," replied the press secretary. "I would advise against that, Mr. President," she added.

Spencer said, "I think a national address would be in keeping with your personality and would present a strong image. My question is more about timing. Wouldn't it be better to take some time to collect as much data as we can so that we can present a more complete narrative to the country?"

"Lisa?" next asked the president.

"I agree with Sterling. I think we need time to gather intelligence, weigh our various response scenarios, and then share that with the public," said Collins, supporting the chief of staff's recommendation.

The president looked down at his hands and turned his wedding ring as he considered the counsel he had just received.

"We'll hold off on the address for now, but I see doing one in the next day or two. Lisa, call Prince Saud and see what you can find out. Plus, we better put Lauren La Rue under tighter security. Then work with our intelligence agencies and find out the location of the sheik's son. I want assets in place where we hit his location with a fusillade of Tomahawk cruise missiles ASAP. I'll be in the residence. Keep me apprised of all developments."

After the president left the Oval, Collins, Spencer, and the press secretary remained.

"Sterl, it's a bad idea to do a national address on this," said the press secretary.

"I agree," chimed in Collins.

"I understand your concerns, but Andrew Russell has a way of connecting with the American people. As we decided, let's gather more information and then revisit the topic," said Spencer, bringing the meeting to an end.

■

"Prince Saud, please hold for the vice president," said the White House operator.

A moment later Lisa Collins was on the line. "Prince Saud, it gives me no pleasure to make this call."

"Madam Vice President, first let me congratulate you on your history-making confirmation," opened the prince.

"Thank you, but the purpose of my call is not to gain your congratulations," said Collins in a terse tone.

"I understand, Madam Vice President," said the prince.

"Exactly what I said couldn't happen on our last call has happened."

"I understand, Madam Vice President, and let me add those actions were completely against my counsel and command."

"Your government will make a formal public apology to the president and the first lady," ordered Collins.

"I will pass that request on to the king, Madam Vice President, but it is very unlikely we will be able to comply with that," said the prince.

"Prince Saud, let me share with you what is being discussed here. People are remembering that fifteen of the nineteen 9/11 hijackers were Saudi citizens, that the kidnapping of the president's family was carried out by a Saudi extremist group, and that the release of these photos was effected by a Saudi. Nothing short of a public apology will tamp down the anger the American people and this administration is feeling," replied Collins.

"Madam Vice President, I assure you the Saudi government had nothing to do with any of those events. And to suggest such will permanently and irrecoverably damage the relationship that we have worked so hard to build over the many US administrations," responded Saud.

"If the result of our relationship produces the acts that I just enumerated, then it has little value to us. To the contrary, these are acts of an enemy, not a friend. Prince, in the strongest terms, I advise your government to make the apology," said Collins.

"May I suggest an alternative, Madam Vice President?" said the prince.

■

Upstairs in the residence the president asked, "How are the kids?"

"They're fine. Andrew is upset, though," replied the first lady.

"I'll talk to him," said the president.

"And what exactly do you plan to tell him?" came the terse reply. "That this is what comes from being a politician nowadays? Andy, I didn't sign up for this. Nobody would. Our first and foremost responsibility is to the health and well-being of our family. Since moving into this gilded cage, the children and I have been kidnapped. And now these pictures."

Andrew Russell was expecting this response. What husband wouldn't?

"Another five years of this? Imagine what that will do to our family," added Kennedy. "You know what I fantasize about?" she asked.

The president just shook his head.

"I fantasize about when we were in Brooklyn and I could go food shopping or clothes shopping with the kids. We could go out for lunch without a phalanx of security. I could volunteer at their schools without camera crews following my every step. And it's just not me that I'm worried about. It's what this is doing to the kids. How many teenagers have to deal with that sort of stress? Andy, is it worth it?"

And that was the question, wasn't it?

"Do you remember when we were dating and we went ice skating at Rock Center?" she asked.

The president nodded.

"You said, 'It feels like we're dancing through life.' Do you recall that?"

"I do," said the president.

"And as we skated, I replied, 'We're on smooth ice.' Now I feel like we're on shattered ice," said Kennedy.

"You just asked if it's worth it. Maybe it isn't. Maybe I won't run again."

"Oh, Andy. You know that won't happen," said Kennedy.

After a minute of reflection, she added . . . "'How hard it is to keep from being king, when it's in you and in the situation.'"

It would be a matter of just a few hours before the president transitioned from consoling his wife to thoughts of payback. As he lay awake in bed, the president ran through an expansive array of responses.

CHAPTER TWENTY-ONE

A Lie Can Travel Halfway Around the World While the Truth Is Putting On Its Shoes

Sterling Spencer met the president in the Oval Office to review their schedule for the coming days.

"We have the Danish prime minister and state dinner later this week, sir. Any changes you would like to make?" asked the president's chief of staff, indirectly asking whether the first lady would want to make a public appearance.

"No, no changes, Sterl," replied the president.

"Fine, sir. The Greenland negotiating team is set to give you the final readout on the treaty we will be signing during the prime minister's visit. After the Greenland briefing, we have a Sit Room meeting where the Joint Chiefs and intelligence heads will present you with response scenarios, sir," added Spencer.

The president just nodded.

"Sir, have you given the idea of making a national address any more thought?" asked Spencer.

"I have. I'm not doing it. But remember, next week I'll be giving an address at the UN."

"Sir, VP Collins spoke with Prince Saud last night. She demanded they make a formal and public apology."

"What sort of response did she get?" asked the president.

"Just about what you would expect on the apology, but then Saud made an unusual offer. He offered to deal with Salman once and for all."

The president thought about what Spence had just shared with him without replying.

"When is the Greenland debrief?" asked the president.

"At ten, sir."

"Okay, then. Thank you, Sterl," said the president, indicating their meeting was over.

■

In Moscow, Svetlana Ivanovna Zlovna was meeting with her leadership team.

"Have we confirmed that Salman released the photos?" asked the SVR director.

"That is affirmative, ma'am," said the SVR's cyberchief.

Zlovna nodded. "What are the final results of the raid on the Maersk ship?" she asked.

"Madam Director, we suffered four dead from our Special Forces team and three injured," responded the chief of special operations.

"How badly are they injured?" asked Zlovna.

"Two suffered only minor injuries. The other is stable but in serious condition. The doctors say he will live but his career in Special Forces is over," replied the spec ops chief.

"Find him a desk job in the Intelligence Directorate," ordered Zlovna. "And what do we think were the American casualties?" she asked.

"We don't have a clear picture. We believe we injured two of their SEALs, but other than that, La Rue and her partner escaped uninjured, as did the three CIA agents. We deployed Kolokov-5; however, as you know, it doesn't have a lasting effect," said the special ops chief.

"Any injured Maersk personnel?" asked Zlovna.

"One was shot in the leg, but other than that just bruises and shaken up, no injuries."

"And where is the ship now?"

"It put into Aarhus for what we believe are repairs and a change of crew," said the intelligence chief.

"We have to expect some retaliation from the Cowboy," said Zlovna, using her favorite moniker for President Russell.

"If I were him, I would target Nord Stream. For protection we are stationing four Akula's along the pipeline. Tell them to be on high alert for an attack by the Americans," ordered Zlovna.

"Any other actions, Madam Director?" asked her chief of staff.

"Heighten our cyberdefenses as well. We likely will experience some sort of attack by the Americans as well," warned Zlovna.

The briefing over, Zlovna sat alone in the conference room. They never were going to release the photos of the first lady. Their entire gambit was to *threaten* to release them. Now with them posted, the SVR had lost all the advantage the photos represented.

She said aloud, "Salman, you insolent fool."

Salman had created a mess for her that she would now have to clean up.

■

Alice Ahern escorted Ed Holland and Lauren La Rue into the Oval Office to brief the president, Sterling Spencer, and Lisa Collins on the Greenland/Denmark pact.

"Good afternoon, Ed. I heard you had an exciting time in Copenhagen," said the president.

"Yes, sir, a little too exciting for my tastes, but we accomplished our goals," Holland replied.

Turning now to La Rue, the president said, "I don't think we've met yet."

"No, sir, we haven't. I'm with the CIA and work for Director McCauley."

It was important for Collins that the president liked La Rue because she planned to steal her from the CIA and make her a senior member of her staff.

"So, what sort of deal did you commit us to?" kidded the president, as he had been kept abreast of every step of the strategic agreement.

Holland began, "Sir, we have a fifty-year deal with a twenty-five-year out. We'll pay the Danish government $38 billion a year and the Greenland Naalakkersuisut government $2 billion a year for an exclusive license to mine and refine Greenland's rare-earth minerals."

"Forty billion a year; is that a good deal?" asked the president, already knowing the answer.

"Sir," responded La Rue, "at twice the price, it'd be a good deal for us."

"Did you hear that, Sterl, Lisa? We got a bargain," said the president.

Not exactly sure how to take the president's comment, La Rue added, "Sir, with the estimated largest rare-earth deposits on the planet, along with its location and the anticipated opening of the Northwest Passage, this deal with Greenland is a home run."

The president smiled, liking the self-confidence La Rue displayed.

Holland now reentered the conversation, saying, "Other aspects of the agreement you should be aware of sir. We've agreed that Maersk will carry sixty percent of the materials from Greenland. Positioning Maersk to profit from this deal was clearly important to them. In addition, the US will provide a stipend equal to twenty-five percent of the purchase price for any Dane wishing to purchase a Tesla or other EV. It's estimated, sir, that within five years more than half the vehicles in Denmark will be EVs. Going further, we agreed that the only vehicles we'll import to Greenland are EVs. First, passenger vehicles, but as soon as commercial EVs are available, that's all we'll use on Greenland."

The president knew that condition would further ingratiate him to Elon Musk. Not that he needed it.

Holland continued, "We've also committed to a capital program where we'll invest $200 billion over the next ten years to build out Greenland's infrastructure. We've already contracted with the firm that built Denver's airport to build a similar facility in Nuuk. In addition, the Air Force will be significantly expanding our base and facilities at Thule."

"When did dropping our opposition to Nord Stream 2 come into the negotiation?" asked the president.

"Sir, that was one of the last requests," said Holland.

"How is it that point came up so late in the discussion?"

La Rue said, "Sir, I believe that was inserted at the suggestion of the Russians, who had an open channel to the Danish defense minister. Given that they only have 62 miles remaining of the 759-mile pipeline to complete, we didn't think it would be a deal breaker."

Again, the president could see why Lisa Collins was so high on La Rue. Her ability to analyze a situation and distill it to its most important parts was rare and highly coveted at the CIA and the NSA, as well as in the West Wing.

"So, in summary, you're telling me this is the sweetest deal America has done since we purchased Alaska from the Russians?" said the president.

As the meeting wrapped up, the president added, "Ed, Lauren, nice job on this. And I mean that. This will position us to have access to an adequate supply of rare-earth minerals for at least the next fifty years. I look forward to seeing you tomorrow night at the state dinner."

■

Later that day the president met with his team in the Sit Room.

"Okay, people, what are our options?" asked the president.

"Mr. President, we have put together a list of scenarios. First, we will present actions that we can take against Saudi Arabia, and then we will present actions against Russia," replied Lisa Collins, taking on a leadership role in the meeting.

The NSA deputy director of intelligence, Kristin Bartlett, was the first to present. "Mr. President, we have a number of offensive cyber actions for your review. We can disrupt their Internet communications for the next thirty days. This would impact all social media and e-commerce, as well as electronic banking. Going further, at your command we can bring down the three leading wireless networks in Saudi."

The president did not react; he just listened.

"What can we do to impact their oil production?" asked Spencer.

"We have a range of actions from slightly impacting their ability to refine crude to completely stopping their ability to refine. We can do this all via a cyberattack. No boots on the ground," added Bartlett.

The president asked, "What would that do to the markets?"

The secretary of the treasury, who was bridged in, responded, "It would wreak havoc with the markets. Oil would probably shoot up to $120 a barrel. The markets would sell off. Gas would go up to $5 a gallon. It could cause a recession depending on how long the supply was disrupted for."

The chairman of the Joint Chiefs took over. "Sir, from a military perspective, we have the ability to strike anywhere in the kingdom on your orders. Any one of their landmarks, commerce centers, or mosques can be precisely targeted and taken out."

The president grimaced and tightened his lips together, not liking any of the general's ideas.

Bartlett returned with, "Sir, in addition to disrupting their IT infrastructure, we can stop their commercial air traffic. We can effectively shut down all their airports."

"For how long?" asked the president.

"Indefinitely, sir."

"Won't they be able to work around our cyberattacks with time?" asked the president.

"Not our attacks, sir. Yes, they can defeat one of our attack vectors, but we can dynamically shift the attack pattern, staying ahead of any of their defensive actions. We can keep them off the air for as long as you order," said Bartlett.

"Lisa, where are they on the public apology?" asked the president.

"I'm going to get a draft of their proposed wording today, sir, but I don't think it will be satisfactory to you in the least," replied Collins.

"Put plans in place to disrupt their Internet and air traffic control. Also, plan to impact their oil refineries for one day, just to show them that we can do it. I'll review the final plan tomorrow. Now, what about Russia?" asked the president.

"Similarly, Mr. President, we have a number of options for your consideration. The first and most obvious is Nord Stream. It would be rather easy for us to sabotage the pipelines. We could take out both or just one, sir," Bartlett said.

"Kristin, if we were to do that, we'd create an enormous problem with Germany. Not to mention with Denmark, whom I plan to sign a treaty with at the end of this week."

"Very well, sir. We have several ideas that make use of our underwater mine capabilities. Sir, we have what we call 'splat mines,'" said Bartlett as she brought up a slide.

"Sir, these mines are about the size of a hatbox and can be deployed from one of our subs. We could attach, say, twenty or so to the hull of any Russian icebreaker and at a designated time we could set them off. They possess a small charge, so the probability of any casualties would be very minimal, but with twenty splats we would sink the target, sir," said Bartlett.

This idea got the president's interest. "So, theoretically, we could take out their fleet of super-icebreakers with these splats?" he asked.

"Not theoretically, sir. We could do it," replied Bartlett.

The CNO asked, "Wouldn't they detect twenty mines on the hull of their ship by the increased drag?"

"They would be detected if we put them on a sub's hull and possibly on a warship's, but their icebreakers are so loud and travel at such slow speeds we doubt they'd notice. Bear in mind they're very small, sir," replied Bartlett.

"Mr. President," continued the CNO, "the problem with this proposal is it isn't that hard to do and I wouldn't want to lose one of our carriers by similar means."

The president considered the CNO's comments. The idea *was* too simple and easily copied. As a result, he dismissed it.

"What's next, DDI?" asked the president.

"Sir, staying with mines, we have reproductions of World War II mines. They are perfect duplicates. We've even covered them with barnacles and seaweed. The only difference is the charge. They're much more powerful. We could release three of these near any Russian ship and have only one blow up. The other two would not explode and could later be found by the Russians. Of course, those two mines would be exact duplicates with the old explosives in them. The belief would be that the Russian ship ran into a random World War II relic. It gives us deniability, sir," concluded Bartlett.

"Comments?" asked the president.

"Sir, I think it's fine if our goal is to blow up one of their ships. But is that our goal?" asked Spencer.

"I'd like to hear the other options, Mr. President," said VP Collins.

Nodding to Bartlett, the president said, "Next."

"Sir, we have a biological weapon that can disable a ship over time. The people at the NSA call it Project Tribble."

That caused everyone in the room to look at one another.

Noting the reaction, Bartlett said, "We have a lot of *Star Trek* fans at the NSA. With this concept a submarine deploys basically large dissolvable bags containing biological material via remote control. We guide the material to the ship's intake ports. Once in position, the bags dissolve and the material gets sucked into the ship's engines."

The president asked, "Won't the ship's filters catch the material?"

"That's the beauty of this, sir. The material is so fine no filter will catch it. In addition, since the material is biological, it grows over time. In a matter of weeks, the engine components will become gummed up and disabled. The projected time to clean and overhaul the engines is substantial. Our engineers think it would take at least a year."

"What about our ships? Would our filters block this type of material?" asked the CNO.

"Not today, sir, but we're working with the Navy on a next generation of filters that would," replied Bartlett. "Finally, sir, that brings us to cyber activities. As you just heard regarding Saudi, we have the ability to implement similar attacks on Russia. That said, we've narrowed down our list to just a few for your review," continued Bartlett. "Sir, much depends on just how much disruption you wish to cause."

"For now, let's focus on government and military targets," responded the president.

"Sir, we can deploy an e-pulse weapon whereby we basically destroy every computer chip within a set radius. We could set off e-pulses at the SVR headquarters or at the Kremlin. Sir, at the same time we could also set off e-pulses at their prisons or at their refineries," said Bartlett.

"Sir, we could come up with a list of other strategic targets for the e-pulses as well," added Collins.

"We could melt down their submarine bases at Severomorsk or Polyarnyy," added the CNO.

"Again, if we take this action, can they do the same to us?" asked the president.

"Mr. President, our intelligence indicates that at least seven countries have e-pulse capabilities, and that list includes Russia, China, North Korea, and India, as well as our allies the UK, France, and Germany," replied Collins.

"What about Saudi Arabia?" asked the president.

"We don't think they have e-pulses currently, but it wouldn't be hard to purchase them from one of the countries that do have them," answered Collins.

"Beyond the e-pulses, sir, we have back doors into their three major wireless providers: MTS, MegaFon, and PeterStar. At your command we can take down those networks," said Bartlett.

"Taking down their networks would be akin to taking down Verizon, AT&T, and T-Mobile here. I don't want some mother giving birth not to be able to call for an ambulance. Take it off the list," said the president.

"Yes, sir," responded Bartlett.

"We also have the capability to disrupt their stock markets, banks, and television broadcasting capabilities," added Collins.

"Our dispute is not with the Russian people. It's with their leadership. I don't want to punish their citizens. Is that clear?" asked the president.

"Keeping with that vein, I suspect, sir, you don't want to involve our Space Force and take out any of their satellites," asked the Space Force four-star general, who was a new addition to the Joint Chiefs.

"Let's leave space out of this," guided the president. "So far the idea that appeals to me most is using the biological material to disable their entire fleet of icebreakers," said the president.

With that the chairman of the Joint Chiefs said, "Thank you, Mr. President, we'll work on operational plans for your review and have them to you shortly."

"Thank you, everyone. Kristin, stop by the Oval before you leave," said the president, and they all stood as he and Sterling Spencer exited the Sit Room.

■

The Marines opened the White House doors, and the president and first lady welcomed the Danish prime minister and her husband at the semicircular driveway of the North Portico. The schedule called for the official signing of the US/Denmark Greenland Pact, an Oval Office meeting, and a photo op, followed by the state dinner that evening.

Attendees from Denmark, of course, included the prime minister and her husband. They also included Crown Prince Frederik of Denmark, who was the heir apparent of Queen Margrethe II, who was now too elderly to travel. In addition, the Danish ambassador, some of the prime minister's cabinet members, and the members of the Danish Parliament who represented Greenland and the Faroe Islands, as well as the senior staff from their embassy, were all attending. Also joining were the CEOs of Maersk and Lego, which were Denmark's premier companies.

The administration's guest list for the evening's event included Lisa Collins, Sterling Spencer, Ed Holland, and Lauren La Rue, as well as a handful of senators and cabinet members.

The US guest list from industry included Elon Musk, Larry Ellison, Jeff Bezos, and Tim Cook. Representing academia were the president of Caltech, Thomas Rosenbaum; Georgetown University's John J. DeGioia; Boston College's William P. Leahy; and NYU's Andrew D. Hamilton.

Also attending by special invitation of the president was His Eminence Cardinal George Deas.

Rounding out the evening's guest list were the Joint Chiefs and the directors of the CIA, NSA, and FBI, as well as three Supreme Court justices.

In preparing for his toast, the president's staff had provided him with two choices. First, the simple "Skoal," or if the president wished, he could use, "Bunden i vejret eller resten i håret," which roughly translates to *Bottoms up or the rest in your hair.*

"Really, Sterl, this is the best the staff could come up with?" asked the president as his chief of staff sighed, agreeing with the president that the choices were "weak."

Where the staff had excelled was in the State Dining Room. The staff had brought in Lego models of the White House, the Lincoln Memorial, and the Capitol, as well as important Danish buildings such as the Amalienborg and Christiansburg Palaces and the Tivoli Gardens.

As the Marine White House band played "Hail to the Chief," the president and the Danish prime minister descended the ceremonial staircase and entered the State Dining Room.

But it was Kennedy Russell who drew the most attention. This was her first public appearance since the release of the photos.

Entering the ballroom behind the president and the prime minister, the first lady dazzled in a strapless silver figure-hugging Versace dress. Kennedy had decided she wasn't going to demure or hide from the public. If anything, she was going to use the release of the photos to augment her standing as a spokesperson for women's rights.

The applause grew as Kennedy stood alone in the center of the ballroom, with the president and prime minister joining in as well.

Fate can be a funny thing. It never would have occurred to Kennedy Russell that the release of these photos would help her to embark on a lifelong mission. This was highlighted by a temporary tattoo she wore on her right arm in the shape of a *G* with a plus sign, the symbol of the Girls' Globe organization, which fought against revenge porn and other abuses against women.

As nights went, this was a great success and did, in fact, elevate Denmark's standing in the diplomatic world. But the star of the evening, and many more to follow, was Kennedy Russell.

Later, back in the residence, Andrew Russell asked his wife how she enjoyed the evening.

"I thought it went well. We haven't had a state dinner in months," said the first lady, expressing both her pleasure and her relief.

The president then said, "Alexa, play 'Wonderful Tonight.'" Turning to the first lady he asked, "Can I have this dance?"

Kennedy Russell smiled and said, "Sure, why not, fly-boy."

CHAPTER TWENTY-TWO

The UN

The next morning the president was preparing for the following week's address to the UN General Assembly. Taking a break, the president placed a call to the CNO, Admiral Brian Jacobsen.

"What do you think about sending a carrier group into the Baltic with planned port calls for Finland, Latvia, and Estonia?" asked the president.

The CNO did not immediately respond and just listened.

"Who do we have deployed in the Atlantic now?" asked the president.

Checking his ships-at-sea screen, Admiral Jacobsen replied, "Sir, we have Carrier Strike Group (CSG) 12, USS *Gerald R. Ford* (CVN 78) along with Carrier Air Wing (CVW) 8, with Destroyer Squadron (DESRON) 2. It's Rear Admiral Craig Clapperton's group."

The president was aware the USS *Gerald R. Ford* was the newest carrier in the fleet.

"Brian, start working out the details for what it would take to send them to the Baltic, but hold short of issuing the order," instructed the president.

"Understood, Mr. President. We'll start working on a plan and report back to you, sir," said the CNO.

Hanging up, the president reflected that when growing up in Brooklyn, he learned the old adage, "If you take a punch, you throw a punch." The president needed to respond to Russia's recent aggressive actions beyond just cyber- or biological actions. Knowing the Russian president, to do less would be to invite more aggression on his part. Russell wasn't going to start a war, but he was going to throw a punch.

■

Next the president placed a call to his alma mater in Brooklyn— Xaverian High School.

Sitting in his office, which overlooked New York Harbor, was Robert Alesi, president of Xaverian.

"Please hold for the president," said the White House operator.

"Bob, how are you?" asked the forty-sixth president of the United States.

"Very well, Mr. President," was all Alesi could get out.

"Bob, I have a treat for you and the students of Xaverian," said the president.

A few minutes later Bob Alesi hung up the phone trying to absorb what he had just heard.

■

It was now Tuesday morning as the president and his team boarded Air Force One for the flight to New York City, where he would be addressing the UN General Assembly. The president invited Prime Minister Henriksen, who would also be attending the UN session, to fly on board Air Force One as a courtesy.

As scheduled, Air Force One took off at 7:45 a.m. on the dot for the one-hour flight to New York City.

The White House Communications team, who had been briefed on the president's flight and sworn to secrecy, had film and photo teams set up at various locations around New York City in preparation for the president's arrival.

When Air Force One entered New York airspace, it descended as it approached the Verrazano Bridge. Now flying at an altitude of one thousand feet, which was about seven hundred feet above the roadway, the massive 747 steadied on a course over the president's hometown of Bay Ridge, Brooklyn.

Heading north, Air Force One executed a flyby of the Statue of Liberty, where the three escorting Super Hornets separated from the president's jet.

Heading back to the harbor, the president ordered Air Force One down to two hundred feet and slightly increased its speed to three hundred knots. As Air Force One approached Brooklyn, the president could see out of the left side of the plane the Sixty-Ninth Street Pier, which was something of a landmark in the Bay Ridge neighborhood where the president grew up.

As Air Force One drew closer, the president could see the entire student body of Xaverian High School standing on the pier. At the president's order, the full-bird colonel flying Air Force One slightly moved his control yoke right to left, causing his wings to rock as he flew by the cheering Xaverian students.

With the aerobatics out of the way, Air Force One pulled up hard and entered the Newark Airport pattern, where they would be landing.

Some would say it was nothing more than a stunt, but for the students at Xaverian or for the millions of New Yorkers who witnessed the president's arrival on Air Force One, it was a once-in-a-life-time event.

After landing at EWR, the president and his party were taken via a high-speed motorcade into Manhattan and to the UN.

Before the president addressed the General Assembly, he met with James King, the prime minister of the UK, as well as with the president of France and the chancellor of Germany. All expressed their disgust over the release of the photographs of the first lady and offered the cooperation of their intelligence agencies to defeat the spread of them.

The president thanked the close allies and made his way to the General Assembly Hall for his anticipated address.

Addressing the General Assembly, the president said:

> Today, I come to this assembly to present a plan for the future. We are announcing two major new trade pacts that will benefit every country whose leaders are in attendance today.
>
> The first pact we are announcing today is the Northwest Passage Free Transit Treaty. Working together with our partners in Canada, the United States will open the Northwest Passage to commerce, providing substantial savings in the movement of goods and materials around the world. Not since the opening of the Panama Canal has there been such a breakthrough in global transit.
>
> As important as the opening of the Northwest Passage is, it is also equally important that we allow that the transit of this body of water be free. This will not only help promote global trade but will accelerate our goal to becoming a cleaner planet. The Northwest Passage will cut an estimated 30 percent of the fuel needed to move products between Asia and Europe. By

significantly cutting our use of fossil fuels, we all will derive the dividend of cleaner air and water.

The other trade agreement we are announcing today is the US/Denmark Treaty that will open Greenland to controlled and careful harvesting of rare-earth minerals. This is critical to ensure the world will have adequate access to the resources we need to save our planet.

As each of your nations rush to migrate to EV vehicles and adopt new technologies, we run the real risk of incurring major shortages of critical resources such as lithium, cobalt, and other elements with exotic names such as neodymium and dysprosium. All of these are essential not only for the batteries that power EV vehicles but also to the motors they employ. In addition, rare-earth minerals are essential for the production of everything from smartphones to solar panels to the sensors that manage our everyday lives such as automatic teller machines, retail store scanners, and a wide variety of medical devices.

Unleashing the resources of Greenland will provide the world's economies with a stable and adequate supply of these critical minerals. We are grateful for the participation and assistance we have received from Denmark in making this historic trade agreement a reality.

However, these steps, with their accompanying advances, are still not enough.

This very day more than 9 percent of the world's people live in poverty. Almost 700 million people around the globe today will suffer from hunger.

And while we have countries in this forum who have infant mortality rates of less than 2 percent, which is certainly enviable, we also have countries in this room who experience infant mortality rates in excess of 14 percent. Why is that? Why do we allow that to persist?

How can we tolerate such blight, pain, and suffering?

The answer is: We cannot and should not.

In addition to the two new trade pacts, the United States is introducing a policy to the General Assembly whereby every member nation agrees to gradually reduce its military spending.

The United States proposes that going forward military spending be cut at a rate of 1 percent per annum. And we continue to cut that rate, every year, for the next thirty years. Think of what could be accomplished if every country in this assembly reduced its military spend by 30 percent over the next generation.

Imagine how your own countries could redeploy those budget dollars. And the amount of good that the reallocation of dollars would do.

As many of you know, I am a strong advocate of the US Navy. Having been a naval officer and fighter pilot, I know firsthand the importance our military represents. And that our capabilities are second to none,

That said, we can be a better and smarter nation. We can be a better and smarter world. So, today I ask you to join the United States in making the pledge to cut your military spending going forward by the very manageable amount of only 1 percent per year.

By setting out on this goal, every nation in this body can repurpose those dollars to fight poverty, eliminate hunger, advance medical care, and speed up your transition to clean fuels.

This is what the charter of this assembly was envisioned to do—to reduce the risks of war and to help those in need.

In closing, I call upon you to stand with the United States and implement these advances.

Together, we can do what is hard. Together, we can achieve what is great. And together, we can build a safer and cleaner planet divorced from hunger and disease.

And together, we can do what is right.

Thank you, and may God bless you. May God bless the United States and may God bless all the people of the world.

It was one of those rare moments. At first, there was just silence as everyone in attendance took in what had just happened. It was history in the making.

Then it started. At first, there were just a few, but it then swelled and grew into a cacophony of applause and cheers that filled and spilled out of the UN's General Assembly Hall.

Lisa Collins applauded, too, as she now saw the full measure of the man who was Andrew Russell.

"Well done, Mr. President," said his chief of staff, joining the president as he made his way to a special meeting of the US's close allies to gauge their reaction to his speech.

"Thank you, Sterl. But the real test now is to see how China reacts to the proposed reduction in military spending," remarked the president.

"Exactly, sir. I do believe your speech will put pressure on them to respond."

"If we can get China to agree to reduce their military spending, then we will have achieved a great win not only for the US but for the world," added the president. "And if China doesn't agree, we can use that to justify our own military expansion. Either way we win."

VP Collins joined the president and Spencer.

"Sir, I'm getting questions from the press regarding the numbers."

Sterling Spencer had anticipated that, and with his figures ready, he went to address the press.

Lisa Collins then excused herself to depart for her afternoon meeting downtown at the New York Foundling at Sixteenth Street and Sixth Avenue. The Foundling, a New York institution and treasure, was founded on October 11, 1869, when Sister Mary Irene Fitzgibbon and two other Sisters of Charity placed a cradle on the doorstep of their brownstone on East Twelfth Street. When they awoke the next morning, they welcomed their first orphaned baby—a girl named Sarah.

Fast-forward to today, the sisters' ministry had evolved from a home for abandoned children to now providing a comprehensive array of child welfare services to the children and families of New York.

It was at the New York Foundling's headquarters offices where Lisa Collins met Sister Doris Smith, the Foundling's president and CEO.

Lisa Collins, herself a product of Catholic education and a graduate of Georgetown University, said, "Sister Doris, I am overwhelmed by the work you and the sisters are doing here."

Sister Doris responded, "Madam Vice President, I assure you the credit belongs to our wonderful staff and to our generous benefactors."

Lisa Collins just nodded, knowing full well just how much of the credit belonged to this capable and holy woman.

"Madam Vice President, after we concluded our tour, I've arranged for us to have lunch in my office," said Sister Doris.

"That would be lovely," replied the vice president.

With that, they embarked on a tour of the facility and then to Sister Doris's office.

Upon entering, Lisa Collins recognized the woman sitting in one of the chairs across from Sister Doris's desk. It was Svetlana Ivanovna Zlovna.

Sister Doris said, "Just let my secretary know when you are done." She then nodded to both women and exited her office.

Vice President Collins held out her hand to the SVR director. "Madam Director, it is a pleasure to finally meet you."

"Likewise, Madam Vice President," said Zlovna, accepting Collins's handshake.

VP Collins took a seat and said, "Director Zlovna, what did you think of the president's speech?"

"Before I answer I'd first like to comment on his entrance in Air Force One. Does President Russell suffer from a self-esteem issue?" asked Zlovna.

Smiling, Collins responded, "Madam Director, I can assure you President Russell does not suffer from any shortage of self-esteem."

"Then why all the aerobatics?" asked Svetlana Ivanovna Zlovna.

"I suppose I could ask the same of you. How many photos do we have to endure of your president shirtless, hunting, or playing hockey? Why don't we both agree to leave the personalities of our superiors as a discussion for another time?" replied Collins.

"As you say," said Zlovna, nodding. "I think the president's speech was clearly meant for China, not the Russian Federation. I think the Chinese will see it for what it was, as an attempt to rally world support to reduce military spending. I think it was a political speech and will not result in any significant reductions in military budgets," said Zlovna.

"Perhaps, but in order to implement change, it takes someone with vision, and President Russell has vision," Collins responded.

Now getting to the matter of importance, Collins questioned, "The photos of the first lady. Did you really think your obtaining them would cool the tensions between our two countries?"

The SVR director replied, "We never were going to release them. Your issue is with Salman Rahman and Saudi Arabia, not with the Russian Federation."

"So, you were never going to release them?" asked Collins.

"Madam Vice President, like you, I would rarely ever say 'never,' but no, that was not our intent."

Pivoting, Collins said, "Director, the sonic attack on our embassy, procuring of these photos, the attack on the Maersk container ship—can you explain what you hoped to gain from these actions other than provoking us?"

"One could ask what the US hoped to gain from installing a sonar network in the Arctic," suggested Zlovna.

"As we just announced, we intend to open the Northwest Passage to free transit and that requires a certain amount of security and defense systems. That is why we are installing the sonar network. But I have a question for you. Can you make the same commitment? Should Russia open the Northern Sea Route, will its passage also be free?" asked Collins.

"Those discussions are currently underway at the highest levels of our government, but I can assure you opening the Northern Sea Route is a strategic imperative for Russia and we will defend those waters as our territorial waters," replied Zlovna.

"No one will dispute that the waters of the Northern Sea Route are your territorial waters. That said, our analysis indicates that the ice there is thicker and opening the Northern Sea Route will be much more difficult and costly than opening the Northwest Passage," replied Collins.

"Perhaps, but we have invested heavily not only in a fleet of state-of-the-art icebreakers but also in ice management systems. Can you claim the same?" asked Zlovna.

"My message, in closing, is that it would be helpful for both countries to turn down the temperature," said Collins.

"Madam Vice President, that, too, was my main reason for agreeing to meet with you. It may surprise you to hear this, but I, too, wish to de-escalate the tensions between our two countries," replied Zlovna.

Collins didn't know if she could trust Zlovna, but she listened intently to what the other woman had to say.

The meeting continued for another few minutes before adjourning, with Svetlana Ivanovna Zlovna departing via the rear entrance while Vice President Collins, accompanied by Sister Doris, emerged onto Sixth Avenue into the awaiting gaggle of reporters.

■

The next morning in the Oval Office, Vice President Collins debriefed the president and Sterling Spencer on her meeting with Zlovna.

"I found the SVR director to be very forthcoming regarding their recent actions, sir."

"Well, I'm glad she was forthcoming, Lisa. Where do we go from here?" asked the president.

"Sir, Zlovna believes their president is trying to goad you into a crisis that will shore up his popularity at home," stated Collins.

"Goading? Lisa, just to be clear, America sustained casualties as a result of their actions," replied the president.

"Sir," said Spencer, "if Zlovna can be trusted and her message is valid, sending a Carrier Group into the Baltic would be just the sort of response they would hope from us. Any visible act of aggression will play into their hands."

Thinking it over, the president said, "We'll keep CARGRU-12 out of the Baltic, but we're going forward with the Tribble Project against the Russian icebreakers."

"On another matter, Mr. President, Zlovna expressed concerns about Salman Rahman. Do you have orders regarding Rahman?" asked Collins.

"He should have been dealt with long ago," replied the president.

"Sir, why don't you let me handle this? I think my CIA background equips me well to deal with him," Collins responded.

The president looked at Spencer, who nodded. They both knew Collins had begun to form a relationship with Saudi Prince Saud, so it made sense.

"Okay, Lisa, it's yours, but if the Saudis offer to deal with Rahman, don't take them at their word. Tell them we'll need proof," declared the president.

"Understood, sir."

With the debriefing now completed, Vice President Collins added, "Mr. President, have you ever met Sister Doris Smith of the New York Foundling?"

"I did when I was a congressman in Brooklyn. We worked together to open a foster care facility in downtown Brooklyn," recalled the president.

"Having met her, it occurred to me that she would be an exemplary and worthy candidate for consideration for a future Presidential Medal of Freedom," suggested Collins.

The president thought about it and then responded, "I can see that. Have the medal panel look into it. Knowing Sister Doris, she'd be mortified to receive such an honor. Just one of the many reasons why she probably deserves it."

With that item covered, Collins left to arrange another call with Prince Saud.

CHAPTER TWENTY-THREE

Happy Trails to You

S alman Rahman walked into the sitting room of an ancient house in the port city of Jizan on the Red Sea. He had holed up there since releasing the photos of Kennedy Russell. He was practicing the best safety measures he could knowing that he was being hunted by the Americans, the Russians, and his own Saudi Secret Police.

He nodded to the woman of the house, who brought him a tray of sweet tea.

As he poured the tea into the glass cup with its ornamental silver handle, he heard a voice say,

"How is your tea?"

A look of panic came over Salman's face as he considered his escape options. Salman's eyes darted from left to right. He knew he had a semiautomatic pistol in the table drawer. But he knew he could never get there in time.

"I will let you pray the Asr," said the Saudi agent, referring to the Muslim afternoon prayers, which took place at 4:45 p.m. Jizan time.

Salman nodded, placed the prayer rug on the floor, and knelt.

In the distance he could hear the call to prayers broadcast over loudspeakers throughout Jizan.

A few minutes later, with the prayers completed, Salman said, "I can offer you money."

The Saudi agent replied, "How much?"

Salman, pleased by his response, said, "I have cash here. I can offer you one hundred thousand euros to leave."

"I need to see the money," replied the agent.

Salman thought about his next move. He could try for the hall table where his pistol was, or he could get the cash. He chose the latter.

"It's in the bedroom," said Salman.

"Get it," said the agent, holding up his Beretta M9A3 equipped with a suppressor.

Salman came back into the room with the euros and placed the stack of currency on the table.

The Saudi agent nodded and said, "The son of a sheik and your life is only worth one hundred thousand euros?"

This was the opening Salman was looking for. "I have more."

"Then, get it," ordered the agent.

Salman turned his back on the Saudi agent and went to the hall table. Opening the drawer, he reached for his Glock 17.

But he never got the chance to pick it up. The Saudi agent placed three rounds in a tight circle in Salman's back.

The assassin then walked over, reached down, and pulled the gold chain off Salman's neck. Leaving him to die in a pool of his own blood, he stuffed the cash in his jacket pockets along with the Glock and exited into the busy streets of Jizan.

Once outside, he pulled out a satellite phone, which was the only type working now that the Americans had disrupted the local cellular networks.

When his call connected, he said, "It's done."

"Very well," came the response. "Now go to the airstrip and board the jet. Call me once you arrive at your destination."

The Saudi agent got on his moped for the short trip to the local airstrip. With commercial flights canceled due the American cyber-attack, the agent boarded a private Gulfstream for his flight to Rome. Once in Rome, he would board a commercial flight to America.

∎

The Russians had a fleet of five of the Project 22220 icebreakers of the *Arktika* class.

Two of the massive icebreakers were in the yards in St. Petersburg for maintenance—the *Yamal* and *Ural.* That left the *Arktika, Sibir,* and *50 Let Pobedy* (*50 Years of Victory*) homeported out of Murmansk, but now all at sea as targets of Operation Shattered Ice.

Admiral Jacobsen briefed the president along with the Sit Room occupants. "Sir, Operation Shattered Ice will be carried out by the *Illinois, Colorado,* and *Vermont* Virginia-class attack submarines. They've been fitted out with the General Dynamics Bluefin-21 unmanned underwater vehicles," also known as UUVs. "The Bluefins will be launched from our submarines, where they will cruise under the hulls of the Russian icebreakers and deploy the biologic material, what the DARPA calls "goop," into their intakes. Within three weeks the goop will incapacitate the engines of the ships."

"What are the risks?" asked the president.

"Deployment requires a series of tight and exact maneuvers. The Bluefins only have a top speed of four and a half knots, so we need to deploy them when the Russian icebreakers are in the ice, going slow.

In the open sea, they travel too fast for the Bluefins to catch them," the CNO said.

"And where are the three icebreakers presently?" asked the president.

Bringing up a real-time chart on one of the large Sit Room screens, the admiral used his laser pointer to highlight the positions of the three targets,

"Sir, the *Sibir* is in the ice in the Barents Sea, the *50 Let Pobedy* is also north of Russia in the Kara Sea, and our old friend the *Arktika* is still in the Northwest Passage, approximately two hundred miles north-northwest of Baffin Bay."

Lisa Collins wanted to show that she had been studying up on submarine technology and asked, "Admiral, you're sending two Block III Virginias and a Block IV boat—while they are all exceedingly quiet, what are the acoustic signatures of these Bluefins?"

The question caused the president to smile and look at his chief of staff.

"Excellent question, ma'am. In general, the icebreakers put out so much noise that we don't think it will be an issue. But to answer your question, the Bluefins do not have the acoustic stealthiness of our submarines. They are operated by electric motors that are relatively quiet, but nowhere near the level of, as you say, our Flight III boats."

"If there was an Akula or Yasen in the area, would they detect the Bluefins?"

Now the president was impressed. It had only been two weeks since Lisa Collins was confirmed as VP, and she was showing her well-earned reputation for being prepared for meetings.

"Possibly, but intelligence indicates that four Akulas are tasked with defending the Nord Stream pipeline, as they think that is our likely target. So, their submarine force is stretched thin," answered Jacobsen.

"Admiral, I think we should schedule Vice President Collins for a tiger cruise on one of our attack boats," kidded the president.

But the subject was a serious one and he added, "The goal here is to inflict damage to the Russian icebreaker fleet without them being able to tie it back to us. So, if there is any risk of detection, make sure our sub commanders know they are to scrub the mission."

"Aye, aye, sir. That will be in the operational order," replied the CNO.

"What is the timeline?" asked the president.

"Sir, the subs are currently at sea. They are drilling on the mission right now. The plan calls for simultaneous attacks on the three Russian icebreakers. We estimate our boats can be on station in the next day or two."

"Admiral, you have a go on Operation Shattered Ice," said the president.

CHAPTER TWENTY-FOUR

You Don't Tug on Superman's Cape

On board the *Colorado*, Submersible Specialist First Class Tony Gonzalez was running diagnostic checks on the Bluefin-21 UUVs.

Captain Matt Pryor checked with his navigator, asking, "Time to intercept target?"

The *Colorado*'s assignment was to attack the *Arktika* as she sheared through the ice far above Canada in the Northwest Passage.

"Sir, on current course and speed we'll intercept Sierra One in five hours and seven minutes.

Pryor left the bridge to join his other officers in the wardroom, where Specialist Gonzalez briefed them all on the mission's steps. "Sir, once we're on a matched course and a couple of boat lengths ahead of Sierra One, we'll deploy the UUVs from torpedo tubes one and four. Once launched, the Bluefins will slowly close the range with Sierra One until they are tracking on either side of Sierra One's hull. Once in position we will discharge the goop. Then we will give the order for the Bluefins to dive into the depths. Captain, once we launch the Bluefins, we should clear the area to ensure we do not ingest any of the goop," Gonzalez said.

"How long do we expect the entire operation to take?" asked Pryor.

"Sir, it should only take ten minutes assuming Sierra One doesn't alter his course," said Gonzalez.

Pryor asked, "What speed and course is Sierra One traveling?"

The XO, who was given the task of tracking Sierra One along with the sonar crew, responded, "Sir, she is traveling at three knots and has been on a heading of 283 degrees for the last three hours."

"And what are the currents?" asked Pryor.

"Sir, we're detecting a current of one to one and a half knots."

"Can the Bluefins deal with that?" asked the captain.

"Sir, the Bluefins have a top speed of only four and half knots. It would be helpful if Sierra One was going a little slower, but I've drilled on the maneuver. I'll get them there, sir," replied the petty officer first class.

Pryor nodded, adding, "Stealth is our order, gentlemen. We need to keep our ears peeled for any Russian subs. We scrub the mission if we detect a Russian boat in the vicinity. Is that clear?"

With that the XO added, "Sir, the scope is clear. No contacts other than Sierra One in the area."

"Very well. Keep your sailors on their toes," ended Pryor. As he exited the wardroom, the captain patted the state flag of Colorado, which hung on the wall near the exit. In turn, each officer patted the flag of the Centennial State as they exited, which had become a tradition on the attack submarine.

■

The Saudi agent landed at Dulles on a rainy April evening and made his way through customs.

In Georgetown, Lauren La Rue went to her garage to start her BMW M8 Coupe, which was not exactly the typical ride for a CIA employee, but La Rue had amassed a fortune while working in Dubai and could afford it.

"Chris, my car won't start," said La Rue, calling him on his cell. They had a date planned for the evening.

"That's what you get for buying a foreign car. I can swing by and pick you up. That is, if you don't mind riding in a Ford Bronco?"

After Chris had picked La Rue up at her tony P Street town house, they only had a short drive until they reached Cafe Milano on Prospect Street.

"So it seems, once again, you came to my rescue, Agent Dunbar. Just like when we were in Dubrovnik and then in Copenhagen," said La Rue.

"It does seem to be a habit that I can't seem to avoid," retorted Dunbar.

Being careful not to discuss too much "business" in a public restaurant, Dunbar said, "Perhaps our next adventure will be in Greenland. I'd like to visit there."

"I'd like to visit the Faroe Islands too. They seem so undiscovered and undeveloped," said La Rue.

"I've never been there. I've been to McMurdo, though, at the South Pole," added Dunbar.

"Really, what was that like—other than cold?"

"Well, it was cold, but it's a very tight-knit community. The C-130s are our main lifelines. Whenever they flew in, we would get 'greenies,'" said Dunbar.

"Greenies? What are those?" asked La Rue.

"Fresh fruit and vegetables. It was always a treat to get a good salad at McMurdo. So much of what we ate was out of a can," replied Dunbar.

"Salad? Really? I see you more as a burger-and-fries guy," said La Rue.

"I do like my burgers, but only on occasion. How else do you think I keep this physique in shape?" teased Dunbar.

"Just remember, I beat you swimming in Dubrovnik, and I bet I can beat you on a Peloton too," returned La Rue.

"You think so?"

"I know so," said La Rue. "You may be able to outlift me, but I bet all that muscle slows you down on a bike."

"Well, we'll have to arrange a time at the gym and see who's faster," said Dunbar.

"Other than greenies, what else do you remember from the South Pole?" asked La Rue.

"The drinking," said Dunbar. "Especially during the dark season. It was and is a real problem."

"Really, I didn't know that," La Rue replied.

Just then a man approached their table. "Miss La Rue?" asked the stranger with Middle Eastern features.

La Rue responded with a simple, "Yes?"

Chris Dunbar immediately placed his hand on his 9mm, which he always carried, whether on duty or not.

"I have gift for you from Prince Saud," said the agent as he placed a gold chain with a gold pendant featuring the House of Saud symbol of two crossed swords under a palm tree on her plate.

La Rue looked down at the gold chain and immediately recognized it. It was the chain that Sheik Abdul Er Rahman, her old boss, gave to each of his children on their eighteenth birthday.

With that, the Saudi agent nodded to La Rue and Dunbar and exited the restaurant.

"What does it mean?" asked Dunbar.

La Rue said, "It can mean only one thing. That Salman Rahman is no longer alive."

Chris Dunbar processed the information. "He said it was from Prince Saud, didn't he?"

La Rue nodded.

The message was clear that Prince Saud had taken out Salman Rahman.

"Chris, I need to report this right away," said La Rue.

Even though they hadn't ordered yet, Dunbar left a sizeable tip for the waitress and then quickly drove La Rue back to her town house.

In a matter of minutes La Rue was connected to Vice President Collins.

"And you're certain that's what it means?" inquired Collins.

"One hundred percent ma'am," responded La Rue.

Riyadh was seven hours ahead of Washington, but Collins needed to confirm La Rue's information.

It was four in the morning when Prince Saud's aides informed him that the American vice president was on the phone.

"Thank you for taking my call, Prince Saud," Collins said.

The prince, who had been expecting the call, responded, "You received my message, then."

"Yes, I did."

"I took this action, as difficult as it was, to strengthen our relationship, Madam Vice President."

"I understand," replied Collins. "My next call will be to the president to share this news with him."

"And I hope this news will motivate your president to put a stop to the cyberattacks against my country," added the prince.

"Give me a few minutes and I will call you back," said Collins. It only took a few minutes before she called him again.

"Prince Saud, within the hour you will see a restoration of your Internet and e-commerce, and all disruptions regarding your air traffic control systems will cease," said Collins.

The prince replied, "I will pass that information on to the king. I hope this begins a new era of trust between our two countries."

"I believe it is a very good start," said Collins, "Good evening, Your Highness."

■

Captain Mike Lanam and his crew on the *Vermont* drew the most difficult assignment, targeting the *50 Let Pobedy*, which was cutting through the ice in the far northern reaches of the Kara Sea, approximately three hundred miles east-northeast of Severny Island.

Because submarines spend most of their time submerged, they cannot rely on the typical celestial navigation systems that surface ships use. This requires submarines to leverage inertial navigation systems that can estimate to a high degree of accuracy the position of a submarine.

Voyage management systems utilize digital charts as well as data provided from an array of sensors on the submarines, including bottom contour mapping systems and fathometers to measure depth above and below the submarines.

In addition, navigation systems process pitch, roll, and ocean current data to precisely pinpoint the exact location of the submerged submarine.

Lanam's navigator was feverishly checking and double-checking the readings from an array of sensors to maneuver the *Vermont* toward the *50 Let Pobedy*.

"Icicle dead ahead," called out the navigation petty officer.

"Come right to 096 degrees, make your depth 317 feet smartly, ahead one-third," called the navigator.

The officer of the watch (OOW) and chief of the boat (COB) repeated the orders.

Captain Lanam supervised all activities in the control room of the Navy's newest and most advanced Virginia-class attack submarine.

"Sir, we need to go around that icicle. Tracking Sierra Four bearing 011 degrees at twenty-two miles."

"Time to intercept Sierra Four?" asked Lanam.

"Sir, at current course and speed we will intercept Sierra Four at 04:23 Zulu. In one hour and seven minutes," called the navigator.

"Con, Sonar. Broadband contact bearing 188 degrees," called the sonar operator.

At the sonar station the senior enlisted sonar operator looked at the waterfall image on his BQQ-10 bow-mounted spherical sonar array.

"I'm starting a tape on Sierra Five," called the sonar operator.

Captain Lanam scanned the screens of his AN/BYG-1 system, which integrated the data feeds from his tactical control system (TCS) and weapons control system (WCS). These systems gave Lanam the most advanced and precise view of the ocean surrounding his submarine.

"Con, Sonar. The BBQ-10 is identifying Sierra Five as Typhoon-1. It's a Russian boomer," called the operator, correctly classifying the contact as a Russian ballistic submarine. And not only that, but it was also the first Typhoon of the class, the TK-208, the *Dmitriy Donskoy*.

The *Donskoy* was propelled by two seven-blade screws. As much as every shipyard looked to produce perfectly balanced propellers, they never could get them perfectly balanced. Sure, they could get the blades within one-one-hundredth of an inch tolerance, but when it came to one-one-thousandth, every blade produced a unique signature, especially when rotated at high rpms. The US Navy's ultrasensitive sonar detects, classifies, and records each submarine's unique acoustic signature, enabling them to identify and track them.

The Typhoon class were Russia's premier ballistic missile submarines. Massive in size, they measured 175 meters (574 feet) in length with a gross tonnage of forty-eight thousand tons, making them the approximate size of a World War II battleship.

"Con, Sonar. Sierra Five is bearing 005, range twenty-eight miles, depth seven hundred feet, speed ten knots," relayed the sonar operator to the control room.

"Rig for ultraquiet. Deploy the thin-line," ordered Lanam.

The thin-line referred to the TB-33 fiber-optic thin-line towed array, which would be deployed from the side of the *Vermont* and streamed behind the submarine to provide enhanced sonar detection.

"Aye, aye, rigging for ultraquiet. Streaming Tabby-33," called the OOW and COB.

The tactical situation for Lanam had his target, the *50 Let Pobedy*, twenty miles to his north and now a Russian boomer twenty-eight miles to his south and headed his way. Given its speed, it would join up on the *50 Let Pobedy* in six hours.

Lanam turned to his XO and said, "What do you think?"

"A loose deuce?" replied Lanam's second-in-command. The XO was referring to a well-known Russian tactic where one of their ballistic submarines would sail under a surface ship to help disguise it. The loud Russian icebreaker would provide a cacophony of sound to mask the Typhoon.

"That's what I was thinking too. I'm going to inform SUBLANT," replied Lanam.

■

Entering the Sit Room, the president and Sterling Spencer took up their seats.

"What do we have?" asked the president.

The CNO replied, "We wanted to give you a status update on Operation Shattered Ice. The *Illinois* and *Colorado* will be deploying on schedule. The *Vermont* has encountered a complication that we want to make you aware of, sir."

The commander of submarine forces (COMSUBFOR), a three-star vice admiral, said, "Sir, the third Russian icebreaker, the *50 Let Pobedy*, is in the Kara Sea just north of Russia." A staff commander brought up a plot on the Sit Room screen.

COMSUBFOR continued, "The *Vermont* has also detected a Russian Typhoon ballistic boat in the area. We believe it will join up with the icebreaker in a standard Russian maneuver that we call a 'loose deuce.'"

"What exactly is a 'loose deuce'?" asked POTUS.

"Sir, the Russian boomer sails under the surface ship with the expectation that the sound from the surface ship will help hide the sub. It is a common tactic for the Russians. Especially with their icebreakers, since they throw off so much sound. The captain of the *Vermont* believes not only can he still carry out his mission, but he thinks he could also contaminate the Typhoon with the biological material."

"What do we know about the skipper?" asked the president.

COMSUBFOR nodded to the commander, who brought up the *Vermont*'s captain's jacket. "Sir, he's academy grad, class of 2004. His fitness reports are 4.0s across the board. He's been CO of the *Vermont* for two years, so he knows his crew well. The *Vermont*, as you know, is the newest of the Virginia-class attack boats, so it's capable of the mission. I have complete trust in Commander Lanam," finished the vice admiral.

"Take me through their proposal," said the president.

"If Lanam is correct and it is a 'loose deuce,' the Russian boomer will form up right under the icebreaker. The *Vermont* would travel just ahead of both and deploy the Bluefins. Once in position, the Bluefins would discharge the material and the cloud would get sucked into both the icebreaker's and the Typhoon's intakes. The *Vermont* would then clear the area as per the original plan."

"This proposal has two subs and an icebreaker within a ship length or two of each other. Seems like pretty close quarters, Admiral," commented the president.

"If I may, sir. I suggest we issue updated orders to the *Vermont* where we underscore the importance of stealth and allow 'captain's prerogative,'" said the commander of all the US Navy's submarines.

"And you're sure this captain isn't a cowboy?" asked President Russell.

Lisa Collins, who was also in the meeting, thought to herself, *That's exactly the same term Svetlana Zlovna used to describe the president.*

"Absolutely, sir. Captain Lanam is no cowboy. If he feels he can perform the maneuver, then I recommend we empower him to make the call. We trust the captain."

The president thought about it for a minute before he said, "Agreed, Admiral. We aren't going to micromanage ops from here. As you do, I, too, trust our commanders in the field. Issue the order, Admiral," said the president, standing up in order to get to his next meeting.

∎

The radioman on the *Vermont* handed Lanam his new orders. As he read them, Lanam knew this would be a make-or-break moment for him and his career.

"Con, Sonar. We're right under Sierra Four. We're tracking his bearing of 050 and matching his three knots. Typhoon-1 is dead astern, range three hundred yards, speed four knots. Sir, she's forming up on Sierra Four," called the sonar operator.

"Sonar, Con. I want continual readings on Typhoon-1's course and speed," ordered Lanam. "OOW, increase speed to four and a half knots, smartly bring us ahead of Sierra Four, maintain depth of one hundred feet, and prepare to launch the UUVs."

The submersible specialist was stationed in the *Vermont*'s Torpedo Room sitting in front of his control consoles.

"Captain, recommend flooding torpedo tubes one and four and opening outer doors," advised the UUV specialist.

Lanam wanted to double-check the location of his target before flooding his torpedo tubes, which produced a slight acoustic signature.

"Con, Sonar. Typhoon-1 range is 325 yards and widening, sir," called the sonar operator.

Lanam called, "Sonar, Con. What is the plot of Sierra Four?"

"Con, Sonar. Sierra Four is 150 yards dead astern of us, bearing 050 degrees, steady at three knots. Typhoon-1 is closing 250 yards now."

"OOW, increase speed to 4.75 knots smartly, maintain course and depth," ordered Lanam, whose blue jumpsuit now showed signs of perspiration under his arms, as it did on most of the control room crew.

"Weps, Con. Flood tubes one and four. But do not open doors," ordered Captain Lanam.

"Con, Weps. Aye, aye. Flooding tubes one and four," came back the precise repetition of the captain's command, which was the protocol on all US Navy submarines.

Lanam knew that if for any reason the Typhoon decided to do a sprint forward, they would run right into the stern of the *Vermont*. Lanam wanted to vacate this position ASAP, but first he needed to launch the Bluefins.

Lanam called to the torpedo room, "Specialist Williams, once we launch the Bluefins I am going to sharply clear baffles and dive away. Copy?"

"Con, Torpedo Room. Copy, Captain. Recommend maintain current speed so as to not create any wash for the Bluefins," replied UUV Specialist Williams.

"Con, Sonar. Sierra Four's dead astern at 220 yards. Typhoon-1 is 275 yards in trail."

"OWW, dead stop now," ordered Lanam.

"Dead stop, aye, aye," came back the response from the control room team, who were expecting the order but nevertheless were hanging on every command, knowing the tight quarters they were in.

This maneuver only provided a thirty-second margin of error.

The XO was calling out the seconds.

Lanam didn't delay. "Torpedo Room, Con. Open doors one and four and launch the packages."

"Con, Torpedo Room. Opening doors one and four. Launching packages," came the response.

Launching the Bluefins wasn't like launching Mk 48 torpedoes, which were the Navy's front-line torpedoes and launched under high pressure and at high speed.

The sixteen-foot Bluefin-21s exited the torpedo tubes slowly under their own electric motor power, accelerating to their meager top speed of only four and half knots.

The diameter of the unmanned underwater vehicles, twenty-one inches, was the exact same diameter as the Navy's Mk 48 torpedoes, but the UUVs were three feet shorter. As a result, Specialist Williams had no problem launching the Bluefins from the *Vermont*'s bow torpedo tubes.

"Con, Weps. Packages away," called Williams.

The XO continued his count, which now had reached fifteen.

"Shift your rudder hard to port, ahead one-third, ten-degree down bubble, make your depth four hundred feet, EXECUTE," yelled Lanam, which told his crew to just perform the order and not repeat it.

The pilot, with the COB standing behind him with his hand on his shoulder, quickly turned his control yoke full to port until it hit the stops, and then he pushed it forward to steer the submarine to the ordered depth of four hundred feet. Seeing the rudder hard over, the helmsman turned the dial on his speed indicator to ahead one-third.

The XO count was now up to twenty-two seconds.

"Con, Sonar. Sierra Four is one hundred yards bearing 050. Typhoon-1 is 127 yards same bearing."

The 377-foot, seventy-eight-hundred-ton Navy attack submarine turned hard left and dove from its current depth of one hundred feet to its ordered depth of four hundred feet.

OOW called, "Thirty seconds."

"Con, Sonar. Sierra Four is bearing 050 at 192 yards and opening, as is Typhoon-1."

Specialist Williams in the Torpedo Room now guided the two Bluefin-21s to a parallel course on either side of the hull of Sierra Four. The beam, or width, of the Russian icebreaker, Sierra Four, was thirty-three meters, as compared to the beam of the Typhoon-1, which was narrower, at twenty-three meters.

Talking quietly to himself, Williams operated his joystick to control the Bluefins. "Okay, there you go, now just idle back a little to the aft portion of the target."

On board the Russian ballistic submarine, no one even picked up the sound the Bluefins made as *50 Let Pobedy* was crunching through six-foot-thick ice.

Williams called the control room. "Skipper I'm ready to deploy the goop."

"Sonar, Con. Range and bearing of targets," called Lanam before answering Williams.

"Con, Sonar. Sierra Four is 422 yards on continued course of 050 degrees, Typhoon-1 range 429 yards, similar bearing, speed three knots."

"Very well. Weps, Con. Deploy the material," ordered Lanam, not able to convince himself to utilize the term "goop," though Williams used it freely.

"Aye, aye, sir. Deploying goop now. Mark," replied Williams.

"OOW, increase speed to two-thirds steady on course 270, maintain depth at four hundred," called Lanam.

Just then the sonar operator on the *Vermont* called, "Sir, I'm picking up a scraping sound, sir."

"Scraping? What scraping?" asked Lanam.

"Sir, it's the Bluefins. One of them is scraping against the hull of Sierra Four," replied the sonar operator.

"Weps, Con. You're hitting Sierra Four," stated Lanam.

In the Torpedo Room Williams was intently working the joystick that controlled the UUVs, and sweat rolled down his face.

"Sir, we're encountering a strong current. It's pushing the port drone into the icebreaker's hull."

"Steer it away," Lanam instructed him.

"All stop," yelled Lanam, not wanting to add any additional sound to the ocean.

On board Tk-208 *Dmitriy Donskoy*, the sonar operator called, "Comrade Kapitan, I am detecting a sound from the *Let.*"

"What sort of sound? Is it ice?" asked the Russian captain.

"Negative, sir. It's a metal grinding sound."

The Russian captain gave his subordinate a puzzled look.

"Misha, what would cause metal grinding?" asked the captain.

"Some sea debris?" answered the number two.

"Way up here? We're far from a shipping lane, and the *Let* is breaking through six feet of ice," said the captain.

"Sonar, are there any other contacts?" asked the captain.

"Negative, sir. The only contact I have is the *Let*. The grinding is gone now, sir," replied the sonar operator.

On the *Vermont* Williams had finished deploying his goop. He wasn't sure how effective the port Bluefin would be, as he had put it hard over after sideswiping the Russian icebreaker. Williams was much more confident about the starboard Bluefin.

"Con, Weps. I've completed deploying the goop, ready to dive the Bluefins," Williams stated.

The Bluefins had a certified depth rating of forty-five hundred meters, or just over 14,700 feet; however, Williams's plan was not to drive them to that depth but rather to idle the motors on the UUVs and defeat the buoyancy system, which would have the effect of allowing the Bluefins to slowly drift to the ocean's floor. Williams opted for this approach, as it was the quietest way to dispose of the UUVs.

"Weps, Con. Approved. Dive the UUVs," ordered Lanam. "OOW, ahead dead slow. Get us away from the material," he instructed, which would have his state-of-the-art $3.4 billion submarine creep away from the Russian icebreaker with its shadowing ballistic submarine at an imperceivably quiet three knots.

They had no way of knowing if the Bluefins had delivered their biological weapons effectively, but their mission was completed now, and they exited the Kara Sea in stealthy silence.

CHAPTER TWENTY-FIVE

Help Only Comes from the Lord

Cardinal George Deas entered the White House, but this afternoon he was escorted to the East Wing, to the office of the first lady.

"Your Eminence, thank you for coming," said Kennedy Russell as she showed the cardinal to her couches, which would be the setting for their meeting.

In addition to the psychological counseling Kennedy had been receiving ever since the kidnapping on Nantucket, she also sought out the cardinal's advice and guidance as part of her dealing with the release of the photos two months earlier.

"And how are the children?" asked the cardinal.

"Very well. Andrew is beginning to think about colleges and Katie is consumed with her passion for track and cross country," replied the first lady.

"If I can be of any assistance on the college selection, please do not hesitate to let me know," said the cardinal.

Kennedy thanked him, knowing full well that gaining admission to the college of his choice would not be a problem for the son of Andrew Russell.

"Your Eminence," Kennedy began, but she was interrupted by the cardinal.

"Please, it would make me feel more comfortable if you called me Father George."

"Very well. Father, if you had told me two months ago, after the release of these photos, that I would feel the way I do now, I never would have believed you. I was understandably mortified, and I had some very direct conversations with Andy about whether staying in the public eye was worth it."

The cardinal just nodded, having learned one of the best attributes of a priest was to be a good listener.

"But now I see the release of the photos, while a great embarrassment and a violation of my privacy, as having given me a new focus and purpose in life. Andrew has often heard me refer to living in the White House as being in a gilded cage, and in many ways it really is like that," continued Kennedy. "But because of the ordeal I've been through, I've adopted this mission to help women and even girls around the world who suffer from abuse and mistreatment," she added.

"The Lord works in mysterious ways sometimes, doesn't he?" Deas said quietly.

"I understand that, but this was so profound. I came from such a dark place to where I am now. I am stunned and overwhelmed by it, Father George."

"We all face tests in life. Often, it is how we respond to these tests that defines our faith. You were tested and, if you don't mind me saying, I believe it was your faith that saved you. And not only your faith but also your strength. You could have easily retreated, but instead you have found a new and expanded purpose. And this purpose is born out of your firsthand experience. By taking this path, Kennedy, you have become an inspiration to many," said the prelate with a genuine smile on his face.

"I think you're right," she said. "Andrew and I look forward to seeing you at the dinner next week," Kennedy added.

"I wouldn't miss it," replied the cardinal, referring to the dinner where Georgetown University was bestowing an honorary doctorate on Kennedy, something that the cardinal had more than a little input in making happen.

"Your Eminence, can I ask for your blessing now?" asked the first lady.

With a smile the cardinal stood and held out his hands over Kennedy's head and began:

I raise my eyes toward the mountains.
From whence shall come my help?

My help comes from the Lord,
the maker of heaven and earth.

He will not allow your foot to slip;
or your guardian to sleep.

The Lord is your guardian.
The Lord is your shade at your right hand.

By day, the sun will not strike you,
nor the moon by night.

And may the blessing of Almighty God, the Father, Son, and Holy Spirit descend upon you and remain with you forever and ever.

Amen.

■

A Russian admiral was giving Svetlana Ivanovna Zlovna a briefing on a mysterious event that the Navy was confronting.

"Madam Director, four weeks ago three of our Arktika-class icebreakers as well as one of our Typhoon ballistic submarines all suffered similar and almost simultaneous mechanical issues. All four vessels have had their internal engine components fouled by some sort of bacterial growth," said the Russian admiral.

"All four coming down with the same problem at the same time? Were they operating in the same area?" asked Zlovna.

"No, ma'am. One was operating above Canada, one in the Barents, and the other two in the Kara Sea. Other than being in the Northern Hemisphere, they were thousands of miles apart from each other."

"Do our people think this 'fouling,' as you call it, was triggered by natural causes or some sort of weaponized biologic?" asked Zlovna, already suspicious.

"We're not sure. We're analyzing the material. It's organic, we know that, but we do not know yet if it was engineered or not," stated the admiral.

"Comrade Admiral, keep me apprised of the outcome of the analysis. What's the time estimate to get the ships repaired?"

"The engines need to be completely disassembled and cleaned, then reassembled and tested. It will take a minimum of nine months for each icebreaker. The Tk-208 will take over a year, given it is our oldest Typhoon submarine in service. Bearing in mind the TK-208 was set to be decommissioned in 2026, a decision will need to be made whether it is worth it to effect the repairs," the senior officer replied.

A few days later a report came to Zlovna's desk indicating that the organic material that disabled the ships was deemed to be an engineered material given its genetic sequencing.

■

Lisa Collins's secretary entered the vice president's office and announced, "This package just arrived by diplomatic courier from the Russian embassy."

The fact that it arrived by the diplomatic courier meant it did not go through the typical X-raying and scanning that was required of all packages that came to the White House.

"What is it?" asked Collins.

"I'm not sure," replied her secretary. "It's from Svetlana Ivanovna Zlovna of the SVR."

Collins read the short note:

Madam Vice President,
It was a pleasure to meet with you while in New York.
I hope you enjoy the enclosed gift.
I consider the score even now. I hope we can now move forward.

SIZ

The VP's secretary held up a small box with the following labeling:

Chia Pet

Icebreaker and Submarine Edition.

Watch It Grow!

Inside was a Chia pet molded in the shape of a Russian icebreaker. Collins just smiled and thought, *Yes, it is time to move forward.*

■

The night had arrived. It was the evening that Georgetown University was bestowing an honorary doctorate on the first lady for her work defending women's rights.

As gatherings went, it was not large, at just slightly over two hundred people. At 8 p.m. the group of dignitaries filed into historic Healy Hall on the Georgetown campus. Constructed between 1877 and 1879, Healy Hall, with its dark paneling and High Victorian Gothic style, made for a perfect backdrop for tonight's ceremony.

Guests at the president's table were Sister Doris Smith of the New York Foundling; Captain Mike and Kristin Bartlett; Captain Amy Bauer; Thomas Rosenbaum, president of Caltech, and wife, Kathy Faber, professor of materials science; John DeGioia, president of Georgetown University, and his wife, Theresa Anne Miller; and, of course, Cardinal George Thomas Deas.

With everyone now seated, a US Navy staff lieutenant commander approached the lectern, from which the presidential seal hung, and announced, "Ladies and gentlemen, the president of the United States." Everyone stood while the Marine Band, shoehorned into the corner of the great room, played "Hail to the Chief" as the forty-sixth president of the United States entered the grand room.

Cardinal Deas offered an opening blessing, and then President Russell made his way to the podium.

Thank you, everyone, and please be seated. This evening I have the honor and pleasure to introduce our honoree.

But before I get to our honoree, I would like to take a moment to introduce three other exceptional women who are with us this evening.

First, I would like to introduce Sister Doris Smith of the New York Foundling. The New York Foundling was started in 1869 when Sister Mary Irene Fitzgibbon put a cradle on the front stoop of their brownstone on the Lower East Side of Manhattan. The very next morning the sisters found a baby girl in it. And that began a tradition of helping the children of New York, which Sister Doris, along with the other Sisters of Charity, continue to carry on—a mission that began 151 years ago.

Applause broke out as the president extended his arm to ask Sister Doris to stand.

Another remarkable woman I would like to introduce you to is Captain Amy Bauer. Having just recently assumed command of the USS *Abraham Lincoln*, Captain Bauer is our first female commanding officer of a US aircraft carrier.

Again, the crowd applauded as an embarrassed Captain Bauer stood to acknowledge the audience's applause.

And, of course, I want to recognize and congratulate our newly confirmed vice president, Lisa Collins. Lisa has made a career of breaking glass ceilings as the first woman to lead the CIA and now as the first woman to hold the office of vice president. And let me take a moment also to extend our combined best wishes to Vice President Jack McMasters and his family.

Again, applause broke out as the crowd acknowledged the fiftieth vice president of the United States.

Our country is blessed to have had some great first ladies. Eleanor Roosevelt was a national treasure who helped a nation dealing not only with a Great Depression but also a world war. And many of us remember Jackie Kennedy, who demonstrated an unmatched gracefulness as she helped not only a nation but also her family heal from unimaginable sorrow and loss. And the list goes on to include Mary Lincoln, Nancy Reagan, and many others.

Which brings us to our guest of honor this evening.

I don't think anyone would argue that the events our first lady has had to face over the last three years were unrivalled and daunting. Yet, despite these trials and challenges, of having her children kidnapped and her personal dignity violated, she has been a beacon of strength not only for me and our children but for our country as well as for people around the world.

Applause broke out again.

It may surprise you to learn I first met our first lady when I was in the Navy. "It was during Fleet Week in New York and we met in a West Village bar that unfortunately no longer exists. But I recall when we met the Berlin song—'Take My Breath Away'—was playing.

She did then, and she does today.

And so, it gives me great pride as well as an enormous sense of honor and privilege to introduce our honoree—the first lady of the United States, and my wife, Kennedy Preston Russell.

■

Sergey Latsanych was again meeting with Zlovna on a brisk April morning in Moscow, where winter had not yet given way to spring, bringing to mind the famous T.S. Eliot line, "April is the cruelest month."

"Madam Director, what is my next assignment?" asked Latsanych.

Svetlana Ivanovna Zlovna, now sporting a short pixie haircut, which allowed her blond hair to cut sharply across her forehead, said, "How do you feel about Hanoi? We need to shore up our relations there, especially with China making such aggressive moves in the region."

"I'll pack my bags immediately," said the SVR's top agent.

"Yes." Zlovna smiled. "But not before we first have our breakfast, Sergey," said the head of the SVR.

EPILOGUE

Three Months Later

In a meeting of the president's senior advisers, Secretary of State Mark Holloway was briefing the president.

"Mr. President, the Chinese have not commented on your UN proposal to reduce defense spending. Which is to say, they will not support it," said Holloway.

"However, the Europeans are all in on it," added Holloway.

"Of course they are," replied Spencer. "They're for anything that can reduce their defense spending and their commitments to NATO."

"We all knew it was a long shot that China would agree to the reduction. Which brings us to the topic of Taiwan," opened the president.

"Sir, a free Taiwan flies in the face of China's 'One China' doctrine. A little background, sir. Japan took the island from the Chinese in 1895 at the end of the first Sino-Japanese War but gave it back again at the end of World War II. At that point the Chinese Civil War resumed between the Nationalists, led by General Chiang Kaishek, and the Communist Party, led by Mao Zedong. In 1949, after suffering several losses, Chiang evacuated his Nationalist government to Taiwan, making Taipei the capital of the Republic of China.

The fact that Taiwan remains independent is a bitter reminder to the Chinese of their chapter of civil war."

"And if President Eisenhower didn't dispatch the Seventh Fleet in 1950, China would have taken Taiwan back then," added the president, signaling that he was not unfamiliar with the history of Taiwan.

At this point Secretary of Defense Graham Petersen joined the conversation. "Mr. President, the Pentagon has conducted eighteen war games that involve China moving on Taiwan. In each China has prevailed, sir."

"Sir," said the CNO, "on that point, China has thirty-nine bases within five hundred miles of Taiwan. On the other hand, our presence is limited to bases in Guam, Japan, and the Philippines and our ability to sortie carrier strike groups to the South China Sea."

"And then there is the issue of the DF-26," added the CNO, referring to China's rumored anti-ship ballistic missiles, which were believed to be capable of sinking a US aircraft carrier with a single shot, which precipitated their being labeled "carrier killers."

"Sir, half our high-tech companies are reliant on Taiwan Semiconductor chips in one way or another," added Spencer, referring to the Taiwan-based chip manufacturer with a market capitalization of more than ½ a trillion dollars.

"Going further, sir. No one doubts that China would choose war over losing territory it considers historical theirs and vital to its national interest," added Holloway.

And with that Taiwan was about to become Andrew Russell's next crisis . . .

ACKNOWLEDGMENTS

For their aid in contributing to technical accuracy and story development, the author wishes to thank the following individuals.

For assistance and help with my knowledge of the periodic table and overall support and advice, a special thanks to Dr. Philip M. Neches, distinguished Caltech alum.

My deep appreciation and respect is extended to the officers and sailors of the USS *Carl Vinson* (CVN-70), USS *Abraham Lincoln* (CVN-72) and USS *John C. Stennis* (CVN-74) for hosting me onboard their mighty warships as I conducted my research. It is because of their courage, dedication, and steadfast commitment to their missions that we are kept safe.

I owe a debt of gratitude to the many dedicated members of the United States Coast Guard, both active and retired, who contributed technical input and authenticity to this plot.

Special thanks to Command Master Chief Chris Swiatek, BMCM, USCG.

And to Vice Admiral Steven D. Poulin, Atlantic Area Commander, whose idea it was, in the first place, to write about the Northwest Passage.

Semper Paratus

This work could not have been completed without the significant editorial and production assistance provided by Jennifer Fisher, Chris Berge, Eileen Chetti, and Deborah Perdue.

And lastly, to Jean, Andrew, and Katie for their never-ending support, encouragement, and love.

Lightning Source UK Ltd.
Milton Keynes UK
UKHW010037280721
387881UK00007B/410/J